THE AUTHOR

Sinclair Ross was born on a homestead near Shelbrooke in northern Saskatchewan in 1908. He dropped out of school after grade eleven to work in a bank. After working in many small-town banks in Saskatchewan, he transferred to a bank in Winnipeg in 1933. In 1941 he published his first novel, *As for Me and My House*, with its evocation of prairie life during the Depression. The prairie is the major setting for his two collections of short fiction, *The Lamp at Noon and Other Stories* and *The Race and Other Stories*.

From 1942 until 1946 Ross served with the Canadian army in London, England. In 1946 he returned to Winnipeg. Later that year he moved to Montreal, where he continued in banking until his retirement in 1968.

Ross's later novels, *The Well*, *Whir of Gold*, and *Sawbones Memorial*, continue his exploration of prairie life and its power to challenge as well as sustain its inhabitants.

Upon his retirement Ross lived in Greece and then in Spain.

He returned to Montreal in 1980, and two years later moved to Vancouver.

Sinclair Ross died in Vancouver in 1996.

BY SINCLAIR ROSS

FICTION

As for Me and My House (1941)
The Well (1958)
The Lamp at Noon and Other Stories (1968)
Whir of Gold (1970)
Sawbones Memorial (1974)
The Race and Other Stories [ed. Lorraine McMullen] (1982)

As for Me and My House

SINCLAIR ROSS

PENGUIN MODERN CLASSICS EDITION, © 2018

New Canadian Library editions published 1989, 2008.

Library and Archives Canada Cataloguing in Publication Data is available upon request.

ISBN 978-0-7352-5288-2

This is a work of fiction. Names, characters, places, and incidents either are the product of the author's imagination or are used fictitiously. Any resemblance to actual persons, living or dead, events, or locales is entirely coincidental.

Front cover design: Five Seventeen
Cover images: Shutterstock.com
(Church © Scott Prokop; clouds © Evannovostro)
Printed and bound in the U.S.A.

Penguin Modern Canadian Classics
Penguin Random House Canada Limited,
a Penguin Random House Company

www.penguinrandomhouse.ca

2 3 4 5 22 21 20 19 18

Saturday Evening, April 8

Philip has thrown himself across the bed and fallen asleep, his clothes on still, one of his long legs dangling to the floor.

It's been a hard day on him, putting up stovepipes and opening crates, for the fourth time getting our old linoleum down. He hasn't the hands for it. I could use the pliers and hammer twice as well myself, with none of his mutterings or smashed-up fingers either, but in the parsonage, on calling days, it simply isn't done. In return for their thousand dollars a year they expect a genteel kind of piety, a well-bred Christianity that will serve as an example to the little sons and daughters of the town. It was twelve years ago, in our first town, that I learned my lesson, one day when they caught me in the woodshed making kindling of a packing box. "Surely this isn't necessary, Mrs. Bentley – your position in the community – and Mr. Bentley such a big, able-bodied man –"

So today I let him be the man about the house, and sat on a trunk among the litter serenely making curtains over for the double windows in the living-room. For we did have visitors today, even though it was only yesterday we arrived. Just casual calls to bid us welcome, size us up, and see how much we own. There was a portly Mrs. Wenderby who fingered my poor old curtains and said she had better ones in her rag bag I could have; and there was a gray-haired, sparrow-eyed Miss Twill who looked the piano up and down reprovingly, and all but said, "If they were really Christians now they'd sell such vanities and put the money in the mission-box."

She introduced herself as the choir leader, and in expiation of the piano the least I could do was consent to play the organ for her. All the musicians in the town, it seems, are a backsliding lot, who want strange new hymns that nobody knows at an ungodly pace that nobody can keep up with. In Miss Twill's choir they sing the old hymns, slowly.

It was about tomorrow's hymns that she came, and Philip, his nerves all ragged, and a smear of soot across his face, didn't make a particularly good impression.

"Any ones you like, Miss Twill," he tried to be pleasant. "I'm sure you'll make a better choice than I could anyway." But with her lips thin she reproved him, "Other ministers we've had have considered the musical part of the service rather important. Of course, if it doesn't matter to you whether the hymns are in keeping with the text or not –"

"You'll understand tomorrow when you hear his sermon," I slipped in quickly. "It's a special sermon – he always preaches it on his first Sunday. Any good old-fashioned gospel hymns will do. I think, though, he would like *The Church's One Foundation* to start off with."

So we got rid of her at last, and steeled ourselves for the next one. Poor Philip – for almost twelve years now he's been preaching in these little prairie towns, but he still hasn't learned the proper technique for it. He still handicaps himself with a guilty feeling that he ought to mean everything he says. He hasn't learned yet to be bland.

He looks old and worn-out tonight; and as I stood over him a little while ago his face brought home to me how he shrinks from another town, how tired he is, and heartsick of it all. I ran my fingers through his hair, then stooped and kissed him. Lightly, for that is of all things what I mustn't do, let him ever suspect me of being sorry. He's a very adult, self-sufficient man, who can't bear to be fussed or worried over; and sometimes, broodless old woman that I am, I get impatient being just his wife, and start in trying to mother him too.

His sermon for tomorrow is spread out on the little table by the bed, the text that he always uses for his first Sunday. *As For Me and My House We Will Serve the Lord.* It's a stalwart, four-square, Christian sermon. It nails his colors to the mast. It declares to the town his creed, lets them know what they may expect. The Word of God as revealed in Holy Writ – Christ Crucified – salvation through His Grace – those are the things that Philip stands for.

And as usual he's been drawing again. I turned over the top sheet, and sure enough on the back of it there was a little Main Street sketched. It's like all the rest, a single row of smug, false-fronted stores, a loiterer or two, in the distance the prairie again. And like all the rest there's something about it that hurts. False fronts ought to be laughed at, never understood or pitied. They're such outlandish things, the front of a store built up to look like a second storey. They ought always to be seen that way, pretentious, ridiculous, never as Philip sees them, stricken with a look of self-awareness and futility.

That's Philip, though, what I must recognize and acknowledge as the artist in him. Sermon and drawing together, they're a kind of symbol, a summing up. The small-town preacher and the artist – what he is and what he nearly was – the failure, the compromise, the going-on – it's all there – the discrepancy between the man and the little niche that holds him.

And that hurt too, made me slip away furtively and stand a minute looking at the dull bare walls, my shoulders drawn up round my ears to resist their cold damp stillness. And huddling there I wished for a son again, a son that I might give back a little of what I've taken from him, that I might at least believe I haven't altogether wasted him, only postponed to another generation his fulfillment. A foolish, sentimental wish that I ought to have outgrown years ago – that drove me outside at last, to stand on the doorstep shivering, my lips locked, a spatter of rain in my face.

It's an immense night out there, wheeling and windy. The lights on the street and in the houses are helpless against the black wetness, little unilluminating glints that might be painted on it. The town seems huddled together, cowering on a high, tiny perch, afraid to move lest it topple into the wind. Close to the parsonage is the church, black even against the darkness, towering ominously up through the night and merging with it. There's a soft steady swish of rain on the roof, and a gurgle of eavestroughs running over. Above, in the high cold night, the wind goes swinging past, indifferent, liplessly mournful. It frightens me, makes me feel lost, dropped on this little perch of town and abandoned. I wish Philip would waken.

It's the disordered house and the bare walls that depress me. I keep looking at the leak in the ceiling, and the dark wet patch as it gradually seeps its way towards the wall. There's never been a leak before, Mrs. Finley told me this afternoon, reproach in her voice that set me fiddling with my apron like a little girl. "Only last week we papered this room for you" – she's President of the Ladies Aid, entrusted with the supervision of the parsonage – "Only last week, and it's worse now than before we touched it. I don't know when we'll be able to do the ceiling over for you. Couldn't your husband get up on the roof and put a few new shingles on?"

She met us at the train yesterday, officially, and took us home with her for dinner. There's one at least in every town, austere, beyond reproach, a little grim with the responsibilities of self-assumed leadership – inevitable as broken sidewalks and rickety false fronts. She's an alert, thin-voiced, thin-featured little woman, up to her eyes in the task of managing the town and making it over in her own image. I'm afraid it may mean some changes for Philip and me too, for there's a crusading steel in her eye to warn she brooks no halfway measures. The deportment and mien of her own family bear witness to a potter's hand that never falters. Her husband, for instance, is an appropriately meek little man, but you can't help feeling what an achievement is his meekness. It's like a tight wire cage drawn over him, and words and gestures, indicative of a more expansive past, keep squeezing through it the same way that parts of the portly Mrs. Wenderby this afternoon kept squeezing through the back and sides of Philip's study armchair. And her twelve-year-old twins, George and Stanley, when they recited grace in unison their voices tolled with such sonority that Philip in his scripture reading after dinner sounded like a droney auctioneer. Philip at the table, I noticed, kept watching them, his eyes critical and moody. He likes boys – often, I think, plans the bringing-up and education of *his* boy. A fine, well-tempered lad by now, strung just a little on the fine side, responsive to too many overtones. For I know Philip, and he has a way of building in his own image, too.

It was a good dinner though, and after breakfast on the train, of milk and arrowroot we found it hard to keep our parson manners uppermost. They're difficult things at the dinner table anyway, eating with a heartiness that compliments your hostess, at the same time with a reluctance that attests your absorption in the things of the spirit. Often we have lapses. Our fare at home is usually on the plain side, and the formal dinner of a Main Street hostess is invariably good. Good to an almost sacrificial degree. A kind of rite, at which we preside as priest and priestess – an offering, not for us, but through us, to the exacting small-town gods Propriety and Parity.

Mrs. Finley, for instance: she must have spent hours preparing for us, cleaning her house, polishing her cut glass and silver – and if I know anything at all about Main Street economics she'll spend as many more hours polishing her wits for ways and means to make ends meet till next allowance day. Yet as President of the Ladies Aid, and first lady of the congregation, she had to do the right thing by us – that was Propriety; and as Main Street hostess she had to do it so well that no other hostess might ever invite us to her home and do it better – that was Parity.

But just the same they're a worthy family, and Philip and I shall be deferential to them. Feeble as it is, we have a little technique. Philip will sometimes have them help pick out the hymns, and I'll ask Mrs. Finley about arranging the furniture in our living-room; and in two or three weeks, when we're settled, our first social duty will be to return their dinner. Ours, of course, a simple, unpretentious meal, for of such must be the household of a minister of God.

Sunday Evening, April 9

The rain has kept on all day, a thin, disheartening drizzle. The leak in the roof is worse. The dark sodden stain has crept across the ceiling and down the wall right to the floor. Now a steady drip has set in. I've put out a pail to catch it, and every few minutes I find myself waiting and listening for the splash. The hollow little clink emphasizes the inert and chilly stillness that has locked the room, gives it a kind of rhythm, makes it insistent, aggressive. The furniture looks older and shabbier than ever as it stands huddled among half-emptied barrels and packingcases. Each time we move there are a few more dents and scratches. Philip will have to wire up his study chair again, and put some kind of brace on the kitchen cupboard. I dread asking him. It always spoils a day. He has the hands for a brush or pencil, not a hammer.

We left at ten o'clock this morning in a rented car for Philip's country appointment, a schoolhouse called Partridge Hill, eleven miles south of Horizon. On account of the heavy roads Mr. Finley was to have come along to show us the way and steer us clear of mud holes, but at the last minute Mrs. Finley needed him, and in his place he sent the schoolteacher, Mr. Kirby.

Mr. Kirby was a nice, quiet-spoken young man, who asked us earnestly to call him Paul. Sandy-haired, blunt-faced, rather small and plain beside Philip, with slow steady eyes that stay right with you till they're satisfied.

"No trouble at all," he assured us as we slithered off through the rain. "I used to teach at Partridge Hill before I got the school in town. That's why Finley asked me to come – thought I might like to see some of my old friends again. Country boy myself, you know – still really belong there."

It turned out, however, that there had been a mistake in dates somewhere, and his country friends weren't expecting us for another week. "You can't always depend on the clocks out here," he said as Philip started fidgeting. "Wait till half-past eleven anyway. I'll get some kindling and start a fire."

It was a fine, crackling fire, and it kept us there till after twelve. We sat round the stove, quiet a few minutes, oppressed a little by the big vacant stillness of the place, listening to the windy lash of rain against the windows.

"I rather like a schoolhouse when it's empty," Paul said presently. "Full of ghosts. You hear whispers. The first school I went to was a little country place like this. We were ranchers, and I had to come on horseback five miles. I used to stop and look back at it, perched up alone on a little hill, prairie stretching round for miles. There were ghosts even then, and somehow it was because of them I became a schoolteacher myself. I never quite understood."

There was a short silence; then noticing the book of organ music I had with me he said abruptly, "Did you know that *offertory* comes from a word meaning *sacrifice*?"

I said I didn't, and rather apologetically he explained that he couldn't help himself – he was a philologist at heart if not any other way. "Philologist, you know – lover of words."

Then as it got warmer I went to the wheezy little organ and played some hymns for him and Handel's *Largo*. Then the *Largo* a second time, because it was simple and steadfast, and good for a man. That's the way he talks, with a wise, innocent solemnity. "Not that I'm at all a religious man," he explained conscientiously. "I wouldn't want to give you a false impression. It's just the music – and the way Mrs. Bentley plays."

I liked him for that. The musician in me dies hard. and a word of praise still sends my blood *accelerando*. "Come then and spend an evening with us soon," I invited recklessly. It was dangerous, but with my vanity up that way I didn't care. "I'll play the piano for you if you like – and then you can go off with Philip and look through his books. He has a few good ones."

Dangerous because Philip these last years grows more and more to himself. At times I find even myself an outsider. He retreats to his books and wants no intrusions. No little Main Street intellectuals to air their learning and discuss theology. No bright young modernists to ask him what he thinks of evolution. I have invited other Pauls to see his books, but not many of them have come a second time.

Today, however, he at least acquiesced in the invitation, and while we talked began to draw our pictures on the blackboard. Good likenesses too they turned out, all three, except that he screwed Paul's face up a little, and by way of contrast, for my benefit, made his own expressionless and handsome like an advertisement for underwear or shaving cream. Underneath he wrote *The New Preacher, His Wife, and Paul. Next Sunday in Person, at 11 a.m.*

On the way home we stalled in a bad mudhole. I took the wheel while Paul and Philip got behind and pushed, but after badly spattering themselves they had to walk nearly a mile for a team to pull us out.

It was hard on Paul, the sticky ploughed field they cut across, and Philip's stride such an unmercifully long one. He climbed into the car looking glum and out of sorts, but brightened presently to say, "I just remembered – such an odd coincidence – *weary*, you know, comes from an old Anglo-Saxon word, meaning to walk across wet ground."

It cost us two dollars to get pulled out, and with rent for the car, gasoline and oil, we find ourselves financially close to breaking-point again. Right away we must see about a car of our own. Our old one brought us sixty dollars last fall, which just cleaned up our coal and grocery bills before we left for Horizon. Philip drums his fingers about it tonight, says that early this week he must find out if the garage here will give him credit.

The real trouble is Philip himself. Not many of these little towns can afford a minister, and if a man is willing to take just what it's convenient for them to give him, he's going to be close to financial breaking-point all his life.

And Philip, because he feels he doesn't belong in the Church, won't insist on his salary. I try to tell him, sometimes, that he earns it, that he doesn't need to feel ashamed or look upon himself as a kind of parasite. Presiding at bazaars and drinking tea with old ladies is what they expect of him. If he doesn't do it someone else will, likely not half so conscientious. I know – and he knows – but when I've said it all he looks at me quickly, then away, and the arrears of his salary are never collected.

From our last town alone there is seven hundred dollars owing, and altogether, for the twelve years that he's been preaching, more than three thousand. And at best his salary is little enough. We wear threadbare clothes, eat rice and porridge by the ladleful, in winter sit close to a dampered little fire. I flare sometimes, ask why we can't live decently like other people, but it never helps. He just winces a little, looks at me quickly, then away again.

It's eleven now, but I'm too restless and tired to sleep. The first Sunday is always hard. Three little false-fronted towns before this one have taught me to erect a false front of my own, live my own life, keep myself intact; yet tonight again, for all my indifference to what the people here may choose to think of me, it was an ordeal to walk out of the vestry and take my place at the organ.

In a little church like this the choirs aren't gowned, and there I sat in plain view of the congregation, miserable with a sense of inferiority, conscious of nothing but appraising eyes on my shabby old hat and coat.

It isn't the hat or coat themselves I'm concerned about; it's what Philip must think sometimes when he looks from me to other women, women who rouge a little, have their hair marcelled, wear smart, mail-order-catalogue clothes. The disturbing part is that likely he doesn't think at all, doesn't take time to be fair. Instead he just sees us, makes a comparison, carries away an impression. First an attractive, well-groomed woman, then a frumpy, plain one.

And himself, he's thirty-six. A strong, virile man, right in his prime. Handsome too, despite the tired eyes, and the way his cheekbones sometimes stand out gaunt and haggard. Looking back, in every town we've lived in it's been his face and stature, not his sermons, that have made us popular at first, then brought dissatisfaction and resentment, finally an attitude that called for our resignation. Horizon, I suppose, will be no exception. People in a little town like this grow tired of one another. They become worn so bare and colorless with too much knowing that a newcomer like Philip is an event in their lives. He's an aloof, strong, unknowable man. In his eyes sometimes there's a hungry, distant look that women in their humdrum forties think appealing, that they don't know the meaning of. Lured by it for a while they flock faithfully to church, outdo one another in Christian enterprise, drop into the parsonage to say how stimulating they find his sermons. And since it's a case of *Love me, tolerate my wife*, they're kind for a while to me, too. For a few months, perhaps a year – till gradually it begins to dawn on them that in his own aloof way he still must care a little for his dowdy wife. Then his sermons become tedious, he hasn't the interests of the community at heart, I turn out to be a snob and troublemaker. Eventually they make it clear to us. We crate our furniture again and go.

That it has happened in three other towns should reassure me. I should count each town, I suppose, as a feather in my cap. But somehow, with a man like Philip, you don't predict the future from the past. I've always been a little afraid, right from the day we met. He keeps withdrawn, yields himself grudgingly. Twelve years with him now, quiet, eventless years, each like the one before it, and still what is between us is precarious. I'm sure that he's as devoted to me as he ever could be to any woman. I know that as wives go I'm a fairly good one and, so far as he'll permit it, a fairly good companion – know, too, that he knows it – but just the same, if ever we reach our hundredth Horizon, I'll still sit looking up and down the pews exactly as I did tonight. Frightened a little, primitive, green-eyed.

Not that there was anyone tonight. After the congregation had gone we sat a few minutes getting acquainted with the choir, and it would have taken an imagination livelier even than mine to find much to be afraid of there. They were four matrons, middle-aged and on, Miss Twill, a shy, white-faced young woman called Judith West, three baritones who sang the soprano part right through the hymns, and several young couples with no voices at all but who came to feel important.

"Some book on popular psychology that the last minister had been reading," Miss Twill explained afterwards. "He said that the only way to bring the young people out to church was to give them something to do – make them feel important. It didn't matter whether they could sing or not, or knew a note of music. Along they came anyway, to sit holding hands and smirking down at the congregation. Just an excuse, of course, for his own incompetence. The right kind of sermon and they'd have all come fast enough. People who are brought close to their Maker can't help feeling important. I hope Mr. Bentley soon puts a stop to it."

And I have to agree with her, for even as Main Street choirs go it's a particularly bad one. The only voice is Judith West, a full, deep contralto, untrained but sensitive, incredibly powerful for such a white-faced slip of a girl. Miss Twill and the matrons, however, don't quite approve of her, and there was a tight-lipped silence for a minute when I remarked after service how well she had sung her solo. She herself broke it at last, saying awkwardly and nicely that she'd rather be like me and play an instrument.

She gives a peculiar impression of whiteness while you're talking to her, fugitive whiteness, that her face seems always just to have shed. The eyes are fine and sensitive, but you aren't aware of them at first. Her smile comes so sharp and vivid that it almost seems there's a wince with it. I mentioned the whiteness to Philip when we came home, and he had noticed it too. He tries to find words to describe it, and wonders could it be put on paper.

I think I'm going to like Judith. Maybe because she looked as if she thought I played the organ rather well; maybe because I sensed an attitude towards her a little hostile and contemptuous, and because there's a perverse, rebellious part of me that instinctively feels it must be against Horizon rather than with it in its dislikes and prejudices.

On the church steps Mrs. Finley told us that she comes from a family of shiftless farmers up in the sand hills north of town. Instead of trying to help them, though, she went out working when she was about seventeen, sometimes as a servant girl, sometimes stooking in the harvest fields like a man. With her savings at last she set off to the city to take a commercial course, only to find when it was finished that little country upstarts aren't the kind they employ in business offices. Now Mr. Wenderby, the town clerk, gives her twenty-five dollars a month and board for typing his letters in the afternoon, and helping Mrs. Wenderby in the morning and evening. They encourage her in the choir because she needs a steadying influence. In summer she's been heard singing off by herself up the railroad track as late as ten o'clock at night. Naturally people talk. Mrs. Finley wishes she would go home and marry some good, hard-working farmer with a background like her own.

Which means that I'll have to be friends with Judith warily. In Main Street society, Mrs. Finley and her kind are the proverbial stone walls against which unimportant heads like mine are knocked in vain. We'll see. In the meantime it's nearly twelve o'clock, and two lamps burning. Horizon will be reminding us of our extravagance.

Tuesday Evening, April 11

We get settled slowly. Philip, his nerves on edge, is hard to live with. This morning it was the kitchen cupboard that had to have one of its legs braced, and this afternoon we tried to paste a strip of clean white paper over the rusty-looking streak that the rain has made across the ceiling. It's on, but we'll have to get up and take it off again. We were such a long time climbing on to the table and sideboard with the long slithery length of it between us that by the time we finally did get started the paste was nearly dry. There's a loose end now, I see, drooping over the window, and a sag in the middle like a little hammock.

Worse still, we got paste on two of Philip's best books. They were the top ones in a box he had just opened, two expensive volumes of French reproductions that he skimped hard for in his student days, and it's perhaps because they are thus a survival of the young Philip, the Philip before the Horizons, that the blobs of paste I dropped on them depressed him so unreasonably.

He went out for an hour after supper to walk it off, but now he's retreated again to the little room we've fixed up for him as a study, the door closed significantly.

It's a depressing house anyway. The ceilings are low, the windows small and mean. White would have been just as cheap and washable, but they've painted the kitchen and Philip's study gray. By way of contrast the bedroom wallpaper has a design of insistent little bright pink roses that stare at you like eyes. They're there, I imagine, to report to Mrs. Finley if the minister isn't careful always first to say his prayers.

And most depressing of all is the smell of the place. Not a bad, aggressive smell, just a passive, clinging one – just the wraith of a smell. Stop a minute deliberately to sniff and it isn't there; go on with what you're doing and it's back to haunt your nostrils with a vague suggestion of musty shelves, repression and decay.

Philip says it's my imagination, but I catch him sniffing too. In a combative mood this morning I washed the floors with a strong carbolic disinfectant; but now as the reek of cleanliness subsides it comes again, this same faint exhalation of the past.

For it is the past, of course, and with a morbid kind of satisfaction I go exploring it, looking at the faded old carpets, trying the hard, leathery easy chairs with broken springs, opening little closets where so many well-brushed, shiny clothes have hung. Then I look round and make comparisons with us, wonder what kind of exhalation it will be when we have gone.

The piano faces me across the room, but I think of Philip in his study, and sit still. When he's in a mood like this it always sets him pacing. There's a chill in the air anyway, and my hands are cold.

After supper when he went out I played a while. Sedately, though, with the soft pedal down, for the house sits so close to the sidewalk that I could hear every footstep going past. Some of them stopped to listen, and until they went on again I barely nibbled at the keys. It's a big, fifty-foot lot, so they must have built the house up close to the street like this in order to learn a little about the occupants. Anyway I feel exposed, catch myself walking on tiptoe, talking to Philip in half-whispers. And it won't do. We're down-in-the-mouth enough already. Tomorrow I must play the piano again, play it and hammer it and charge with it to the town's complete annihilation. Even though Philip slams a door or two and starts his pacing. For both our sakes I must.

It's a small, squat, grayish house, and pushed up against the big, glum, grayish church it looks so diminutive that I'm reminded of the mountain that did all the fussing and then gave birth to a mouse. There's no veranda, just a big flat step where callers scrape their feet and introduce themselves. On each side of it is a stunted, bedraggled little caragana, and farther along a flower bed marked off neatly with whitewashed stones. On the side away from the church there's a vacant lot, and then the Ellingsons in a stuccoed, hip-roofed house; at the back a good-sized garden, with a little sidewalk running down the middle of it to the woodshed, outdoor privy, and garage.

The privy leans badly, fifteen or twenty degrees anyway from the perpendicular. Last Hallowe'en it was carried off by the hoodlums of the town and left on the steps of the church with a big sign nailed to it *Come Unto Me All Ye That Labor and Are Heavy Laden*. They haven't been able since to get it straight again, but Mrs. Finley says that we can use it with assurance.

My neighbor, Mrs. Ellingson, came over this morning to tell me how she and her husband laughed when they saw me go in the first time. "Sven say she look so scared I maybe tank she vaste her time."

She's a large, Norwegian woman, in shape and structure rather like a snowman made of three balls piled on top of one another. Her broad red face is buttoned down like a cushion in the middle with a nose so small that in profile it's invisible. Her hair is flaxen, as if bleached that way by the radiations of her ruddy cheeks. She keeps boarders and chickens, and brought us over two fresh eggs for supper. It seemed a pity to waste them on supper though, the paste and the ceiling having spoiled it anyway, so I've put them away for Philip's breakfast. Meals are a problem these days. I haven't much to tempt him with, and he's been running too long on nerves and coffee as it is.

Friday Evening, April 14

I found an old pipe today when I was cleaning the little back porch. It was hidden so well in a cranny up near the ceiling that the Ladies Aid must have missed it when they were here to do the papering. A black, well-seasoned pipe like Philip's used to be. It brought a little tightness to my throat for a minute, the old smoky smell of it, the thought that we aren't the only ones. I started off to show it to Philip, then changed my mind and put it in the fire instead.

It was easier when Philip smoked. The silences were less strained, the study door between us less implacable. The pipe belonged to both of us. We were partners in conspiracy.

I used to fill it for him, light his match, and then draw up a stool. It was always late at night, when there was no chance of anyone coming to discover him or smell the smoke;

and together like that for a while we would get the better of the day. It was a strong, reassuring knee to lean against. I used to feel myself a match for all the Main Streets in the world.

It's a good many years now since he stopped. The secrecy and furtiveness at last began to spoil it for him. Hiding the pipe in the back shed so there wouldn't be a trace of smell when callers came, burning coffee on the stove to kill imaginary traces, sending out of town for tobacco, on tenterhooks till it came lest they overlook his instructions and use a mailing wrapper that would reveal the contents to the postmaster – gradually it wore at his self-respect till at last one night he flared, said that since he couldn't smoke in daylight like a man he wouldn't smoke at all. And then white and bitter he seized the pipe, slammed out to the kitchen with it, and threw it in the fire.

I thought it was just a tantrum though, and promptly ordered him another. But when it came he flared a second time, and because his jumpy nerves had been making mine as bad I flared in turn, and said that so far as hypocrisy went the pipe didn't make much difference one way or another. It was no worse smoking on the sly than taking out his spleen and temper on his wife.

We stood glaring at each other a minute, trying to keep our eyes hard and unyielding; then he swung away and shut himself in his study till suppertime. But all afternoon I could feel him there, and the stillness through the house was screwed down tight upon us like a vise. Every time I took a step I imagined him listening, his lips set, his eyes dry and hurt. I rehearsed things to say to him, to make amends, but it was no use. At the table his voice was neat and brittle, his eyes aloof. All through the meal I seesawed with him in the same dry guarded tone.

It's difficult at times anyway, just two people in a house. They become sensitive to each other; a sullen or irritable mood always communicates itself. The words they find are stilted, lifeless. Every clink of a dish or fork is solitary and foreboding like a chip off the crack of doom. I remember how I ran to him at last as he started back to his study, how I sobbed against his coat and said I hadn't meant it. And how he tried to laugh, and made me blow my nose, saying he couldn't kiss me while I had the sniffles.

I remember as if it were today. Somehow, because of the pipe I found, I can't help feeling that it really was today. For there's been little change since then. I sobbed and blew my nose and cleared *my* trouble up, but his is a tougher kind. It persisted, and persists.

For hypocrisy wears hard on a man who at heart really isn't that way. As far back as I can remember it's always been there, darkening, draining him, but with Horizon now it seems to be gathering for a crisis. So often he looks past me, so often his lips are white, strained with a suffering, back-to-the-wall defiance. Only last night I was lying half-awake, thinking about him, a little uneasy; and then drowsing off I seemed to see him in the pulpit, turning through the pages of the Bible. The church was filled. I was sitting tense, dreading something, all my muscles tight and aching. It seemed hours that he kept on, searching vainly for his text; and then with a laugh he seized the Bible suddenly, and hurled it crashing down among the pews.

I sat up, wide awake, too frightened for a while to understand I had been only dreaming. He was muttering in his sleep, and when I settled down at last against his arm I could feel it give a steady little twitch. I can still see him, standing there so fierce and dishevelled, the Bible upraised in his hands. It makes me wonder had he been dreaming too, had my mind as I lay there half-asleep been sensitive to the rage and bitterness racking him. He's the kind that would never speak of it himself. But he's a poor actor, and his voice and look speak for him.

We're getting on – thirty-six and thirty-four. Getting to the place, I'm afraid, where it's not enough to put a false front up and live our own lives out behind it.

At least where it's not enough for him. I don't need any more. The hypocrisy and shabby clothes and small-town social round – none of it matters very much when he takes time off to be aware of me. I can stand apart, look on the Horizons with detachment. But to him I'm less than that.

It's a man's way, I suppose, and a woman's. Before I met him I had ambitions too. The only thing that really mattered for me was the piano. It made me self-sufficient, a little hard. All I wanted was opportunity to work and develop myself.

But he came and the piano took second place. I was teaching and saving hard for another year's study in the East, wondering if I might even make it Europe; and then I forgot it all, almost overnight.

Instead of practice in my spare time it was books now. Books that he had read or might be going to read – so that I could reach up to his intellect, be a good companion, sometimes while he talked nod comprehendingly.

For right from the beginning I knew that with Philip it was the only way. Women weren't necessary or important to him as to most men. He was the kind to stand back and appraise them, make his decision reflectively. For a while, before understanding the lie of the land, I even read theology. Submitting to him that way, yielding my identity – it seemed what life was intended for.

But he through it all kept his own stature. He lost the career he wanted. but he retained himself. Untouched by me he kept on struggling, his own, unsharable struggle with things out of reach of a woman or his love for her.

He's a failure now, a preacher instead of a painter, and every minute of the day he's mindful of it. I'm a failure too, a small-town preacher's wife instead of what I so faithfully set out to be – but I have to stop deliberately like this to remember. To have him notice, speak to me as if I really mattered in his life, after twelve years with him that's all I want or need. It arranges my world for me, strengthens and quickens it, makes it immune to all other worlds.

I've just come from him. There's his sermon for Sunday beside him on the table, but he's been drawing again. A cold, hopeless little thing – just the night as he left it at the front door. The solitary street lamp, pitted feebly and uselessly against the overhanging darkness. A little false-fronted store, still and blank and white – another – another – in retreating, steplike sequence – a stairway into the night. The insolent patch of the store is unabashed by the loom of darkness over it. The dark windows are like sockets of unlidded eyes, letting more of the night gape through. Farther on is a single figure, bent low, hurrying, almost away. One second more and the little street will be deserted.

Something has happened to his drawing this last year or two. There used to be feeling and humanity in it. It was warm and positive and forthright; but now everything is distorted, intensified, alive with thin, cold, bitter life. Yesterday he sketched a congregation as he sees it from the pulpit. Seven faces in the first row – ugly, wretched faces, big-mouthed, mean-eyed – alike, yet each with a sharp, aggressive individuality – the caricature of a pew, and the likenesses of seven people. Seven faces more in the second row – just the tops of them. Seven faces in the third – seven in the fourth – just the tops of them. Seven until they merged – brief, hard pencil flecks, nothing more, but each fleck relentless, a repetition of the fleck in front of it, of the seven faces in the front row, of all that he saw there contemptible and mean.

Something has happened to his drawing, and something has happened to him. There have always been Horizons – he was born and grew up in one – but once they were a challenge. Their pettiness and cramp stung him to defiance, made him reach farther. Now in his attitude there's still defiance, but it's a sullen, hopeless kind. These little towns threaten to be the scaffolding of his life, and at last he seems to know. He tried to do better. He never spared himself. He kept the struggle up at clenched white heat for years. And now, withdrawn, he seems to feel that the responsibility for what's ahead is no longer his. He's finished. This one, the next one, it's only Main Street anyway.

And there's the strange part – he tries to be so sane and rational, yet all the time keeps on believing that there's a will stronger than his own deliberately pitted against him. He's cold and skeptical towards religion. He tries to measure life with intellect and reason, insists to himself that he is satisfied with what they prove for him; yet here there persists this conviction of a supreme being interested in him, opposed to him, arranging with tireless concern the details of his life to make certain it will be spent in a wind-swept, sun-burned little Horizon.

It isn't an attitude either that he's encouraged just as an excuse for himself. He's not the kind to shift the blame for his failure to an Almighty. It's just that with something deeper than his intellect he believes that Horizon is his due. He wanted to paint; the Church offered itself as at least one step away from the prairie town where he had spent his boyhood. It was against his convictions, against all his instincts of what was decent and honorable. He went, though, undeterred. He believed he could paint with the passion and extravagance that are natural to a boy sometimes, believed that he was meant to paint. The important thing was to fulfill himself, let the end justify the means.

That the means at hand were distasteful and humiliating didn't matter. He was going to be an artist – he couldn't afford fastidiousness. He may have dramatized himself a little – looked upon the Church as a challenge to the artist in him. Supposing for a few years he did profess what he couldn't believe – after all, could the pebbles of his disbelief do any real harm to an institution like the Church? Wasn't it only his smug self-righteousness that was at stake? His own smug satisfaction with himself at being an outspoken, honorable boy? Could he be an artist and afford such luxuries?

Had he succeeded, had he not put his books away one night and gone to a concert with a friend, then I suppose he would look back now complacently and feel that the end had more than justified the means. The struggle would still seem a dramatic one. The lad who had plunged into and emerged from it would come striding up the years with a hero-air about him, one of the few real dreamers who make their dreams come true.

But having failed he's not a strong or great man, just a guilty one. There are plenty of others to whom the Church means just bread and butter, who at best assert an easy, untried faith, but that's no solution for him. His guilt is that emphatically he does not believe. His disbelief amounts to an achievement.

He made a compromise once, with himself, his conscience, his ideals; and now he believes that by some retributive justice he is paying for it. A kind of Nemesis. He pays in Main Streets – this one, the last one, the Main Streets still to come.

Sunday Evening, April 16

We went to Partridge Hill schoolhouse this morning in our own car. Philip spent the biggest part of yesterday sandpapering and painting it, but it still looks like ten dollars down and ten a month till a year this coming June. "They say in the garage the engine's good," he said apologetically. "And the tires back and front are just six months old."

Paul Kirby, the schoolteacher, was with us again, and as I stood making my dubious inspection he hurried on tactfully to say that the word *automobile* is a very corrupt one, a hack and unscholarly job of splicing a Greek prefix to a Latin root, the sort of thing that in the best philological circles simply isn't done. Himself he prefers *car*, a good, straightforward Celtic word, that originally meant *war chariot*. And I said unkindly, "It does look battle-scarred, doesn't it?"

Philip preached well this morning, responding despite himself to the crowded, expectant little schoolhouse. They were a sober, work-roughened congregation. There was strength in their voices when they sang, like the strength and darkness of the soil. The last hymn was staidly orthodox, but through it there seemed to mount something primitive, something that was less a response to Philip's sermon and scripture reading than to the grim futility of their own lives. Five years in succession now they've been blown out, dried out, hailed out; and it was as if in the face of so blind and uncaring a universe they were trying to assert themselves, to insist upon their own meaning and importance.

"Which is the source of all religion," Paul discussed it with me afterwards. "Man can't bear to admit his insignificance. If you've ever seen a hailstorm, or watched a crop dry up – his helplessness, the way he's ignored – well, it was just such helplessness in the beginning that set him discovering gods who could control the storms and seasons. Powerful, friendly gods – on his side. And if they were more powerful than the storms, and if they were concerned with him above all things, then it followed that he was really more powerful and important than the storms, too. So he felt better – gratefully became a reverent and religious creature. That was what you heard this morning – pagans singing Christian hymns . . . *pagan*, you know, originally that's exactly what it meant, *country dweller*."

After the service the women came up fidgeting with their ungloved hands to invite us soon to visit them. They were all wind-burned, with red chapped necks and sagging bodies. For a quarter of an hour they stood round the steps in sharp-tongued little groups, heartened by the spring again, discussing crops and gardens. It was a clear, still morning. There was a bright fall of sunshine that made the dingy landscape radiant. Right to the horizon it winked with little lakes of spring-thaw water. The sky had a fragile, crystal look, as if a touch of breath might bring it round our heads in tinkling ruin.

We went home for dinner with a couple about our own age by the name of Lawson, where Paul used to board when he taught at Partridge Hill. Mrs. Lawson is a sharp, stirring, rather pretty woman, hurrying and managing her long lean husband like a yelping little terrier round a plodding Clyde. Joe Lawson looks like Philip. He has the same turn and gestures, the same slow strength. Sky and weather have put the same look of stillness in his eyes.

"Joe's such a farmer," she kept saying at the table. "Town folks, Joe, don't pitch in themselves and eat. They take encouragement!" And then round she would come to fill our plates herself, and ask in exasperation couldn't he let his own stomach wait just once.

But she likes being exasperated with him, and perhaps he knows. What woman doesn't like being exasperated with a man and finding that he pays no heed, pitting herself against him, finding him too strong for her?

They have a thin, delicate-looking boy about twelve, Peter, who limps a little still from a runaway two years ago. He plays rather well by ear, and because of the way his father sat watching him, proud, fearful, exactly like Philip if he had a boy, I told him to bring Peter to town whenever he could and I would give him lessons.

Then it was my turn. I played quietly at first, for his father's sake not wanting to outshine the boy, then gradually forgetful of my good resolve, releasing myself after so many pent-up days in this tight, depressing little parsonage.

It was a fairly good piano, that Paul told us later they got for Peter after his accident, and that they will likely lose this fall unless the crop is good. I played old-fashioned *Hymns with Variations* for them, a southern medley; then for Lawson a country hoe-down.

"The minister's wife, and Sunday afternoons," Mrs. Lawson snapped at him. "Can't you ever wake up and catch on?" But her foot the next minute was tapping out the rhythm too.

When I finished, it was time to start for home. They gave us a bowl of butter and a dozen eggs, and at the last minute took us off to the stable to see twin calves that were born just yesterday. In the car Paul said thoughtfully that that was the worst penalty inflicted by education, the way it separates you from the people who are really closest to you, among whom you would otherwise belong. Himself now, a ranch boy with a little schooling, he fits in nowhere.

Wednesday Evening, April 19

I had a call this afternoon from Mrs. Bird, the doctor's wife. "I heard the piano, my dear," she announced herself, walking in without knocking. "I'll just sit still if you don't mind and listen. No – not the rocking chair – it's sure to creak. I don't want to be a distraction."

She's a short, round, tubby woman, with horn-rimmed glasses and an air of erudition. She had on an odd, old-fashioned little tweed hat, and a khaki-green tweed jacket buckled in so tight above her hips that the tail stood out as if she were going to use that side to make a curtsy.

"I'm fond of tweeds," she caught my glance, taking off the hat and handing it to me. "It's nine years old and the coat's twelve. Good to begin with. I was brought up that way."

I nodded. "You can see the difference all right."

"Background, my dear. Not what you wear, but how. Look at all the new spring outfits walking round the streets these days. Mail-order-catalogue ladies complete for nineteen ninety-five. The doctor looks at me and says thank God Josephine that you're not that way."

I smiled my pleasure at the doctor's discernment. She continued, "We serve the town, but we don't submit to it. Our private lives are our own. Remarkable man, Dr. Bird. Capable of anything, anywhere – but Horizon needs him. That's just how remarkable he is."

"It will be made up to him though," the parson's wife remembered to say. "It always is, you know. I'm sure Horizon itself is very appreciative."

She smiled graciously and unbuckled her jacket. "Still I get tired sometimes. Such an ugly barren little town. I simply wasn't meant for it. Just today I started thinking of spring in other places – birds, flowers, aromas. Expatriate – I couldn't help myself.

Oh to be in England, now that April's there,
And whoever wakes in England –

Well, whatever it is the English do when they get up in the morning. No my dear, I'm not English, and as a rule I don't indulge in feeling sorry for myself –"

She sat a moment looking melancholy through her glasses, then rallied: "That's why I dropped in on you, my dear. I heard your piano up on Main Street – young, sparkling, jubilant – and I said, 'There, Josephine – there's an expatriate too. You'll find the spring you're looking for – someone akin to you –'"

She looked at me expectantly a moment, then bent forward and prodded my knee. "Intellectually, you see, the doctor and I are alone here. Provincial atmosphere – it suffocates. The result is it's always a man's world I live in. The dominating male – you'll understand when you meet the doctor. Even worse, a doctor's world. Cold, scientific. I wasn't quite meant for it either. There are days when I positively loathe streptococci. Then an afternoon of bridge or tea and I realize there are things more virulent."

"How nice," said the parson's wife appropriately, "that you and the doctor have so much in common."

"No more than you and I, my dear. The first night you played the organ here – 'Manna, Josephine,' I said. 'Positively manna. You must go and tell her so. She'll understand – speak your own language.' Once, you know, I was a musician too."

It must have been a sickly smile with which I acknowledged the bond between us. With her head at a sudden diagnostic tilt she said, "You don't look very well, my dear. Pale – shadows underneath the eyes. You must drop in and see the doctor right away. An understanding man, and thorough."

"It's just the moving," I replied thriftily. "Tired, you know – but we're all nicely settled now."

"And Horizon's such a difficult town. You must help Mr. Bentley by keeping well. I'll tell the doctor to expect you."

She leaned back reflectively a moment, running her fingers through her short-cropped, slightly graying hair. "There's something about Mr. Bentley that reminds me of the doctor. Not in appearance exactly – the doctor's quite small. Myself I'd say it's spiritual, but the doctor's such a scientific man he'd never tolerate the word. Mr. Bentley, too, could go anywhere, only he knows it's little towns like ours that need him. Noble sermons, both of them. And I'm so glad he's one of us, doesn't wear his collar the wrong way round. Makes you feel quite free to take all your problems to him."

I sat still, nodding politely. She proceeded. "Mrs. Finley of course doesn't approve – says her little Horizon isn't what it used to be. Distressing woman. I met her on the street this afternoon, and told her that I'll take the Ladies Aid at my place next time. Just to show my appreciation of you and Mr. Bentley. Ordinarily I don't have much to do with them. But if you can stand them so can I. We must be loyal to each other."

At the supper table I started to tell Philip about her, but frowning after a minute he asked wasn't it bad enough to put up with such people when we had to – did we have to have them every mealtime, too?

Then white-lipped he excused himself and went into his study. I waited a few minutes before following him. He was standing at the window, the curtains pushed back, his face against the glass. When I touched his arm he swung round almost angrily, then took my hand and turned again to look through the window at the ugly little roofs of Horizon.

I glanced up and saw a twitch to his lips. There were lines around his mouth that made him seem spent, almost broken. His hand stayed quick and strong on mine as if he wanted me there – as if he were trying to tell me so.

It was more of him than I had had in weeks, but afraid to be spendthrift with such a moment I slipped away from him again. For when he gives himself to me like that, when we come close to each other, always to follow is a sudden mustering of self-sufficiency, a repudiating swing the other way. He resents his need of me. Somehow it makes him feel weak, a little unmanly. There are times when I think he has never quite forgiven me for being just a woman.

So while his hand was still warm and insistent I left him, put my hat and coat and rubbers on, walked into the town and then away from it.

I had to. The house was too small, too oppressive with its faint old smell of other lives. And the little town outside was somehow too much like a mirror.

Or better, like a whole set of mirrors. Ranged round me so that at every step I met the preacher's wife, splayfooted rubbers, dowdy coat and all. I couldn't escape. The gates and doors and windows kept reminding me.

Hurrying along I had a curious sense of leaving imprints of myself. I crossed the town, took the road that runs beneath the five grain elevators, left it for drier walking on the railroad track – but all the way back to the parsonage, no matter how fast or far I walked, the imprints still were there.

I went perhaps a mile, then stopped to rest. The sun was low now, and its slanting light hung over the fields like yellow mist. There was a smell of thawing earth, and somewhere near a meadowlark.

Then the sun went down, and some clouds that had been lost in the light came out on the sky in bright little flecks of red and gold. Like the incredible clouds young artists sometimes paint before they learn restraint or discipline. Like the ones I've known even the austere-eyed Philip to do. Before he lost the enthusiasm and zest for such things. Before the Horizons and the pulpits.

I stood a long time thinking of him, of us. The little lights in town were beginning to stretch and glimmer through the dusk when at last I started home. He was waiting for me, worried that I had stayed so long, penitent at the thought it was because of him I had hurried away.

He didn't say anything. It was just the way he helped me off with my coat and rubbers, shook up the fire in the kitchen stove, and made me sit down to warm myself. I told him about the clouds and the meadowlark, and said that some evening soon we would maybe go together for a walk. And then, still to be frugal with the moment, I let him go back to his study.

Thursday Evening, April 20

Mrs. Ellingson called me over for coffee this morning, and while I was there gave me some geranium slips and a little fuchsia already coming into bud. For the present, till I can buy some pots, the slips are planted in tomato cans. The fuchsia has a table to itself, close enough to the window to catch an hour or two of morning sun, yet out in the room a little way where I can look up and get the good of it.

That's important. I have a slack, perishable feeling tonight, that it's all I have left, that there's nothing else to stave off the town, or help me maintain my own integrity.

I had callers this afternoon, seven of them, lasting from half-past two till half-past five, and all the time I could feel Philip in his study, silent, careful, pretending to be out.

What's a man to do anyway? He can't sit up in the grocery stores or barber shop trying to be a man of the people every afternoon, and he can't sit here talking with middle-aged matrons about recipes and needlework. It's bad enough when we go calling ourselves, but then we can at least cut each call to twenty minutes. There's a formality about it that saves his self-respect and leaves him intact. But helping his wife entertain with sponge and cake and tea is another matter.

It was a strain on both of us, and supper again was one of those brittle meals through whose tight-stretched silences you can fairly see the dart of nerves. He's in his study now, the door closed, drawing again. I went in a little while ago, determined to break the atmosphere of restraint and calamity that's hanging over us, but he refused to talk, and didn't want me looking on.

It's Judith tonight he's drawing. Or rather, trying to draw, for the strange swift whiteness of her face eludes him. The floor is littered with torn-up, crumpled sketches. He's out of himself, wrestling. There's a formidable wrinkle across his forehead, and in his eyes tense moments of immobile glare.

It left nothing to do but retreat, and come back here to sit staring at the little fuchsia. That's the part about him that hurts, the way he does wrestle, the way he throws himself into his drawing, his fierce absorption till what he's doing turns out right. It doesn't mean that he just has a skill with a pencil. Even though the drawings are only torn up or put away to fill more boxes when we move, even though no one ever gets a glimpse of them but me, still they're for him the only part of life that's real or genuine.

That's why I believe he's an artist, why I can't deceive myself, or escape the hurt of it. Alone in there, hunched over his table, groping and struggling to fulfill himself – intent upon something that can only remind him of his failure, of the man he tried to be. I wish I could reach him, but it's like the wilderness outside of night and sky and prairie, with this one little spot of Horizon hung up lost in its immensity. He's as lost, and alone.

Monday Evening, April 24

I hate this house. I've been trying to shut my eyes to it, trying to tell myself it's just the strangeness, the difficulty and inconvenience of getting settled, but I do, I hate it.

The ceilings are so low; they're such sly, crafty-looking windows. The way we're crowded close against the church the light comes colorless and glum all afternoon. It's hard to laugh or speak naturally. I find myself walking on tiptoe, setting things down with elaborate care lest they let out a rattle or clang. Even the piano, it seems oppressed and chilled by the cold, dingy walls. I can't make it respond to me, or bring it to life.

There's the smell too, vague and musty and pervasive, like some illogical dread or worry that you can't bring clearly into your mind.

I notice how often I sit still, not even thinking. My eyes keep worming their way along the rusty stains that the rain has left across the ceiling. I hate it all, every room. Some part of me is in protest. I can't relax, can't accept it as home. There's something lurking in the shadows, something that doesn't approve of me, that won't let me straighten my shoulders. Even the familiar old furniture is aloof. I didn't know before it was so dull and ugly. It has taken sides against me with the house. I hate it too.

Philip and I had a quarrel this morning. It was my fault today, but ever since we started getting ready to move here he's been sullen and unreasonable. And my nerves sometimes get on edge a little, too. He didn't like the prospect of Horizon, he doesn't like things now that he's here, but what kind of holiday, I wonder, does he think it's going to be for me? I asked him today, told him about his temperamental sulking and his useless hands.

I'm sorry now. I can't forget the hurt, flayed look in his eyes. He just stood white-lipped till I had finished, then slipped outside. Now he won't look at me. I wasn't trying to hurt him, it was just my temper again, but I can't get close enough to let him understand.

I was in a dirty old dress this morning, down on my knees scrubbing the floor again with carbolic disinfectant, when Mrs. Holly knocked. Mrs. Holly is a tall, good-looking young woman. She has yellowish, light-brown hair that goes metallic in the sun, and thin red lips that stand out strong and clear against her fawnish skin. Fawnish, somehow, because of big pale yellow freckles that seem to lie just underneath the surface. I kept staring at them, thinking how lovely they would be if she weren't a woman. She wore a green, freshly-laundered dress, and a green ribbon binding down her hair like a schoolgirl. She smiled at me, and said it was to see Mr. Bentley she had come.

I called him; and then as he came into the room and stood silent a moment, looking at her, I became conscious of my own hot face, and the dirty-water rim around my wrists. My sleeves were rolled up; there were splashes on my apron. When I sat down I caught her eyes for a moment on the scuffed old slippers I keep for wearing in the morning round the house. I tried to tuck them out of sight underneath my chair, and sat with my hands spread carefully across my apron where the spots were thickest.

It wasn't me, though, she was interested in, and sitting there ignored, I had time to think that with clothes like other women I might be just as attractive. A clench of self-pity came into my throat. She had come to discuss her Sunday School class with Philip, to ask languid, unnecessary questions, but he wasn't curt or irritable as he nearly always is with me. I sat still a few minutes; then my throat grew tighter, and abruptly I left them and went back to my scrub-pail in the kitchen.

He had to call me when she was ready to go, and I was steeling myself so hard against his anger that it was all I could do to be civil. As soon as we were alone he said I might have tried to endure them a few minutes longer. Hardest of all, he knew why I hadn't stayed. "It's nobody's fault but your own that you aren't more presentable in the morning. And when somebody catches you it doesn't help to go off about it in the sulks."

That was when I lost my temper. He tried to quiet me, seized my arms, said there were people going past, to control myself, and for answer I mocked him, jeered at the good, God-fearing man who was afraid the town might hear him quarreling with his wife. I told him about my old clothes, our ugly furniture, these dark, dingy-smelling little rooms. My voice was nearly a shout; the sound of it goaded me on. I said that when I married him I didn't know it was going to mean Horizons all my life. I had ambition once too – and it was to be something more than the wife of a half-starved country preacher.

He went out at last. It was noon when he came back, but he went straight to his study, and when I told him dinner was ready said he wasn't hungry. Suppertime again it was the same. I prepared a tray for him, hoping he would see I was sorry, willing to make amends, but I took it three times as far as his study, and three times carried it back to the kitchen.

Everything's quiet now – so quiet and spent it's hard to believe that only this morning I was making the windows dance as if I loathed the sight of him. There's rain again, and I've set a pail out in the middle of the floor to catch the drip. Between the clinks I hear a fretful swish against the windows, and a crushed, steady murmur on the roof. It's getting late, but still he doesn't stir. I think of the things I must say to him, walk across the room, knock at his door, go in and say them – and all the time keep sitting here. my flesh and ears strained, waiting for the little clink of drip.

The lamp is burning dry. As the light contracts, the room becomes enormous, its shadows merging with the night and rain. He won't come out till I'm in bed long enough to be asleep; yet I can't go leaving things as they are between us now.

Tuesday Evening, April 25

We've made it up again.

I sat waiting for him and listening to the drip last night till finally the room was quite dark, with only the lamp wick glowing through it like a coal; and then I put on a raincoat and his old felt hat, and went out for a while to walk my spirits back.

It was cold and drizzling, with a gusty wind that made the rain against the skin like needles. There was no one out. I walked back and forth, up one street and down another, then finally along the railroad track a little way till I reached the last grain elevator.

I crept close against the sheltered side, and stood there a long time looking back towards the town. The high expanse of wall was like a sounding board on which the beat of rain became a deep, husky sound, that hushed and eased a little. I thought of the times we used to go walking in the rain together, and I tried to imagine him there with me again, his arm against mine warm and strong. For of all weathers there's none so good for two as rain. It draws you closer to each other. With its wet and chill it proves how good another arm is, warm and dependable against your own.

But presently I began to think of him coming out of his study, finding me gone and the house in darkness; and I hurried home, and was just in time to meet him in the doorway, starting out to look for me.

It made me glad to see how his face was white and anxious. I flinched a little when he looked at me, then half-defiant said, "I like walking in the rain. You remember, don't you?"

He set his lips and nodded. We faced each other, listening to the driving gusts of rain against the windows; then I broke and went to him, and pushed my face in close against his vest. For a minute he stood erect, unyielding, then drew me to him tight and hard, and said I was a little fool.

For a long time we lay awake, quiet, aware of each other; and then for a long time I lay awake alone, grudging the way a child does the waste of such a night in sleep.

At last I did sleep though, and woke to find that through the night the rain had turned to snow. Thick, slow, smothering snow, a stealth about its silent pile, as if ashamed for leaving us to dirty streets and dingy fields it were back to make extravagant amends.

We watched it this morning from window to window, room to room, quiet and companionable again.

Even inside we could feel the silence of the street. Sometimes a figure slipped past, but blurred by the thick heavy flakes, and without sound of footsteps. Reality had given way to the white lineless blend of sky and earth. Across the street we could see the walls of the houses, and a little higher the chimneys; but between them were the white rooftops, merging scarless into the white air; and know what we would, the eye was not to be told that chimneys and walls belonged to one another.

"It's a day for walking," I said at last, early in the afternoon. He nodded; we put our things on, and went into it.

The snow spun round us thick and slow like feathers till it seemed we were walking on and through a cloud. The little town loomed up and fell away. On the outskirts we took the railroad track, where the telegraph poles and double line of fence looked like a drawing from which all the horizontal strokes had been erased. The spongy flakes kept melting and trickling down our cheeks, and we took off our gloves sometimes to feel their coolness on our hands. We were silent most of the way. There was a hush in the snow like a finger raised.

We came at last to a sudden deep ravine. There was a hoarse little torrent at the bottom, with a shaggy, tumbling swiftness that we listened to a while, then went down the slippery bank to watch. We brushed off a stone and sat with our backs against the trestle of the railway bridge. The flakes came whirling out of the whiteness, spun against the stream a moment, vanished at its touch. On our shoulders and knees and hats again they piled up little drifts of silence.

Then the bridge over us picked up the coming of a train.

It was there even while the silence was still intact. At last we heard a distant whistle-blade, then a single point of sound, like one drop of water in a whole sky. It dilated, spread. The sky and silence began imperceptibly to fill with it. We steeled ourselves a little, feeling the pounding onrush in the trestle of the bridge. It quickened, gathered, shook the earth, then swept in an iron roar above us, thundering and dark.

We emerged from it slowly, while the trestle a moment or two sustained the clang and din. I glanced at Philip, then quickly back to the water. A train still makes him wince sometimes. At night, when the whistle's loneliest, he'll toss a moment, then lie still and tense. And in the daytime I've seen his eyes take on a quick, half-eager look, just for a second or two, and then sink flat and cold again.

He grew up in one of these little Main Streets, rebelling against its cramp and pettiness, looking farther. Somewhere, potential, unknown, there was another world, his world; and every day the train sped into it, and every day he watched it, hungered, went on dreaming.

I know it only in fragments, pieced together through the fifteen years I've known him. Before we were married he told me who he was and what he came from, his head set defiant, his voice quick and hard, warning me, asking nothing. Once he tried to write, the second year we were married, and all through his clumsy manuscript I read himself. That was what spoiled it, himself, the painful, sometimes bitter, reality. Even I might have done it better. There's another reality, kindlier, that he's never seen or understood. It's his way to look through himself, always to see just the skeleton.

His mother was a waitress in a little Main Street restaurant. His father, a young student preacher, died without marrying her before Philip was born.

His mother's family were the owners of the restaurant; to help earn his living Philip worked in the kitchen and helped wait on customers. They were drunken customers sometimes, who laughed suggestively about his mother and his birth. Gradually he came to feel that for all the ridicule and shame he was exposed to, it was his mother to blame. Too young to understand emotionally what had happened, he recoiled from her with a sense of grievance and contempt. She died when he was fourteen, but it made no difference. The early years had left an imprint that was not to be erased by sentiment or reason. Towards even her memory he remained implacable.

His father had lived for a few months in the restaurant, and pushed out of the way in the little room that later they gave to Philip was a trunkful of his books. There were letters and photographs among them. When a lad still, Philip discovered his father's ambition to paint, that he had been as alien to the town and Philip's mother as was Philip now himself. The books were difficult and bewildering, more of them on art and literature than theology; but only half-understood, beyond his reach, they added to the stature of the man who had owned and read them.

And because of this he made a hero of his father, and in lonely, childish defiance of his surroundings, resolved to be another like him.

It became a kind of worship in which there was an effort perhaps to maintain his own self-respect, a belief in his own importance. He was the son of this hero: there was some compensation, at least, for being the son also of a common waitress. In his taking sides it never seems to have occurred to him that if these two were really as he thought, then the moral responsibility for his existence could hardly have been where he placed it. But he was just a boy then, and even now he feels a situation better than he can think his way through it. And his father all this time belonged to the escape world of his imagination, and his mother to the drab, sometimes sordid reality of the restaurant.

He still has the photographs, and among them there's a face you might take to be his own. The same aloof, self-sufficient eyes, the same half-sensitive, half-haughty lips. Yet he says that as a boy he was thin and puny, so self-conscious that he always walked with a sidle, his eyes cast down. They say let a man look long and devotedly enough at a statue and in time he will resemble it. Perhaps that accounts for what he grew to be.

He was seventeen when a preacher who had gone to college with his father came to town. Philip at this time was a serious-minded, presentable enough lad, and the preacher suggested his entering the ministry. The Church would educate him, and in the summer, between college terms, give him a rural appointment where he could earn a little towards his next year's expenses. He accepted. He didn't know about me then. He thought that at the longest it would be for three or four years.

The restaurant where he lived faced the railway station. At six o'clock the train came in and stayed half an hour for supper. There was a bell for him that he had to stand out on the sidewalk ringing to attract the passengers. Sometimes, because he looked timid and uncomfortable, the passengers jeered a little; and because there was the glamor of distance about them, because they came out of the unknown, went into it again, their laughter was harder than the town's. It passed sentence on him. It said that the outside world had no place for him either, that there too he would be unwanted and deplored.

His dream must have been hard building. Lonely and embittered, he must have often come close to breaking point.

If his father's books gave life a purpose, quickened his imagination, they crushed him too, sometimes, brought home to him his insignificance. He condemned himself because they were difficult, because he was too immature to master them. He read on doggedly, but he wondered if all he was fit for was peeling potatoes and ringing his bell. Likely he often felt defeated, that it wasn't much use trying to make a stand against the town.

And then, offering escape, there was the Church.

He had grown up feeling it hostile, a force aligned against him. In Sunday School, where they sent him regularly, he was tolerated, left on the edge of things. Another might have forced himself forward, insisted on his place, but he was of a less aggressive grain. Whatever it might profess, he soon found, the Church was for only the approved and respectable part of the town. Little Main Street churches, no bigger than their Main-Street-minded members, are like that sometimes, and a little Main Street church was the only one he knew. Right or wrong, he made it the measure for all churches.

He began to realize, too, that his father's attitude had been almost the same as his own. There were letters to prove it, the books on everything but theology. It had been his father's first pulpit, the first real test of his convictions. Just a few months and he was realizing it was not the work he was fitted for. At bottom, I suppose, it was a matter of temperament, not convictions anyway. But the thought that here at least he and his father were together encouraged Philip, made him unyielding in his defiance. The very way they put their eyebrows up in Sunday School brought out his pride. They could deplore his bastardy no more than he despised their Main Street minds.

There were no suspicions of this when he made application to enter the ministry. It was enough that he was studious, quiet, hard-working. These were the virtues of the bitter, solitary existence forced on him by the Church's very attitude of condescension, but to the Church they were only evidence of its own fine, uplifting influence.

The plan was practicable. The Church was willing to lend him what he needed, repayable on convenient terms after he was ordained. Fifteen and twenty years ago in the West, with fewer men available and a university education more difficult to obtain, it was only by making such assistance possible that the Church could keep its pulpits filled. He was young, had no responsibilities. There was only himself to stand in his way.

It was a hard acceptance. This Church that had tolerated him, that stood for the respectable, self-righteous part of the town, that all these years he had pitted himself against; he was to turn to it now, be humble about it, pull a grateful face.

It was his pride against what he wanted most from life, his instincts to be frank and upright against his instinct to fulfill himself. Days when to go was sane and right, against days when he dared not go and face himself. And always the urge to create, the belief that he could create. Always the encroaching little town, always the train, roaring away to the world that lay beyond.

He was in his fourth year at college when I met him. Still friendless, solitary, his lips cold with dogged iron. The outside world, that the train came out of, went into again, it had disappointed him. Now he was straining towards still another outside world, farther than the little university city, than the Middle West.

The new life around him, that he had spent all his life hungering for, he was no more a part of it than he had been of the old. He had expected too much. In the little town he had been alone with his books, no one to pace himself against, and in an effort to prepare himself for what he imagined the standards of the outside world to be, he had attained an intellectual maturity that in college isolated him from his fellow-students.

He had never learned to play or relax. He wanted friends but had been too long alone, already was a little darkened. After living so long and intensely in the future he couldn't accept a reality which, instead of the new way of life he had been striving for, turned out to be just an extension of the old. When he did try to make friends it was in the wrong places, among people who seemed to possess and offer this new way of life, who deceived him with a shallow poise and sophistication. His naïve, country-town eyes saw a kind of glamor, I suppose, and for a while believed in it.

He was forever being disillusioned, forever finding people out and withdrawing into himself with a sense of hurt and grievance. The only artistic life he could make contact with was genteel and amateurish. It wasn't what he expected or needed; he went on studying alone.

He had confidence now. The new life had been a disappointment, but it had made him aware of himself. Had I not met him then he might have got away as he planned, eventually realized his ambitions.

For a long time he held aloof. At heart, I think, he was distrustful not only of me but all my kind. It was friendship he wanted, someone to realize in flesh and blood the hero-worship that he had clung to all through his hard adolescence. He would just half-yield himself to me, then stand detached, self-sufficient. It was as if this impulse to seek me out made him feel guilty, as if he felt he were being false to himself. Perhaps, too, he knew instinctively that as a woman I would make claims upon him, and that as an artist he needed above all things to be free.

I was patient. I tried hard. Now sometimes I feel it a kind of triumph, the way I won my place in his life despite him; but other times I see his eyes frustrated, slipping past me, a spent, disillusioned stillness in them, and I'm not so sure. It's hard to feel yourself a hindrance, to stand back watching a whole life go to waste. Sometimes Philip himself seems to know what I feel, and in his awkward way tries to make me understand it's not his wife that keeps him a small-town preacher, but the limitations of his hand and eye. Only I'm not so sure about that either. Sometimes I wish I could be.

Anyway we were married. The next year there was a baby, stillborn. Philip still owed the Church; debts started piling up. He had counted on a salary of at least fifteen hundred dollars once he was ordained, but hard years and poor appointments kept it to a thousand.

That was when he tried to write. He had no literary ambitions – it was just that he hoped to earn enough writing to escape the Church before it was too late – but still the artist in him was uppermost, and instead of trying to make his story popular and salable, he pushed it on somberly the way he felt it ought to go.

It was a failure, of course, and it exhausted him. We just went on. Tillsonborough, Kelby, Crow Coulee – now Horizon. There hasn't been much change, either in the towns or in us. He still draws, cold little ghosts of his dream that are stronger than their uselessness. He's alone in his study with them now, quieter even than he usually is. It was the train today, reminding him again of the outside world he hasn't reached.

Wednesday Evening, April 26

It's been warm and sunny today; the snow already is disappearing fast. Philip has a cold after our walk in the snowstorm yesterday, but manfully he won't be put to bed or nursed, and coughs on dry and hacking like a martyr.

Mrs. Ellingson heard him this mornmg when she was over with two fresh eggs for breakfast. Later, up in Dawson's store, she told Mrs. Finley, who told Mrs. Pratt, who told Mrs. Wenderby. By early afternoon I was entertaining six of them.

It was awkward for a while. Arriving with offerings of soup and jelly and cough sirup for an invalid, they were rather put out to find him up on the roof robustly shovelling off the snow before it melted. I showed them the leak in the ceiling, explained he was up there of his own free will, but they wouldn't be convinced. Mrs. Pratt said colds in the spring were often dangerous. Mrs. Bird, with a wither in her voice, said professionally that colds were always dangerous. I smiled, asked them in turn wasn't it a lovely day.

Presently Philip came in, and with a curt nod and another cough passed on directly to his study. That wasn't just to their liking either though, and even tea and sponge cake left the atmosphere a little strained. Mrs. Finley thought going for a walk in a snowstorm when we didn't need to was the most ridiculous thing she ever heard of. Mrs. Bird sniffed Mrs. Wenderby's homemade cough sirup, and said it was the sort of thing the medical profession was always up against. I played *Chapel Chimes* for them finally, imitating the sound of bells to everyone's astonishment and my own return to grace. They decided music was nice in the home, and told me what fine musicians their sisters and cousins used to be.

Then Mrs. Pratt, the postmistress, thought I should heat some of her soup for Philip while she was there to see I did it right. It had a gray, gluey look, but she followed me into the study with it, and stood beside him watching till he had it finished. "He's very fond of soup," I assured her. "His throat, though, hurts him still. Yes, I know how to mix a gargle. He has to be careful of his voice for Sunday."

The others didn't like such favoritism, and when we came back were standing up and putting on their gloves. "I'll have to get a chin strap," Mrs. Bird said, pulling her old tweed hat down hard around her ears. "No pins these days – the wind keeps taking it."

And Mrs. Finley smiled at her appraisingly and said, "You'd wonder at the wind."

When they were gone Philip took sick at his stomach, and for supper had nothing but strong black tea and toast. He was a little morose about it, inclined to blame the soup and me. Paul Kirby dropped in later to spend the evening, but I asked him would he come tomorrow for supper instead. "Nausea," I explained. "I'm afraid he wouldn't be very good company."

He looked so severe for a minute I thought I had offended him, but it was just that *nausea* is from a Greek word meaning *ship* and is, therefore, etymologically speaking, an impossibility on dry land. When I promised in future to remember, he was nice again, and with a little bow said he would look forward to partaking of our hospitality.

Thursday Evening, April 27

It's nearly midnight. Paul's gone, and I've put Philip to bed. There's a high, rocking wind that rattles the windows and creaks the walls. It's strong and steady like a great tide after the winter pouring north again, and I have a queer, helpless sense of being lost miles out in the middle of it, flattened against a little peak of rock.

I stood at the door a while after saying good night to Paul. The town, too, seems clinging to a little peak, the rays of light from lamps and windows like so many thin-drawn tentacles. The stars are out, up just above the wind. They light the sky a little, and leave it vast and dark down here.

I spent the whole day worrying about Paul, and then unexpectedly Philip was nice to him. We had sausages and mashed potatoes for supper, and tarts I baked this morning hecause there was the jelly they brought for Philip yesterday to fill them with. Paul never smiles or laughs, but his seriousness is the kind you can relax against. He keeps saying that he's a country boy and always will be, apologetically, yet as if he were proud of it, too.

"Your company manners," I cautioned Philip as he picked a tart up in his fingers, and Paul said quickly, "You use it too? They laugh at that word, but it's really right you know."

"Who?" in the bliss of my provincial ignorance I asked, "Who laugh at what word?"

"People of the world, with background – sophisticates – *company* for *guests* – but actually it means the ones you break bread with – the most appropriate word of all."

There was an inflection to his voice you couldn't define, almost hurt, almost complacent, that made me wonder had a sophisticate one time laughed at him. His eyes were narrowed as he spoke, bitten a little with perplexity at the uselessness of being right against the world.

In appearance he's a farm boy, compactly, sturdily built, with strong, simple hands, and a brown, weathered skin that makes his hair bleached-looking, and his eyes for the first glance or two emotionless and pale. He keeps a horse still, goes riding every morning and afternoon: "A three-year-old bronco from my brother's ranch. I'll ride round some afternoon and let you see him. Harlequin – a skewbald. Fast and smooth – just like a rocking chair. If ever you'd like to take him out –"

I explained that Horizon might not approve, and he went on to tell us about one of the boys at school he lets go riding. Steve was the first name, Rumanian or Hungarian, about twelve or thirteen, his mother dead and his father a laborer on the railroad. Not very well looked-after, living in a little shack near the station with his father and some other woman. Sensitive and high-strung, hot-blooded, quick-fisted.

"The horse means a lot to him. They've baited him so much he seldom fights back now, just tries to slip away by himself. It's the sort of thing that can't be lived down. The boys would forget about it, but their parents won't let them. It's the only case of open immorality in the town. For the sake of their own self-righteousness they've got to make the most of it."

His eyes were fixed on the lamp in the center of the table, the reflection of the flame making them sharp and resentful. "The horse is good for him. Good for his self-respect. You can't ride a horse and feel altogether worthless, or be altogether convinced that society's little world is the last word. If I had a boy of my own that's what he'd do. There's no better way to grow a mind."

We were silent a minute; then a sudden awareness of constraint and tension made me glance at Philip. His eyes, too, were on the lamp. Sharp and resentful with the reflection, just as Paul's had been, but with a combative kind of bitterness that was their own. His lips were thin, curled a little, as if they were drawn that way in scornful suffering. There was something tender in his face, written over with something hard and cruel.

He met my glance and resented it. While Paul went on talking I could feel him flare. It was as if he were helpless for a moment before a spasm of hatred for me. We've lived so long together that we sense and know such things. It was some memory, perhaps, evoked by what Paul had said about the boy, some vague, half-wishful thought for the boy of his own I haven't given him. And then, ill-timed, my glance to make him aware of me – a precipitant, crystallizing to anger whatever there was in his mind just then rankling and unsatisfied, clearing his eyes for a moment so that he could see me in his life for what I actually am. The anger passed, and he sat with his eyes on me, cold, somehow condemning; and then with a deliberate movement, ignoring me, pushed back his chair and invited Paul to go into the study.

And it wasn't just my imagination. Paul felt it too. I saw him look from me to Philip, then drop his eyes. At the study door he glanced back a second, hesitating; but afraid that he might take sides I turned my back, and pretended to be busy with the dishes.

I sat alone out here all evening, trying to read, trying to sew, trying to understand. At ten o'clock I made coffee and took it in to them. "None for you?" Paul asked, and I lied, "I've had mine." Philip kept his eyes down, stirring his coffee round and round till it spilled a little into his saucer.

Watching him I realized he was uneasy and ashamed about what had happened, and when Paul was gone I pretended to be concerned about his cough, said how queer and feverish his eyes had looked at the supper table. It relieved him to think I hadn't really understood what had come over him; for the first time in all our years together he let me put him to bed and rub his chest with liniment. I'm waiting now till he's asleep before going to bed myself. It's quiet for a while, and I'm all ready; then above the wind I hear his hacking little cough again.

Sunday Evening, April 30

The wind keeps on. It's less than a week since the snowstorm, and the land is already dry again. The dust goes reeling up the street in stinging little scuds. Over the fields this morning on our way to Partridge Hill there were dark, foreboding clouds of it.

Service was difficult this morning. They were listening to the wind, not Philip, the whimpering and strumming through the eaves, and the dry hard crackle of sand against the windows. From the organ I could see their faces pinched and stiffened with anxiety. They sat in tense, bolt upright rows, most of the time their eyes on the ceiling, as if it were the sky and they were trying to read the weather.

Lawson, the man who reminds me of Philip, was there. Alone this time; Peter, their boy who limps, had been put to bed again for a few weeks, and Mrs. Lawson was home with him. "We'd like it if you could come round some time and play for him. We've been talking about you a lot since that other day." He was the only one who seemed indifferent to the wind.

Philip and Paul and I stood on the school steps till the congregation were all gone. The horses pawed and stamped as if they, too, felt something ominous in the day. One after another the democrats and buggies rolled away with a whir of wheels like pebbly thunder. From the top of Partridge Hill where the schoolhouse stands we could see the prairie smoking with dust as if it had just been swept by fire. A frightened, wavering hum fled blind within the telephone wires. The wind struck in hard, clenched little blows; and even as we watched each other the dust formed in veins and wrinkles round our eyes. According to the signs, says Paul, it's going to be a dry and windy year all through. With the countryman's instincts for such things he was strangely depressed this morning. Not the history or derivation of a single word.

Tonight again in town it was the same, hymns and sermon lost against the wind. Even though it was a different congregation, that had come intent on its new spring hats and coats, on seeing that all the little proprieties of the service were carried out with nicety. They sat in the same bolt upright rows, listening to the same strum and whimper through the eaves. Their faces, too, were set and drawn, not with the stark anxiety I saw this morning, but with an apprehensive sense of feebleness and isolation.

I found it hard myself to believe in the town outside, houses, streets, and solid earth. Mile after mile the wind poured by, and we were immersed and lost in it. I sat breathing from my throat, my muscles tense. To relax, I felt, would be to let the walls around me crumple in.

The wind was too strong for Philip or the choir, but Judith scaled it when she sang alone again before the closing hymn.

The rest of us, I think, were vaguely and secretly a little afraid. The strum and whimper were wearing on our nerves. But Judith seemed to respond to it, ride up with it, feel it the way a singer feels an orchestra. There was something feral in her voice, that even the pace and staidness of her hymn could not restrain.

"She stood there all the time so white and small," Philip said afterwards. "Unaware of herself."

It's seldom he listens to music, but as soon as she began tonight he turned in his chair behind the pulpit and sat with his eyes fixed on her all the way through the hymn. I could see him in the little mirror over the organ that's there for the organist to watch the progress of the collection plate, and know when it's time to taper off the offertory. Even after she had finished he sat a few minutes without stirring. There was an uneasy clearing of throats and rustling of hymn books as the congregation waited for him. They seemed trying to assure themselves of their existence and reality, to put the walls back in place and brace them there.

Afterwards, she looked so lost and ignored among the rest of the choir, I asked her home with us. But she was too self-conscious to talk, and after an uncomfortable half-hour stood up suddenly, and said Mrs. Wenderby would be wanting her for the children. I felt it had taken her the whole half-hour to muster the necessary courage.

When she was gone I tried to keep Philip out here in the living-room a while, but after pacing a few times in and out he slipped off to his study again, and very quietly closed the door.

Which was worse than if he had slammed it. It implied a pity for me, a regret for the way things stood between us, a helplessness to do anything about it. Not that things between us tonight are much different from any other night; it's just that there's so much of him unyieldable, unknowable, so much that must find or lose its way alone. And tonight, because of the wind, we both seem to know.

It's the most nerve-wracking wind I've ever listened to. Sometimes it sinks a little, as if spent and out of breath, then comes high, shrill and importunate again. Sometimes it's blustering and rough, sometimes silent and sustained. Sometimes it's wind, sometimes frightened hands that shake the doors and windows. Sometimes it makes the little room and its smug, familiar furniture a dramatic inconsistency, sometimes a relief. I sit thinking about the dust, the farmers and the crops, wondering what another dried-out year will mean for us.

We're pinched already. They gave us fifteen dollars this week, but ten had to go for a payment on the car. I'm running bills already at the butcher shop and Dawson's store. Philip needs shoes and a hat. His Sunday suit is going at the cuffs again, and it's shiny at the seat and knees. I sent for a new spring hat for myself the other day, but it was just a dollar forty-five, and won't be much.

There's the dinner, too, that we owe the Finleys still. Even when you have money it's hard sometimes to know what you ought to do. For a plain meal once in Crow Coulee I earned the reputation of being a shiftless housewife; and another time, when I went to more expense, I set our guests talking all over town about my extravagance that they were paying for. In any case I mustn't let it go another week. Every time I meet Mrs. Finley I imagine her eyes are saying When? We can manage a tin of salmon anyway, and trust they leave the twins at home.

Tuesday Evening, May 2

Paul rode round this afternoon to let me see his skewbald bronco Harlequin. A temperamental, knowing little beast, that plunged hysterically halfway across the street at sight of me, and then, after all his histrionic dash had been displayed, came back the best of friends to slaver on my dress and hear me say to Paul how handsome and astonishing he was.

Which was what Paul, too, had come to hear me say, and which, when I said it, made him push his big sombrero back complacently and cock a dextrous leg around the saddle horn. I noticed that he was not without a certain histrionic dash himself today, rigged out in all his cowboy togs, boots, leather chaps, a bright red spotted handkerchief, and giving the temperamental Harlequin just rein enough to make a good display of horsemanship.

"You put all those clothes on every time you ride?" I asked, and leaning down to try the saddle girths he said, "Not every time. Mostly for Harlequin – he's used to them, and sulks a little if I don't. The same with the saddle – not much sense such a big one when you aren't out punching cattle, but he's more himself with it than any other. His mother won it in a race six years ago – they're the only two that have ever had it on. She was a little skewbald too – Annabelle – after a girl the cowboys used to know with yellow moles."

He went philological then – *mustang* meant *stray*, *pinto* meant *painted*, a skewbald was a pinto with markings any color but black – and then as we talked and petted Harlequin a lad came up unnoticed and stood three or four feet away, strong dark eyes fixed on us impassively, waiting to be spoken to or dismissed.

At first glance you would take them for Oriental eyes, a blind drawn over a window, that could be seen through only from inside; and then you saw it was just a feint of indifference, dubious, uneasy, with a natural, boyish eagerness behind.

It was Steve, the boy Paul lets go riding twice a week. He came forward when Paul nodded to him, and with shy, possessive firmness laid a hand on Harlequin alongside mine. After a moment or two he glanced up at me and smiled, companionably, as if to say how good it was to feel him there. Then he started rummaging in his pockets, and brought out two dirty lumps of sugar.

While Harlequin munched them Philip came out of the house. Critically for a minute he and Steve looked each other over. Philip's eyes were narrowed a little, his mouth relaxed and absent, as if his vision just then were taking all his energies of concentration. He didn't see either Paul or me. We waited without a word till they were finished.

I turned then to look at Steve again myself. Something in Philip's expression made me. And this time I saw an ominously good-looking boy. The limbs were free and well-proportioned. The shoulders were broadening a little, establishing a balance with the slender, undeveloped body, giving promise already of form and gracefulness. It took a moment to see it through his dirty shirt and ragged overalls; and another to make allowance for the untidy way his hair hung down around his ears, to see the strength and fineness of his features, decisive already, almost mature.

"It's Mr. Bentley, the minister," Paul said, and without speaking Steve started stroking Harlequin again. I stroked him too, and when he took my collar in his teeth and gave a pull let out a sudden, high-pitched laugh. I remember the laugh, because there was such an abrupt, self-conscious silence afterwards. All four of us for a minute were intent on Harlequin. I ignored Philip, and Philip ignored me. A blast of dusty wind struck suddenly, and we blinked and screened our eyes, and stood uneasily a moment listening to the moan of it across the town.

Then a tumbleweed came bouncing up the street, and veering suddenly struck Harlequin across the flank. With a snort he reared and bolted down the street a little way; then as Paul drew hard on the reins reared a second time, and for a moment hung in mid-air almost motionless.

There was no dash of showmanship this time. They both looked ashamed when they came back, Harlequin's sides jerking in and out as if they were going to burst, Paul leaning over to pat his shoulder, doing his best to be nonchalant.

"Just a colt," he said with an apologetic shrug. "I was harder on him than I should have been. When you're taken off your guard that way you forget how strong you are, and what a brutal thing a bit is."

"I'd like to be on him when he jumps like that," Steve spoke up unexpectedly. "And I wouldn't fall off either."

He spoke the last sentence with a little flare of defiance in his voice, as if it were Paul's way to be somewhat skeptical of his horsemanship; and then turning round and looking up at Philip, "I do go riding – and I don't fall off."

He speaks good English, but with a force and inflection that in contrast to our monotones sounds a little impetuous. His voice was quick and insistent now, as if it were of especial importance that Philip should be convinced. "One day it rained – and we were galloping down a hill, and he slipped three times and once came right to his knees –"

I didn't hear the rest. I was watching Philip. When Steve finished he smiled a little and put a hand on his shoulder and said, "Some day when Mr. Kirby's using his horse you'll have to come for a ride with me in the car. Some Saturday, when I've calls to make in the country. I'll let you know."

I glanced up at Paul, then turned to Harlequin again, and started running my fingers through his mane. I didn't look at Steve or Philip now, but I could feel them standing there, unaware of us, complete for the moment in themselves. I don't know what came over me – maybe just the wind, the plaintive way it whined. I seemed to feel myself vaguely threatened.

Then some boys came along the street, the Finley twins and others that I didn't know. At the sight of them Steve stiffened a second, the corners of his mouth pulled down, then without a word slipped off and disappeared around the church.

"He isn't a coward either," Paul said in a low, dispirited voice. "He was just afraid of what they might say to him in front of you. I suppose that for once he'd like to have someone think really well of him."

Philip at that pulled down the corners of his mouth too. He stood looking in the direction Steve had gone a moment, then gave a curt nod to Paul, and went inside.

He's scarcely spoken since. We had an omelette for supper, and toast and black currant jam and tea, but he ate abstractedly, and left the second piece of toast I forced on him untouched. "The wind gets on your nerves," he said when he caught me watching him. "It's the way it comes round the church, I think. With all this prairie you'd think they wouldn't have had to jam us up so close."

I didn't eat much either. I kept looking at him, trying to find something to say. Steve was on my mind. There was something rankling in me that my reason couldn't justify.

It's eleven now, and the wind has settled to a steady blow. The walls are creaking with the heave of it. To stop the rattling I've wadded rags along the windows, but on the roof there's a shingle working loose, and every few seconds it gives a buzz and stutter. The room is filled with a haze of dust like smoke, and it sways and heaves a little with the vibrations of the walls. The bells of the fuchsia sway a little too. There are seven of them now, and still more buds, and I'm going to need a bigger trellis soon.

A few minutes ago I knocked at Philip's study and went in, but he didn't want me, and I came away again. It's nearly always like that; sometimes I wonder why I go. I put my hand on his shoulder, and in acknowledgment he squeezed it a moment; then without looking up or speaking began to feint some little strokes and rubbings out till I had gone. For while I'm there he's actually helpless to draw a single line. He can't even sit out here in the living-room with me and read or write.

If I ask him he'll come all right and try, but I know him better now and never do.

It's a little street again tonight, false-fronted stores, a pool hall and a wind. You feel the wind, its drive and bluster, the way it sets itself against the town. The false fronts that other times stand up so flat and vacant are buckled down in desperation for their lives. They lean a little forward, better to hold their ground against the onslaughts of the wind. Some of them cower before the flail of dust and sand. Some of them wince as if the strain were torture. And yet you feel no sympathy, somehow can't be on their side. Instead you wait in impatience for the wind to work its will.

Saturday Evening, May 6

It's been a long week. A busy one, too – Ladies Aid at Mrs. Bird's, calls, choir practice, the Finleys for dinner – but all the little events that made it up have been rubbed out by the wind, rubbed out, or perhaps submerged in it, so that there's nothing left but Philip and me alone here, day after day, night after night, tensely aware of each other through the study door, listening to the whimper in the eaves.

So I'm going to have a garden. The way the wind keeps on, and all the signs for drought, it isn't likely anything will grow, but I'd rather be out in the wind and fighting it than in here listening to it creak the walls. It's so hollow and mournful when there's nothing to do but listen. You get so morbid and depressed.

That's why Philip and I must keep out of each other's way. Shutting himself up in his study doesn't help. We can still feel each other. When the wind sends him pacing I glance up as he passes, uncertain whether to speak or not, then twist my face into a feeble smile, and hurry off to the next room with a show of some activity. If I don't have the garden he's going to hate the sight of me by fall.

There's the town, of course, but I can't join in. I might feel different if it were our town, if we had come here years ago when it was just beginning, were part of its growth and struggle, if we owned one of the little false-fronted stores, if we could share in the hopes and ambitions and disappointments of its people.

But we're detached, strangers, seeing it all objectively; and when you see it that way it's just bickering and petty and contemptible.

Mrs. Wenderby, for instance, gave a bridge last week but didn't invite Mrs. Brooks, the butcher's wife, and now Mrs. Brooks is telling up and down the town that the Wenderbys owe a hundred-dollar butcher bill.

I hear it all from Mrs. Ellingson, who won't be snubbed and brings me regularly two fresh eggs. For such is the social hierarchy of a little town that despite her hats the minister's wife goes everywhere, meets everyone. Her prestige is second not even to that of proven leaders like the doughty Mrs. Wenderby. And with social ambitions of her own Mrs. Ellingson is quick to see I may be useful. Some day, with my prestige as a pry, she may work her way through the guarded doors of the elect. Whenever I want to have a tea, she says, she'll bake a cake and come in and help.

And that's why I need the garden. My fingers want to feel the earth, dig in it, burrow away till the town is out of sight and mind. The house huddles me. I need a tussle with the wind to make me straight again.

I had a garden once. The bright seed packages on display in one of the stores this morning reminded me.

It was the year after the baby was born, the year Philip was at work on his book. I used to say to myself, "By the time the poppies are out he'll have his book half-written. By the first snow he'll have reached the end. Next spring maybe we'll be away."

It was such a dark, clenched year for him, and all I could do to help was keep out of his way. That was why I had the garden, because when the dust was blowing, when the sun burned, and my arms were sore and tired, then it seemed that I was sharing in his struggle too. Somehow it brought me nearer to him, made me feel I mattered. The little leaves would shrivel in the heat, one by one curl up against the dusty earth. Sometimes I slanted shingles over them for shade, and every day I carried water for them from the pump three streets away. There were five nasturtiums, four yellow and a red. As fast as they bloomed the poppies lost their petals in the wind.

My present problem, though, is to get the digging done. The proprieties permit the mistress of the parsonage to grow a garden, to sow and weed and water like a lady, but hardly to put her foot to a fork or spade. Philip will have to do it. He's going to say that nothing will grow, and look uncomplimentary things at me, but he'll have to do it anyway. We mustn't stay all summer locked together in these little rooms. Even if I have to drive him to it playing the piano.

Monday Evening, May 8

It's dug. He didn't say much either, almost as if he understood. The fork has given him blisters on his hands, but he's better for the sun and wind. He looks browner, ruggeder. The unaccustomed exercise has tired him out, and made his muscles stiff and sore, but after supper we talked a while, and he's more relaxed than usual in his mind.

I kept watching him out of the window today, thinking how good it was to see the steady ply and rhythm of his body. Sometimes he'd wipe his sweaty forehead with his hand, sometimes he'd stand with his hat off letting the wind blow through his hair. He has the build and stride for out-of-doors. In these little rooms I seldom see him.

And I didn't know until I saw him standing out there straight and hatless in the wind how much of late he's let his shoulders sag, or how his movements in the house or on the street are all constrained. It makes me wish I had a garden for him every day, or a horse to ride, and a hat and chaps like Paul's.

We have two weeks' holidays in July, and Paul says we're to spend them at his brother's ranch, seventy or eighty miles straight west of here. There'll be horses to ride, a river to swim in, and bare wild hills for Philip to draw. Their contours, he says, are so strong and pure in form that just as they are they're like a modernist's abstractions. We'll see. I begin to know Paul, a homesick rancher with a streak of poetry in him posing as philology, and suspect that his enthusiasm oughtn't to be taken too literally.

Saturday Evening, May 13

True to his promise Philip took Steve to the country with him this afternoon. I could feel that he didn't want me along, so at noon I complained of a headache, and stayed home to finish putting in the garden.

At least that's maybe why I said I had a headache. When I think about it now I'm not so sure. He had three sick calls to make, one of them to the Lawson boy who wants to hear me play again, and maybe I was expecting to hear him say the drive would do me good, or that he'd better put his visits off until another time.

He didn't, though, and it was a long afternoon. All the flower seeds I could afford were already planted. There was nothing left but onions and potatoes.

The wind was hot and dry, and the sweat kept running down my face and stinging as it dried. I hoed with firm swift strokes at first, but in a little while my shoulders stiffened and my back began to ache. I kept on stubbornly, though, till the last hill of potatoes was planted, hurt at the unconcerned way Philip had gone off without me, afraid to face myself in the dark little house alone.

Just as I finished Paul came. It was for a book Philip had promised him, so while I washed myself and changed my dress I turned him into the study.

Then I joined him there, and we sat among the books till nearly suppertime. We didn't talk much. I like Philip's study, but I'm seldom in it. Not even when he's out, except to clean and dust. It's reserved somehow, distant, just like him. It's always loyal to him. It sees and knows him for what he really is, but it won't let slip a word. This study and the others before it – they're all the same. You don't obtrude. You don't take liberties. It's like being a child in the presence of grown-ups who have troubles that can't be explained to you. The books understand, but you don't.

They're old books, most of them, that he collected in his student days. We used to go round the secondhand stores together, and when he found something that he wanted I'd take it home with me for cleaning and repairing. I had heavy cloth for pasting on the backs, a hard, leathery finish to it so that I could take white ink and print the titles on again. There were dark red, blue and black, because I knew they'd look better contrasted that way when we had a study lined with shelves of them.

I still give him a book at Christmas and for his birthday. He still manages from time to time a few for himself. I know them all as well as he does – the covers anyway – and sometimes when I'm dusting I discover that he's slipped a new one in.

"For a town like this it's a library," Paul said with enthusiasm. "Everything but theology."

I told Paul then about the secondhand bookstores and the bindings I put on, and showed him some expensive volumes with color reproductions that Philip some way or other saved for when he couldn't even send his laundry out and had to do it in the bathroom basin late at night.

Paul slipped a book away at that, and with a wise look told me that Odin, god to the Norsemen, paid with an eye for a single draught from Mimer's well of wisdom. And the sirens who sang to lure Ulysses from his homeward course, their song was a promise, not of love or wine or idleness, but of knowledge of all things that pass on earth. Faust, too, the early Faust, before they made a tenor of him, it was for knowledge, not a mere comely Marguerite, that he made a compact with the devil and let himself be carried off alive to Hell.

And then we sat quiet a few minutes, while the books and rattling windowpanes continued, thinking impressively of wind and men, and the mystery of passage.

It's easy to sit like that with Paul – easier than with Philip. His hands lie quiet and simple. He's aware of you all the time, but it doesn't worry him, or set him fidgeting.

Then the clock out here struck half-past five, and not expecting that he would accept I invited him to stay for supper. He did, however, and I had to leave him looking at the books, and hurry off uptown for butter and a tin of meat.

I deliberated two or three minutes over some little heads of lettuce, spotted and limp and fifteen cents – made up my mind they weren't worth it, then recklessly went back and blew myself.

I was scarcely home when Philip came, and with him Steve for supper too. The tin of meat was small, so I had to whisper to serve himself and me with just a little, and not take any cake at all. I was glad, though, that I had such things to think about, and that Paul and Steve were there to ease the strain between us. I poured warm water into the kitchen basin for Steve to wash with, then while Philip watched took a comb and brush myself and tried to put a parting in his mat of hair. Over my shoulder I told Philip to go in and talk to Paul until the kettle boiled.

I don't remember much about the meal except that Steve's appetite was good and his table manners bad, that Paul said learnedly *sponge* cake didn't get its name from any resemblance to a sponge for washing with, but was a corrupted form of *Spanish* cake.

I remember, too, catching Philip's eyes on me as I noticed the way Steve used his fingers for his meat, and how with a quick sense of danger I tried to make amends for it by urging Steve to pass his plate for more, and telling him we'd have a better supper when he came to visit us again.

Afterwards Paul asked me to play, and because it had been such a humiliating afternoon I played brilliantly, vindictively, determined to let Philip see how easily if I wanted to I could take the boy away from him.

I succeeded, too. Steve came over and stood at the end of the piano, his face eager, a little flash in his eyes. "Pay us another visit soon," I said. "Philip doesn't care much for music, but we'll send him out and have a concert just ourselves."

It hurt Philip. At the time I approved, remembering the afternoon I'd spent out hoeing in the garden, but I wish now I had spared him. He stood so big and solitary saying good night to Steve, and when he came into the room again his face had such a white, forsaken look. He disappeared into his study, saying he had some changes to make in his sermon for tomorrow, but a while ago when I went in with coffee he was drawing again. There were papers littered on the floor, and just as I opened the door he crumpled up another. So quickly, before I might get a glimpse of it, that I imagine it must have been one of Steve.

"You'd be better with the door open, getting a little breeze," I ventured, but he sipped his coffee and said, "I like it shut."

As a rule he resists me more gently, with a furtive kind of care for my feelings. It must be Steve that's responsible for such bluntness, taking sides with him against a world of matrons and respectability.

Tuesday Evening, May 16

There's a dance in the little community hall tonight, over on the other side of town.

The wind's from that direction, not quite so strong as it has been lately. From the garden I can hear a saxophone, and underneath it every now and then the throbbing of a drum.

For more than an hour I stood out in the back yard listening to it. Through the darkness the saxophone was wavering and slender like a fine thread of light. It was far enough away to be poignant and mellow; and in the drum throb there was zest and urgency.

I imagined the couples moving round the floor, the atmosphere of carefree excitement and enthusiasm. And there was a remoteness about it that made me feel shut away from life, too old, forgotten. It was like standing in the darkness, hidden yourself, watching figures round a fire.

Then Philip came out of the house and stood a few minutes listening with me. "I heard the door," he said. "I wondered if anything was wrong."

"Just listening to the music," I answered, casually edging along the fence a little nearer to him. The foxtrot finished; there was an encore, then a waltz. Finally, in a helpless wooden kind of voice he said, "I suppose, if I knew how, we could dance a little just ourselves out here."

I slipped my arm through his then to let him know that it wasn't the dance I cared about, but he didn't understand. Or at least pretended he didn't understand, for I could feel that his arm was helpless and wooden too. When he went into the house again I walked up the street and across the prairie a little way, and sat down on a stone I found and looked back at the lights and tried to pick out ours. The wind was warm and soft, like the darkness blowing past. I sat there till a car swung out of town and swept me with its glare. There were some youngsters in it who had had a drink too many, and slowing up they called "Hi Lonesome – jump in and we'll take you to a better dance. We don't like this one either."

Which scared me then, and makes me feel how stale and cupboardlike and prim this little house is now. There are dusty, gray-winged moths tonight, that thud on the chimney of the lamp and glance away again with such incessant regularity that you think at last they must be worked on little springs or wires. There are six of them, and one that flew too low through the shaft of heat above the flame, and fluttered away to the floor somewhere with singed and crippled wings.

Friday Evening, May 19

It's Steve again.

There was a fight a few days ago among the section men over the woman that has been living with his father. They left town together yesterday, and Steve's coming here tomorrow morning.

Mrs. Wenderby was in this afternoon with the details. "A low, drunken lot anyway," she summed them up. "The town's well rid of them. We women should have run them out long ago."

I asked what would happen now to Steve.

"They say he doesn't belong to Kulanich anyway. He got drunk one night and told it in the poolroom. The Catholics have plenty of places they can send him to. Just now he's living down in a shack near the railway with a couple of section hands."

At the supper table I asked Philip what he had heard. He finished his tea slowly, and nodded.

"What about Steve? Have you seen him?"

He nodded again, looking past me. "Just for a minute this morning. He wasn't at school."

"And does he know what's going to become of him? Will they send him to an orphanage, or bring his father back?"

"I didn't ask him. He seemed in a hurry."

He gave up the effort of his nonchalance then, and met my eyes squarely. And his face had such a tired, haggard look that all at once I understood. There wasn't time to be discreet or think of consequences. For the moment all I could feel was his pity and hunger for the boy. It came to me the kind of life that as a boy he himself had lived; and guiltily again I remembered the boy of his own that I haven't given him.

So I breathed hard and deep a minute, tried to look casual about it, then said, "It's a pity to put him in an institution. I'd like to take him myself for a while – just to teach him table manners."

He looked up quickly, furtively, to see before he spoke whether I really meant it or not. I caught his glance, held it for a moment, nodded.

"If you think you can browbeat a few more dollars out of Finley and his church board. I noticed the other night that there's nothing wrong with his appetite."

He wrinkled his forehead, trying to be not too eager. "The only thing is we can't take him for just a while. It'll have to be for good or not at all. You know it's a big undertaking."

I do know – now.

At the time I wasn't thinking about Steve at all, just Philip. He was sitting there in front of me with such a white, hopeless look on his face; somehow I knew that what I was doing was the right thing to do.

It still is, maybe, but I begin to have my doubts. Twelve years alone together, just the two of us, all wrapped up in our own little ways, our own little day-to-day routine – and overnight now a son. A twelve-year-old son – twelve years behind him that have been different from our twelve years – twelve years that we'll be a long time wiping out.

Blood, too, behind him that's different from ours. Hungarian, or Rumanian, or Russian – we don't know even that. And whatever crops out, whatever happens, we're responsible. We take him for good, or not at all. And we take him.

To say nothing of what the town's attitude is going to be, and the fact that he's a Roman Catholic, and that Philip's a Protestant minister in a bigoted Protestant town. I'm wondering, too, where the money's coming from – clothes, schoolbooks, a schoolboy's appetite. I know Philip, and if he wrangles an extra ten dollars out of the board he'll think he's doing handsomely. We haven't even a bed for the boy, and Philip's fetching him in the morning.

I'm not saying anything to Philip, though. He's so blissfully unaware of it all – and soon enough he's going to knock his head against realities.

He's in his study now, quiet as usual, but earlier he slipped away for a walk by himself, and then when he came back kept making excuses out here to talk about Steve. This unexpected advent of a son, I must admit, has brought a little life and enthusiasm to his face, taken some of the sag out of his shoulders. He kept pacing up and down when he was out here, and his step for the first time in years had a ring. There was eagerness and vitality radiating from him to make me aware how young he still is, how handsome and tall and broad-shouldered. Which if it lasts is going to make things harder still, I'm afraid, seeing that Steve hasn't rejuvenated me, too.

Saturday Evening, May 20

There's a fretful, high little pull of wind round the corners of the house tonight. The moths are thick; the lamp's burned nearly dry. It was such a tiring day I persuaded Steve to go to bed before nine o'clock, and now, in the long heavy silence, I rather wish I hadn't.

I borrowed a cot and mattress from Mrs. Ellingson this morning, and as it's warm weather now, cleared out the lean-to shed behind the kitchen, and did my best at fixing it up as a little bedroom for him. It's not bad. At breakfast when I suggested it Philip stiffened. It sounded, I suppose, as if I weren't intending to treat Steve with enough consideration, as if I were trying to put him out of the way; and though Philip didn't say a word I could see his lips go white with resentment.

So to redeem myself I had to bring in the woodbox and put it under the kitchen table, right where it's in the way of my feet, find a place for my broom and mop and dusters behind the stove, and for the present anyway take down the curtains on one of the windows in the bedroom.

As soon as Steve came this morning I set him and Philip carrying out trunks and boxes to the woodshed. Then when they were at the barber shop I cleaned and scrubbed and put the curtains up, draped a little chintz round a shelf that's been holding some of my kitchen odds and ends, and replaced them with a lamp and half a dozen books.

Steve thinks it's all right. He says he's never had a room before that he didn't have to share with someone else, and this afternoon without telling us he went home to fetch pictures and a little table.

"How did you get in?" I asked when he came back. Kulanich went off leaving debts, and the house is locked until along with the furniture it can be put up for sale. "I thought Mr. Wenderby had the key."

He winked slyly and rummaged in his pockets. "But they didn't know about this one. I'll go back tonight for some other things if you like."

Philip took the key and promptly went over to Wenderby with it, but he forgot the little table that Steve brought along with the pictures. After supper when he remembered, I argued no; taking it back now would amount to declaring Steve a thief, just when it's so important that the town think well of him. After all it's a nice little table, with a drawer and a shelf and not a scratch, and I don't want to give him the one in the living-room that I keep the fuchsia on.

The pictures aren't the kind that Philip would have chosen, but for the present anyway he's let Steve put them up. I stood a moment looking at a spaniel carrying a gory duck, then smiled round craftily at Philip to remind him how critical he always is of my taste. "Just the same," he countered, thrusting his hands into his pockets and looking incredibly smug about it, "just the same it was what he noticed first, that the walls were bare. Wait a year – and of his own accord you'll see him put some others up."

More disturbing, though, is a Sacred Heart lithograph of the Virgin Mary, and a little crucifix that he says used to belong to his mother. They're both up, too, prominently, the crucifix where he can reach it from his bed. Very fine and broad-minded of us, I have to admit, only what's Horizon going to say?

It's been an expensive day. After they had been to the barber's Philip took Steve into Dawson's store, and the result was overalls, two blue shirts, socks and underwear, a pair of canvas shoes with rubber soles. As outfittings go it's hardly what you would call an expensive one, but I've learned to spend every dollar with such thrift and foresight that when they arrived with all the packages I forgot my prudence for a moment, and failed to look particularly pleased about them.

"Well?" Philip dared me, opening things up. "Don't you think they're all right?" and making a quick recovery I said, "Of course – only you should have told me you were getting them. A man doesn't know – there's not much body to these shirts. It usually pays in the long run to get something a little better."

His eyes had been on me the same way all day, daring me to look my disapproval. And I can't help it. I like Steve, and at the same time I resent him. I grudge every minute he and Philip are alone together.

I knew this morning after he'd had a bath, and Philip brought him out of the bedroom dressed up in his new clothes. He had on one of Philip's ties. His head was up; there was a little glint in his eyes. I saw the shy, self-conscious way he was pressing against Philip, Philip's hands so firm and possessive on his shoulders, and I laughed and said quickly, "What a difference a tie and a haircut can make. You're just as good-looking now as Philip."

Then I hurried with the dinner, a better one than we usually have, and while we ate kept my expression innocent of anything that Philip might think was disapproval of the way Steve used his knife and fork. Manners can come later – even not at all. Philip's jaw is out stubborn already, waiting for the outcry of the town, and the important thing is to convince him that I'm firmly on his side. For a little while anyway, till Steve blows over. If history repeats itself it may not be so very long.

For Philip isn't aware of Steve yet. Not Steve the boy, the whistle and fidgets reality that he's going to have to live with for the next six or seven years.

He hasn't seen him with his eyes yet, just his pity and imagination. An unwanted, derided little outcast, exactly what he used to be himself. It's plain enough: as he thrusts out his chin to meet the town it's his own fight still. As he starts in to dream and plan for the boy it's his own life over again. Steve is to carry on where he left off. Steve is to do the things he tried to do and failed.

For Philip's a born dreamer, and the last few years what with the Church and the Main Streets and me, he hasn't had much chance to dream. That's what has been wrong with him. He hasn't been able to get above reality. Dreams that ignored us were just fantasy. Dreams that included us weren't worthy of the name.

Which explains, perhaps, why Steve just now is so important. Philip has taken him for Pegasus, and gone off to the clouds again.

So instead of resenting Steve I ought really to be sorry for him. When their ride's over and they're back on earth he'll have scant pasturage from Philip. After a while the pity and imagination are going to run out; and there's going to be left just an ordinary, uninspiring boy.

All I have to do is wait. Steve's little whistle and the way he taps his feet will be my allies. In the meantime it's making Philip more like he used to be. His eyes tonight didn't have such a foiled, uneasy look as usual, and the forthright ring in his step that I noticed last night persists. It's something. Even though he doesn't last himself, Steve may help Philip back where he belongs. Initiative, belief in himself – that's all he needs. There's a lot left still for a man at thirty-six. We may be packing our trunks and taking leave of Horizon sooner than we think.

Sunday Evening, May 21

Paul's been shopping too. A new blue suit with a fancy stripe, stunning tan shoes, and a pearl-gray fedora that against such a weather-tanned complexion makes him look like a farmer at a picnic in his Sunday best. He arrived to go to Partridge Hill this morning with a slightly sheepish air, feigned a look of surprise badly when I said how nice he looked, and then went out to the kitchen for a drink so that he could steal a glance or two at himself in the little mirror that hangs above the sink.

How did the coat fit across the shoulders, he asked me presently, and did I like the fedora straight or at a little tilt? I showed him at just what tilt, then on a sudden impulse nipped off one of my precious fuchsias and pinned it on his lapel. He said that fuchsia was called after a botanist with a name something the same, that the suit had cost twenty-five dollars, and the shoes seven. Then I looked round at Steve, and quickly nipped off another fuchsia for him. He had been so proud of his overalls and canvas shoes until Paul came. He thanked me, held out his shirt co-operatively so I wouldn't stick the pin in him – but long before we reached Partridge Hill I noticed that he'd got rid of it.

During the first prayer Paul got rid of his, too. From the organ I saw him bend down low, then slip his hand up stealthily to his lapel. Joe Lawson, the man who looks like Philip, was sitting across the aisle from him, just a freshly-ironed work shirt on, and blue overalls nearly white with washing. And Paul, dressed up so naïvely in his finery, felt it a rebuke. Other times he stands round talking after the service, but in shame for his shoes and fedora today he slipped off to the car and waited in the back seat till we were ready to go.

For the wind and dust keep on, and their faces all are set with a numbness of anxiety. Along the road there are drifts of dust two and three feet deep. Sometimes the fence posts are almost buried. Here and there you can see a faint tinge of green, but most of the seed has been blown out and lost. Some are going to seed again this coming week, in hopes the wind won't last; but most of them think the same as Paul, that it's going to be a dry and windy year all through.

It makes me wonder how things are going to be with us. The crop is the town's bread and butter too; and the first place to feel the pinch is the collection plate. We're behind already with the car, and now that Steve's here the store accounts will climb just twice as fast. I was looking at him in church tonight, and the overalls won't do. I see in the catalogue that suits for boys his age are from seven dollars up, but they're sure to be dearer in the Horizon stores.

And it's the Horizon stores where we're supposed to deal. Mrs. Pratt, the postmistress, must have noticed my hat when it came: I've been hearing all week about people who earn their money in the town but spend it somewhere else. It's all very well sending Philip to the church board, but if he goes too often or becomes insistent they'll know that Steve's responsible. And they're resentful enough of our taking him as it is. There's a storm brewing. In church tonight the atmosphere was already charged with it.

"Of course what we're hearing isn't really true," Mrs. Finley smiled at us after the service. "Stories do get twisted so."

Quickly, before Philip could be untactful, I assured her it was quite true.

"You mean, of course," Miss Twill spoke up, "just till other arrangements can be made. Naturally you wouldn't think of keeping him."

I said we did, though, and to get the upper hand of her, countered quickly, "Why not?"

"The Roman Catholics have so many places of their own that he could go to. If you really want a boy to adopt there are surely enough good Protestants."

"At his age you'll never change him over. Catholics are like that, you know."

"It seems rather dangerous. You've heard, I suppose, what the blood behind him is?"

And all the while Philip stood with his hands on Steve's shoulders, a formidably big, impressive man in contrast, his own shoulders hunched and gathered a little, his lips clenched bloodless with restraint.

One by one they glanced up at him, gave a sickly little smile to finish off their say, and sidled out the door. Presently we were alone except for Judith, who usually stays a few minutes after the choir to gather the hymn books and music. Then she came over and looked up at him for a minute too. He met her glance, and for the first time I saw the whiteness of her face give way to a little flush of color. She turned to go, but I asked her would she like to come with me for a walk. There was something about Philip's expression just then that warned me that it might be to my advantage to leave him and Steve for a little while alone.

So we walked up the railroad track about a mile, and then sat down against a bank where we wouldn't feel the wind. We stayed there till it was dark. I told her about Steve and the store accounts and what Horizon thinks. She sat tossing pebbles at a big white stone across the track, and when I finished said that she thought a man like Mr. Bentley could be trusted to do what was right.

I laughed at her earnestness, and said, "Even preachers aren't infallible. You don't know him yet."

But letting her handful of pebbles fall she insisted, "I think I do, though. And I think I'd trust him."

Then, tossing her pebbles across the track again, she talked about herself for a while, about her family and her childhood, and the neighbor boy who keeps asking her to marry him.

"I'm not a coward for the things I want," she said slowly. "I worked far harder trying to get away from the farm than I ever would just living on it. Dan's a nice boy, with a good house, and a half-section clear. It would be easier than working for the Wenderbys, but it would leave me just where

I started. I'd always feel guilty, I think, that I'd given in too soon. There'd be nothing more that really counted."

"While this way," I said, "the doors aren't all quite closed."

She nodded. "I'm saving a little. Maybe next spring I'll be able to try again."

Intent upon her pebbles she went on to tell me about the years she put in on the farm, cows to milk, pigs and calves to feed, five in the family younger than herself to cook and mend for.

"They say at home I'm too big for my shoes, but it isn't that. I was always sure that there was something more than cows and pigs and people like Dan – even before I really knew. It just wouldn't have been right if there hadn't been."

"You mean, not dramatically right," I suggested. She peered at me a moment, then repeated, "Not dramatically right. I stooked and drove a binder and a grain team, then walked the streets trying to find a job, till everything that I'd saved was gone and there was nothing left but to come back and start working for the Wenderbys. You see, though – even that much is better than staying home like the others. At least a little more dramatically right. You understand, don't you?"

I'd have understood better had it been someone else. She's so slim and frail, and against her white face her eyes had such a childlike, wistful look. The whiteness itself is the only intense part of her. You feel it long after she's left you.

We stopped once coming back to town, and stood a moment looking at the bright little sprinkle of its lights against the darkness. "I used to watch them from the top of the hill in our pasture," she said reflectively, "and go home trying to imagine what it would be like to live in town. Sometimes I'd drive in with my father or brother, and even the people I saw in the stores, the ugly little houses, none of it disillusioned me. When I was sixteen I came in and worked a few months for Mrs. Finley. It wasn't long till I started making excuses down to the station at night when the train came in. Mrs. Finley forbade it, but I would slip out anyway. It always excited me, the glare of the headlight, the way the engine swept in steaming and important, the smoky, oily smell. On the farm, you know, we don't see trains very often. When it was gone I'd stand by myself on the platform watching the green tail light disappear past the elevators, listening to the whistle, two long, two short at every crossing. Finally Mrs. Finley sent me home, with a letter to my father that she was afraid I'd come to no good end. He took my wages as punishment, and bought a mower."

When I reached home Philip was helping Steve with his arithmetic for tomorrow, up to his eyes in the square root of numbers that properly haven't any. Neither of them had noticed that I'd been gone a long time. "Oh, it's you," Philip said absently, and gathering up their books and pencils they went off to continue in the study.

At half-past ten I called Steve and sent him to bed, then went in for a while to talk to Philip. He didn't want me, but I stayed this time anyway. I told him I thought Steve should have more clothes, and suggested he call on Finley first thing tomorrow morning. "After all," I said, "I notice his boys both have good Sunday suits."

It worked. It brought a touch of life for a minute to his face, a quiver to his nerves that I could feel sitting three or four feet away.

Only it wasn't the animated, enthusiastic life that I felt two or three nights ago. Instead it was retaliative, bitter. His jaw set harder than ever. His eyes narrowed, and his lips went white again. "In a week or two," I said, "they'll have forgotten everything. Even the Finleys will accept the preacher's son."

But I came away feeling that the idea hadn't particularly pleased him.

Monday Evening, May 22

Very cool and self-possessed this morning Philip went off to round up the different members of the church board, and a little before noon returned with forty dollars cash.

He didn't speak. He just strode into the kitchen where I was finishing up my washing, counted the bills out onto the table in front of me, five ones and seven fives, then turned on his heel and shut himself up in his study.

He didn't speak because he didn't want me to know how excited and triumphant he was. Suds on my hands I snatched up the money and ran after him, but frowning at me over a newspaper he merely said, "Well, it's coming to us, isn't it?"

"We can pay on the car, and get Steve a suit," I started, "and something on the store accounts, and shoes for all of us –"

He rattled the paper and nodded. "Whatever you think. They'd just made some good collections. All I said was we were getting a little short."

It was a quarter to twelve, so I pushed my tub and rinsing pans out to Steve's bedroom, changed into my good slippers and a dry dress, and hurried uptown to the butcher's for beefsteak. Three thick good ones like those we do well to have for Christmas or Philip's birthday – and then into Dawson's store for a tin of peas and a bottle of ketchup.

Adult to his stomach even, Philip wouldn't deign to join us till it was all ready, but Steve turned the beefsteak for me while I set the table, opened the peas and found out how to work the patent fastener on the ketchup bottle.

It's good to eat well once in a while. Even Philip relaxed a little and enjoyed himself. It occurred to me, though, that making such an event of forty dollars wasn't the kindest thing to do, that it was maybe rubbing in what a church-mouse living ordinarily we get, so to dampen a little the festive air I hazarded a suggestion to Steve that he eat more slowly and more quietly, and then asked Philip didn't he find the steak just a little on the tough side.

When it was over, though, when Philip was in his study again and Steve had gone back to school, there was a curiously unsympathetic stillness through the house. I wanted to celebrate, and the walls disapproved. They seemed to be concentrating on me, trying with all their will power to restrain me to propriety and decorum. Every few minutes the windows gave a little rattle of deprecation. Even the smell, the faint old exhalation of the past – it seemed sharper, more insistent, seemed trying to tell me that this is a house of silence and repression and restraint, that it is stronger than we will ever be, that its past will not be mocked.

And it was so. I hummed a little as I washed the dishes. I brought out the forty dollars and counted it again, smoothed all the bills, arranged them on the table like a game of solitaire, so much for Steve, so much for Philip, so much for me. Then I looked through the mail-order catalogue a while, then I took a pencil and paper, and repeating aloud the figures as I made them, tried to flout the walls, to go on and celebrate in spite of them.

But it was no use. The walls were too much for me. For half an hour they disapproved, looked on reminding me where I was. Then, when that wasn't enough, when still I persisted in my unseemly ways, then they drew themselves up and asked pointblank, Did he ever go out like this and bring forty dollars home for you?

It was my own fault, holding out so long. I left them no alternative.

Anyway I put the money back in one of the kitchen drawers, and unknown to Philip slipped out of the house, and went walking again up the railroad track.

There was a hot dry wind that came in short, intermittent little puffs as if it were being blown out of a wheezy engine. All round the dust hung dark and heavy, the distance thickening it so that a mile or more away it made a blur of earth and sky; but overhead it was thin still, like a film of fog or smoke, and the light came through it filtered, mild and tawny.

It was as if there were a lantern hung above you in a darkened and enormous room; or as if the day had turned out all its other lights, waiting for the actors to appear, and you by accident had found your way into the spotlight, like a little ant or beetle on the stage.

I turned once and looked back at Horizon, the huddled little clutter of houses and stores, the five grain elevators, aloof and imperturbable, like ancient obelisks, and behind the dust clouds, lapping at the sky.

It was like one of Philip's drawings. There was the same tension, the same vivid immobility, and behind it all somewhere the same sense of transience.

I walked on, remembering how I used to think that only a great artist could ever paint the prairie, the vacancy and stillness of it, the bare essentials of a landscape, sky and earth, and how I used to look at Philip's work, and think to myself that the world would some day know of him.

I turned for home at the ravine where we sat in the snowstorm just a month ago. A freight train overtook me, and someone waved a towel from the caboose. When the clatter died away I sat down on a pile of ties to rest a few minutes, and start in spending the forty dollars again. The dust clouds behind the town kept darkening and thinning and swaying, a furtive tirelessness about the way they wavered and merged with one another that reminded me of northern lights in winter. It was like a quivering backdrop, before which was about to be enacted some grim, primeval tragedy. The little town cowered close to earth as if to hide itself. The elevators stood up passive, stoical. All round me ran a hurrying little whisper through the grass. I waited there till nearly suppertime.

Supper was a strained, unappetizing meal. Things hadn't been going very well with Steve at school, and through the silences again I could feel the dart of Philip's nerves. It was the nerves as much as what had happened at school that kept Steve subdued. We had eggs and bread and butter and tea, and a spoonful of honey for Steve. "He ought to have milk instead of tea," Philip said shortly, and I answered that in the morning I'd start taking a quart instead of a pint.

Early in the evening I left the house again and called on Mrs. Bird. She was in slippers and dressing-gown, reading a magazine and eating candy-coated biscuits out of a package. "Not a stitch on underneath," she assured me, parting the dressing-gown an inch or two in proof. "I like it that way – makes me feel elemental. The doctor's away on a country call, but you can wait and have tea with me. So far as he's concerned you're diagnosed anyway. Intuitive. I've seen him look a woman in the eye just like that and say 'What you need is a sedative.' I see you do look pale again. We've heard, my dear – and we both think it's just magnificent."

She's the only one in town I feel safe with. I asked her would she let me order a suit for Steve through the catalogue and have it come addressed to her.

"Order everything that way if you like." She brushed the biscuit crumbs off her fingers and leaning forward gave my knee a prod. "The storekeepers can't tell us that we ought to spend our money in the town. Including the butcher they owe us for eight deliveries alone. Mrs. Pratt by this time knows your writing, though. I'll address an envelope, and in your order sign my name."

I rose to go, and she followed me to the door. "The doctor insists it's environment, not heredity, so when you hear what I've been hearing simply shut your ears. Only today I told Mrs. Finley that worse sins can come home to roost than those of your peasant ancestors. You see I know Mrs. Finley; we've both been here nearly twenty years. 'Such a good woman,' people keep on saying like so many sheep, 'such a good wife and mother!' You'd think the rest of us ran bawdy houses, or fed our husbands powdered glass. But if ever she says too much just bring the conversation round to me. You'll see her start to wonder how much I've been telling you."

Home again I called Steve from his books to let him help pick out his suit. We found a smartly tailored one in blue or gray or brown with an extra pair of pants for eleven seventy-five. The color was a moot point for a while, then Philip came out and cast his vote for blue.

While they got the tapeline and did their measuring I started the order with a bright red tie. It will go well with the suit, I think, and set off his dark hair and eyes. I also put down khaki pants that he can wear to school instead of the overalls, and two more shirts and a pair of Sunday shoes. It's all finished now, sealed up and stamped, and ready to be mailed. I explained to Steve that we're supposed to do our buying here in town, and that he'd better not go out of his way to talk about the suit to any of the boys. As he went off to bed Philip smiled narrowly and said, "You don't need to worry how much he'll tell the boys. I've been talking to him and listening. He has his pride."

His voice had a harsh, contentious tone. I looked at him and saw his jaw clench out the smile. "Kirby's right," he said. "He'd be better with a horse."

Wednesday Evening, May 24

We were out making formal, twenty-minute calls this afternoon, starting with Mrs. Finley as the worst one, and ending up with Mrs. Nicholson, the station agent's wife.

"Of course you know your own minds best – but so sudden – you can't have had much time to think it over."

"No – twelve years just the two of us together – then a son at a few hours' notice – almost as tall as I am."

"That's exactly what we say – he'll never really belong to you. If instead now you'd take a baby –"

"But all along we've wanted a boy. We started in wanting him twelve years ago. As parents, you see, it makes us really twelve years old ourselves."

"Only there are so many deserving cases – our own kind – clean, decent people –"

"We believe in Steve. As to his misfortunes – well, it's the sick, isn't it, and not the whole –"

So I parried them, cool and patient, piety to my finger tips. It was the devil quoting scripture maybe, but it worked. They couldn't answer. They had to curb their resentment to wondering were we wise, to telling us that blood will out and Catholics never change. Philip sat white and clenched, his eyes two little drills of steel. I knew the signs, and for safety talked ahead of him. He looked on, flinching for me, but I didn't mind. I'm not so thin-skinned as he is anyway. I resigned myself to sanctimony years ago. Today I was only putting our false front up again, enlarged this time for three.

Philip, Steve and I. It's such a trim, efficient little sign; it's such a tough, deep-rooted tangle that it hides.

And none of them knows. They spy and carp and preen themselves, but none of them knows. They can only read our shingle, all its letters freshened up this afternoon, *As For Me and My House – The House of Bentley – We Will Serve the Lord.*

Thursday Evening, May 25

It's been nearly dark today with dust. Everything's gritty, making you shiver and setting your teeth on edge. There's a crunch on the floor like sugar when you walk. We keep the doors and windows closed, and still it works in everywhere. I lay down for a little while after supper, and I could feel it even on the pillow. The air is so dry and choking with it that every few minutes a kind of panic seizes you, and you have an impulse to thresh out against it with your hands.

I went into it for a while this afternoon, trying to escape. There's a lumber yard at the edge of the town, and seeing a gate open and no one round I slipped inside. It gave a safe, sheltered feeling different from the house. I found a place with a pile to sit on and a higher one to lean against, and other piles all round to hide me from the office and the street. I sat an hour there, wishing I had an apple and listening to the wind. When finally I came out the dust had thickened so that I could see just the first two elevators. The next two were dim and blurred, as if the first ones had moved and left their imprints behind. I stood a while straining my eyes to make the fifth one out, with an odd kind of satisfaction that I couldn't.

Coming home the wind up the street was so strong that I could lean against it a little, relax and still not fall. When I stopped and turned my back for breath there was a wild little yelp in it, sometimes the way a coyote howls. On the other side of the street I saw a man in Dawson's window watching me; and all the lamps were lit.

Steve was out in it too. It was his day for riding Harlequin, and after school he wouldn't be persuaded that in such a wind for once he'd better miss. He came back so grained with dust right through his clothes that I wouldn't let him go to bed until he'd had a bath. He sulked a little because there wasn't any water, and with the wind whipping it out of the pails it meant he had to bring it from the well three times. I insisted though, lecturing him sternly on habits of cleanliness. My poppies and nasturtiums were drying up, and when he was finished I planned to water them.

My scheming failed, though. I told him to get into bed and leave the tub for me, but at the wrong moment deciding to be a gentleman he emptied it himself. That's the kind of garden it is: I don't want even Steve to know that I still have hopes for it. Yesterday when he found me poking to see if my beans were sprouted yet he looked down his nose incredulous and said, "You should have seen the cabbages my father used to grow."

It wouldn't be so bad if there were even weeds. I could at least weed, then – stay out an hour or two, and still be rational. I wouldn't mind carrying water, but it means passing Wenderbys' and Pratts' each time, and it doesn't do to be too conspicuous.

The wind and the way it creaks the house is making us both nearly desperate. Sometimes Philip goes out to tinker round the garage a while, but his hands are so useless that changing a tire or fixing anything is harder on his nerves than staying in here and putting up with me. I catch Steve sometimes looking at us puzzled and uneasy. The last day or two he's even stopped his little whistle. So far his coming hasn't made much difference.

Friday Evening, May 26

The wind last night blew our privy over, and it took Philip and Mr. Finley the best part of the morning to get it up again. It's leaning worse than ever, but they've wired it to the woodshed and insist it's safe. Steve, who in his geography lessons lately has been studying the architecture and monuments of Europe, came home at noon and called it the Leaning Tower of Pisa. A rather good name too, by virtue of a bad pronunciation.

Saturday Evening, May 27

Philip and Steve went off to the country again this afternoon and left me at home. Steve likes the car, and Saturday is the only day he's free. At noon, when Philip suggested it, I hesitated a moment, thinking of a sick call I'd promised to make with Mrs. Finley, wondering could we put it off till after supper. He saw my hesitation, went on quickly, "It's all right if you've something else to do. Steve and I can go alone. It's just a matter of putting in an appearance anyway. At this time of the year on the farm they've something to do besides talk to the preacher."

I think I started to answer, to tell him that I could hurry and be ready, that the visit I planned could wait – but then I saw his eyes fall, and it flashed on me that he would rather go with Steve alone.

I remember getting out a clean shirt for Steve, brushing his hair at the kitchen sink and putting on soap to make it stay in place. He asked once why I wasn't coming too, and I spun him round so he wouldn't see my face. I laughed as I told him I had other things to do, thinking how strong it was of me, even with such sudden ruin all around, to be so self-effacing and restrained.

But I broke when they drove away. I paced in and out of the little rooms, sobbed and paced again, then at last threw myself across the bed.

We've lived alone too long. I'm not used to coming second in his life. For the first time now I realize that there have been no companions for him in these little towns, that he'd had the poor choice of the barber shop or me. I've just gone on taking for granted that he's stayed at home because he wanted to, because I really mattered in his life, because he couldn't get along without me.

Of course I've been wrong. Sitting here quiet and tired now I understand things better. All these years I've been trying to possess him, to absorb his life into mine, and not once has he ever yielded. I remember the year he was working on his book. It was his book; there was no place in it for me. There used to be something almost threatening in the way he would close his study door. His book – his world. Already I had encroached too far. I was something to be defied, held at arm's distance. He wrote, and I kept out of his way, hoed and weeded in the garden. It was temperament, I said, the artist in him.

His book was a failure; the little world that it had meant for him collapsed. I kept suggesting that there was still my world, kept trying to draw him into it, but he was too strong for me. His own world was shattered and empty, but at that it was better than a woman's. He remained in it. He was no longer young, had nothing much left to dream about, but at least he could shut himself away from me. He worked on stubbornly with his chalk and pencil, intent on his drawings that with every year became a little colder and grimmer. Partly because he was an artist, because he had to draw; partly because he was a man, and the solitude of his study was his last stronghold against me.

I understand it well enough tonight. It's a woman's way, I suppose, to keep on trying to subdue a man, to bind him to her, and it's a man's way to keep on just as determined to be free. I'm wrong when I feel that I've lost him to Steve. He was never really mine to lose to anyone. These false-fronted little towns have been holding us together, nothing else. It's no use a woman's thinking that if she loves a man patiently and devotedly enough she can eventually make him love her too. Philip married me because I made myself important to him, consoled him when he was despondent, stroked his vanity the right way. I meant well. You do mean well when you keep on like that three years, slighted and repulsed, determined not to mind. At the end I thought I'd won. More and more years went by, and still I thought I'd won. Even when he was hard to live with, when he closed the study door on me, and kept himself aloof. I said it was the Church – fell back again on temperament. Not till today, when I saw him driving off with Steve, did I know the worth of what I've always called a victory.

It's the reason perhaps I still care so much, the way he's never let me possess him, always held himself withdrawn. For love, they say, won't survive possession. After a year or two it changes, cools, emerges from its blindness, at best becomes affection and regard. And mine hasn't.

I almost wish it had. It would be easier now. Tomorrow

I'm afraid will be today again – every tomorrow. Not the pacing and sobbing – that was the easy part – but the quietness that came after, when I could think my way through what had happened, see it plain. I tried not to think. I tried to be a fool. I stormed through the house, telling myself I didn't care. A small-town preacher – a hypocrite at that – was he so much to lose? But I only made myself know how unneeded I was, how much I needed him.

It was nearly seven o'clock when they came home. Philip noticed the table with the cloth I had laid over the dishes to keep out the dust, and while Steve was washing explained apologetically that they had had motor trouble coming home. His voice sounded brighter than usual, as if the afternoon had gone well. He told me how popular I was among the farmers: at every place, while he was in the yard or stable talking to the men, the women had come out and made him promise to bring me the next time too. At one place there was a chestnut pony that he would like to get for Steve.

There was a stone in my throat that made it hard to answer. Part of it was pride. I didn't want him to know he had hurt me. At the sight of him, his quietness and sanity, I thought of the weak way I had cried when he went off with Steve, and I was ashamed of myself. But as well as pride there was fear, a kind of instinct, that if I let him know he had hurt me he would withdraw even further than before. For a man I think is like that. Where a woman is concerned he likes to be able to respect himself, feel chivalrous, superior. If instead I make him feel guilty he'll hold a grudge against me for it, stand off wary. So I went on talking as if I were in the best of spirits, as if it had been an afternoon just like any other, and when we sat down to the table started asking Steve about the pony they had been looking at.

A chestnut with a white face, a walleye, and a Roman nose. Ten years old and thoroughly reliable. They want seventy-five dollars for him, so much a month if it's easier, the way we pay for the car.

I chewed glumly a minute, then looked at Philip and said. "You don't know the first thing about a horse. You're likely being taken in. First why not go and ask Paul?"

"That's right." Philip agreed, "and his brother's a rancher raising them. Didn't he say we could go there if we liked for our holidays?"

Which pretty well makes the ranch, I think, a certainty. Steve says he didn't like the walleye very well anyway, and wonders will Paul be able to get him another pinto like Harlequin.

Sunday Evening, May 28

Today was the first time we took Steve to Sunday School, and he celebrated it having a fist fight with one of the Finley twins.

To make matters worse, Mrs. Finley was their teacher. A few rows away with my own class of girls I could see Steve and the twin giving each other furtive digs with their elbows; then – so Steve says – just as Mrs. Finley asked him to stand up and repeat the Golden Text, the twin took a nip at his behind. Anyway, before I could reach them, they were clinched and out rolling in the aisle, the twin with a nosebleed, Steve on top and walloping.

Too quick for me Mrs. Finley jerked Steve up by the collar and struck him across the mouth with the back of her hand. I threw myself between them, pushed Steve out of the way, and swung round and faced her. Nobody was going to strike her boy, she stuttered out excitedly, then lunged past me, trying to reach him again.

But now Philip was there. Everyone else suddenly fell away. He put his hands on Steve's shoulders, and stood with his body buckled forward a little, his own shoulders hunched, his chin drawn in. I never saw him look like that before. He worked his lips helplessly a minute, then said thick and hard, "If ever you dare do it again –"

It was as far as he could get. With a laugh she said she'd let him see what she dared do, and setting her lips for it thin and vicious struck Steve across the face a second time.

Then she fainted, and they carried her outside. The teachers and children dwindled away till the three of us were alone. I closed the organ, walked along the pews putting the hymnbooks in their racks – and still Philip stood there. He kept his hands on Steve's shoulders. His lips were white, and his forehead knotted. When I went back to him there was a glare still in his eyes. I took his arm and we went home. For a few minutes he stood at the window in the living-room, then slipped quietly into his study and stayed there for the rest of the afternoon.

Supper was strained and difficult again. With the aid of biscuits and a tin of peaches that I'd put away for unexpected company I finally succeeded in brightening Steve a little, but Philip spoke in an abrupt, disjointed way, and his eyes kept slipping past me.

Even in the pulpit tonight his shoulders were still set defiant and contentious. His voice had a kind of passion in it, a darkness and boding. It was only Mrs. Finley today, but he's pitted against the whole town. When I tried to tell him he won't be blamed for what happened he shook me off almost as if he found a bitter satisfaction in believing them all hostile, as if he preferred it that way. He hates Horizon, all the Horizons, and he's clinging to the incident today as a justification for his hatred. It frightens me a little. Just a word will touch him off. There were times during the sermon tonight when I bit my lip and waited. It frightens me – and yet I wish he would. I'd be with him. All these years he's shrunk from the Church, been galled by it, and still it's been something to lean on, bread and butter, a roof over our heads. The constant sense of deceit and hypocrisy has been a virus, destroying his will and sapping his energy. Lack of self-respect has meant lack of initiative to try something else – it's been a vicious circle. If he were to break away now it might mean worry and hardship, but it might also mean getting a fresh grip of himself, recovering something of his old independence and ambition. Especially now that there are the three of us.

Tuesday Evening, May 30

My peas and radishes are coming through. I spent a long time up and down the rows this morning, clearing away the dust that was drifted over them; and at intervals, so that I wouldn't attract too much attention, I made five trips for water. My beans are sprouting too – I dug another up to see – but the wind day after day keeps dry and deadly, like the current of heat that rises from a fire.

Mrs. Ellingson took pity on me, and came over with Sven's straw hat and three fresh eggs. "I wouldn't work so hard if I were you," she counseled me. "The last preacher had some beans and peas like you, and he was so mad because my chickens scratched them out he wouldn't speak to me. If I'd thought, I'd have told you just to put in potatoes. The chickens don't bother them."

I went on clearing away the dust from the radishes, wondering what Steve was like with a slingshot. She looked on in silence a few minutes, then gradually worked round to telling me that Mrs. Finley had been in bed since Sunday, and that in a few days she's having the church board summon us before a special meeting.

I'm worrying about it. Mrs. Bird said this evening when she was here with Steve's new suit that I don't need to, that the town knows Mrs. Finley, but I'm afraid for what Philip may do. I haven't told him yet. He's white and pinched-looking, nervous from trying not to be. At the table he forgets and sits staring past us, eyes narrowed, shoulders brooding still. Sometimes when he looks at Steve I see his tight-clenched lips relax, his face take on an eased, grateful look; but in what he feels for him there's such intensity and strain that Steve keeps shy before it, wary and perplexed. Philip never had the opportunity to be a boy himself. When he reaches down now and tries to talk to one he doesn't know the language.

I let Steve dress up in his new suit and red tie when Mrs. Bird was gone. It was a good fit, and the tie touches off his hair and eyes exactly as I thought it would. I worked at his hair for all of five minutes, soaping it down and trying to get the parting straight; then I knocked at Philip's door, and said there was a young man out here to see him.

But he couldn't carry our little comedy any further. The excitement and novelty of getting dressed up in a brand-new suit – for Steve the important thing – he couldn't enter into the spirit of it. I saw something clutch him when he opened the door – pride maybe, tenderness – something so strong and full that it wouldn't let him laugh.

"A boy's new suit ought to have something in the pockets," I said, and fumbling in his own, his eyes still on Steve, he brought out a quarter and a nickel. Steve took the coins awkwardly, and to escape the way Philip was watching him turned round to me and said, "Look – thirty cents!" Then

Philip advanced a step, put his hands on Steve's shoulders and stood like that helpless a minute, not knowing what to say, or how to take his hands away. I made an excuse out to the kitchen, but Steve followed right at my heels. For a minute he stood preening himself at the little looking-glass that hangs above the sink, then without looking round said soberly, "I was wondering if you knew that altogether I've got ten pockets."

I laughed and went to the cupboard for my purse, but he intercepted me, "No, I'll let you work it out instead at the piano. Each pocket half an hour – and you can start right now."

For Philip's sake I played the driest Bach I knew, but Steve was not to be discouraged. Philip listened patiently a while, trying to be one of us, then went on tiptoe back to his study. Conscientiously, I kept on with Bach, but before the half-hour was up Steve interrupted to ask could I play one of his own songs if he whistled it a few times. It was a simple folk tune; just one whistling and I had it. Then, because there's a bit of the showman in me still and admiration's always sweet, I repeated it with arpeggios and ornaments, something in the style of very bad Liszt.

He was so excited when I finished that I forgot about Philip and my good resolves. I brought out a pile of music and played nearly another hour, brisk, lifey marching pieces to suit a boy, Chopin waltzes and mazurkas, finally some of the Gypsy-Hungarian themes from the Liszt rhapsodies.

This time, though, when I finished he sat still a minute, his lips white, and then without speaking slipped away to bed.

I followed him, for the first time realizing what a boy he still is, what strangers we are.

We didn't say anything. I sat down beside him on the cot and he went on unlacing his shoes. He made them last a long time. Finally, when they couldn't last any longer, we looked at each other; then I went sentimental for a minute, and he let me.

I didn't know anything like that could happen to me. It was as if once, twelve years ago, I had heard the beginning of a piece of music, and then a door had closed. But within me, in my mind and blood, the music had kept on, and when at last they opened the door again I was at the right place, had held the rhythm all the way.

He's asleep now. It's nearly twelve, and Philip's in his study drawing still.

Another little Main Street. In the foreground there's an old horse and buggy hitched outside one of the stores. A broken old horse, legs set stolid, head down dull and spent. But still you feel it belongs to the earth, the earth it stands on, the prairie that continues where the town breaks off. What the tired old hulk suggests is less approaching decay or dissolution than return. You sense a flow, a rhythm, a cycle.

But the town in contrast has an upstart, mean complacency. The false fronts haven't seen the prairie. Instead, they stare at each other across the street as into mirrors of themselves, absorbed in their own reflections.

The town shouldn't be there. It stands up so insolent and smug and self-assertive that your fingers itch to smudge it out and let the underlying rhythms complete themselves. Philip himself could feel that there was something wrong, but he didn't know what. He kept giving last little touches here and there, as if it were just a matter of perspective, or a rounder buggy wheel.

The wind's getting up again. It's in the eaves like someone with dry lips trying to whistle. There's a faint haze of dust already, and I see the fuchsia beginning to sway. I've started another little one, and Paul's to come tomorrow after school to widen the window sills. They're too narrow, now that I've put the geraniums into proper sloping pots. He says he likes to work with tools, and for Philip it always spoils a day.

Wednesday Evening, May 31

Paul has his troubles too. He has been telling his pupils that *belly* is a perfectly good, respectable word, to be used whenever it's *belly* they're talking about, but the town is pursing its lips against such sanction of vulgarity. "Cows may have them," says Mrs. Wenderby, "and you, Mr. Kirby, but not my daughter Isobel or I."

He told me while working at the window sills, his forehead screwed up in little wrinkles, perplexed, humorless. He's so humble about being just a country boy, yet so stubbornly proud of it. Humble because it's born in his country bones to be that way, because he still shares instinctively the typical countryman's feeling of disadvantage before town people who wear smarter clothes and write a better hand. Proud because he's come to know these town people and see them for what they really are, to discover that most of his own values have been sounder all the time.

"It's no place in here to bring up a boy," he went on to caution me. "They don't have enough to do – don't take enough responsibility. Long before I was Steve's age I looked after my horse – days I wasn't at school rode fence and herded cattle. It was good for me – toughened me up, taught me self-reliance. There were the cowboys, and I was always trying to hold my own with them. They weren't heroes exactly, but on the average they were pretty fair men. Now Steve here – he hasn't anybody."

I thought of Philip, mounting to his pulpit every Sunday, making his twenty-minute calls, and I didn't answer. He read me, tried to patch it up. "There's Philip, of course – but

Steve – you see a boy – there are only certain qualities in a man he can appreciate. If Philip were doing something else –"

"As he ought to be," I said wryly, forced to it by a feeling that Paul knew anyway. He laid down his hammer and went on earnestly: "I thought that the first time I met him. It's like sizing a horse up as a runner, waiting to see what he can do, and then discovering that he's spavined. You can see it in his face. It seems a pity when there are so many who could take the pulpit and be in their element."

Paul being what he is I might have gone on and told him more, but Philip and Steve came in just then, and we started talking about the ranch and our two weeks' vacation in July. Philip, I think, would just as soon I stayed at home, but Steve and Paul include me. I want to go. I want to get away from the Ladies Aid and this hot, dry, dusty little cupboard of a house. I want to find the trees Paul promises, and paddle in the river, and go off some morning in the hills and lose myself all day. A horse for Steve is practically agreed upon, but there are no more calicoes like Harlequin. Paul says they'll get a fairly good one for a hundred dollars, with some sort of saddle and bridle perhaps thrown in. Philip thinks the price is reasonable, doesn't so much as bat an eyelid. Steve's been out already looking the woodshed over, with an eye to converting half of it into a stall. So far, apparently, I'm the only one who knows about the meeting that they're calling Friday night.

Thursday Evening, June 1

Judith was here for a few minutes this afternoon. She asked me to play for her, but just as I sat down at the piano Philip came out of his study. He nodded and stood staring at her with such a direct, searching look that she flushed again and got up to go.

"He's planning to draw you, Judith," I said quickly. "He's tried it before, but finds there's something about your face that's hard to catch. Come in here a minute and I'll show you."

It was a departure from all precedent. I didn't ask his leave, just sailed ahead of him into the study and rummaged through his drawings till I found the ones of Judith.

She remained quite still a minute, then gave an uneasy glance at Philip. She was white again. She didn't speak. It was his turn now to color. He straightened his tie, fidgeted, looked out the window. But I could tell, just the same, that her admiration pleased him.

"They're like me," she said at last. "They're really like me. I had my picture taken once when I first went to the city – I wanted to send it home so they would think how well I was getting along – but it wasn't half as good as these."

He pulled his tie again, careful not to look at either of us, and then brought out other drawings to show her. She would take a step away from them, her head at an incredulous little tilt, then draw close again and touch them with the tip of her finger, peering into the paper as if to discover how they were done. With a few deft strokes he made a likeness of her while she watched, then from memory another of himself. She asked if she could take them home with her, and I cautioned, "Only don't show them to anyone else. If you do there's the danger that half the women in town will come for sittings – and if they catch him on an honest day some of them might not be exactly pleased."

He gave a grim little smile when she was gone. "You're afraid, aren't you, of what the town thinks?" His lips smacked apart as if he were drawing deep satisfaction from a sudden consciousness of not being afraid. He looked away from me, but the smile persisted. I could imagine him with his fingers on the town's throat, smiling exactly the same way.

As soon as supper was finished he went into his study and drew the door after him, stealthily, so I wouldn't hear it close. Steve asked me to play, but I sent him to see Philip about tomorrow's arithmetic instead. He looked bored a second, then nodded understandingly, and went. It makes me a little uneasy, the way we get along so well together. I have a guilty feeling that our companionship is rapidly becoming a conspiracy.

Friday Evening, June 2

The church board meeting that I've been dreading all week turned out a rather tame affair. Mr. Finley, I imagine, was forced to it against his better judgment by Mrs. Finley. He looked sheepish and uncomfortable as he recited her account word for word of what had happened; then with a deep breath and a smile assured us on his own that the meeting had been called for no purpose other than to help us solve our problems.

Philip didn't like that. He'll never see Steve as just a problem. I clenched my knees together, and tried to look poised as I saw his jaw come out.

Someone said we would remember our position in the community, the example we are setting. Someone else, more kindly, said we might be given time to train the boy. Miss Twill wanted to know was it true that Mr. Bentley had so far forgotten himself as to threaten Mrs. Finley. Still someone else reminded us that bad blood was bad blood and always would be. As Steve Kulanich he had been recognized for what he was and treated accordingly. As the minister's son there was the danger of his vicious habits being overlooked and tolerated. It was to be hoped we realized our responsibilities, and were prepared to measure up to them. Someone else had caught a glimpse of the crucifix above his bed, and thumped on a pew, "No popery."

Then Philip stood up. He spoke with difficulty, trying to be cool and logical so that he might make a better case for Steve; his knuckles white, the veins out purple on his forehead.

He seemed broadening, growing taller. In his tightened, half-closed eyes I could see a little flash that came and went with every breath. His voice was shaking out, hardening. I could feel the hot throb of all the years he has curbed and hidden and choked himself – feel it gather, break, the sudden reckless stumble for release – and before it was too late, before he could do what he should have done twelve years ago, I interrupted.

I took my place beside him, and as he groped for words began explaining the situation as it really was.

I was cool and logical enough. I succeeded in making a good case for Steve. Alone now, watching the little dusty moths go thudding round the lamp, listening to the wind, and the creak and saw of eaves, I'm thinking what a fool I was. If I had only kept still we might be starting in to worry now about the future. We might be making plans, shaking the dust off us, finding our way back to life.

I feel such an ache tonight to be away. I ask myself how many more years like this it's going to be, the little house so still and dead, the door between us closed. All for the sake of a few hundred dollars a year. Four ugly little rooms, a hat that cost a dollar forty-five. I didn't used to be that way.

Tuesday Evening, June 6

The wind keeps on. When you step outside its strong hot push is like something solid pressed against the face. The sun through the dust looks big and red and close. Bigger, redder, closer every day. You begin to glance at it with a doomed feeling, that there's no escape.

The dust is so thick that sky and earth are just a blur. You can scarcely see the elevators at the end of town. One step beyond, you think, and you'd go plunging into space.

The days are blurred too. It's wind in the morning, wind at bedtime. Wind all through the night – we toss and lie listening.

Philip paces; I keep out of his way. I go into the garden and up the railway track for as long as I can stand it. Sometimes he slips away for a few hours too. We never ask each other questions.

The sand and dust drifts everywhere. It's in the food, the bedclothes, a film on the book you're reading before you can turn the page. In the morning it's half an inch deep on the window sills. Half an inch again by noon. Half an inch again by evening. It begins to make an important place for itself in the routine of the day. I watch the little drifts form. If at dusting time they're not quite high enough I'm disappointed, put off the dusting sometimes half an hour to let them grow. But if the wind has been high and they have outdrifted themselves, then I look at them incredulous, and feel a strange kind of satisfaction, as if such height were an achievement for which credit was coming to me.

The wind and the sawing eaves and the rattle of windows have made the house a cell. Sometimes it's as if we had taken shelter here, sometimes as if we were at the bottom of a deep moaning lake. We are quiet and tense and wary. Our muscles and lungs seem pitted to keep the walls from caving in.

A while ago the wind and the crunch of sand on the floor used to put an itch in my fingers. I wanted to tear and shake and crush something. But it's different now. I sit quiet, listening, looking at the fuchsia till it's disappeared. In the last week I seem to have realized that wind is master.

It's the same with Philip. Last night again he drew a Main Street, and this morning I looked at it and then went through his drawers to find another that he did a month ago. In the first one the little false fronts on the stores are buckled low against the wind. They're tilted forward, grim, snarling. The doors and windows are crooked and pinched, like little eyes screwed up against the sand. But in the one last night the town is seen from a distance, a lost little clutter on the long sweep of prairie. High above it dust clouds wheel and wrestle heedlessly. Here, too, wind is master.

My garden keeps coming up and burning down again. Every morning I creep along the rows, scooping away the dust and sand. I slip out usually when Philip's away or busy in his study, for a look comes into his eyes that makes me ashamed for my little yellow poppy and nasturtium leaves. I carried water for them yesterday, but on the second trip met Miss Twill, who asked with a contemptuous little pucker of her lips what my husband and son were doing. Philip, though, doesn't understand the garden, and I hesitate to ask him. Steve makes three trips for a nickel.

There's a change coming over Steve. He's at home with us now. Even in Philip's study, even when Philip is at loggerheads with next Sunday's sermon. I notice his eyes critical as I set the table. He has his preferences and lets me know them. Saturday when I brought out the scissors to trim his hair he made such a fuss about it I let him go to the barber shop. Yesterday at noon he told us rather pointedly about the new trousers the Finley twins are wearing, some that Dawson's store have just got in, navy blue, with a red stripe down each leg, and a broad red belt like a girdle round the waist. After school Philip bought him a pair, and today he's got them on and his new red tie to match. They suit him. In the long trousers, skin tight over his thighs, he looks taller. The touch of color sets his hair and eyes off, gives him an air of braggart insolence. I notice his step a little self-conscious today, shoulders squared, chest out – and the swagger suits him better even than the trousers.

Swagger and trousers, though, are the least of it. Philip is spoiling him thoroughly.

I ought to protest, but I'm too small and selfish. However much Steve begins to mean to me, Philip means more. Perhaps I've lost Philip anyway. Sometimes at night when I lie listening to the wind, and my arm feels the hard wall of his shoulder, sometimes it beats down on me that my day is finished, that the rest has but little meaning. And in the darkness perhaps I see clearly – but I don't admit it.

Don't dare admit it. I must still keep on reaching out, trying to possess him, trying to make myself matter. I must, for I've left myself nothing else. I haven't been like him. I've reserved no retreat, no world of my own. I've whittled myself hollow that I might enclose and hold him, and when he shakes me off I'm just a shell. Ever since the day he let me see I was less to him than Steve I've been trying to find and live my own life again, but it's empty, unreal. The piano, even – I try, but it's just a tinkle. And that's why I mustn't admit I may have lost him. He's spoiling Steve, hurting him, and I must stand by and let him. He would resent my interference. It would make me one with the town then, hostile, critical, aligned against him. He would resent and even hate me if I did, and I'm too small for that, too cowardly.

He's doing his utmost to make Steve scorn and reject the town, and Steve, because all his life the town has done exactly that to him, is learning fast. It's the same scorn that Philip taught himself once, a kind of defense instinct, to protect his self-respect and pride. Only it was necessary for him, and it isn't for Steve. He was alone, and Steve now has us. Philip's stand of scorn and self-sufficiency has hurt him. He has paid in bitterness and isolation. It's warped him with a struggle to prove himself that perhaps he was never strong enough for. He knows, and still will have the same for Steve again. "A horse," he keeps saying, "next month we'll have a horse for him."

Perhaps it's a kind of jealousy. Perhaps instinctively he knows that this way will keep Steve alone too, that Steve, in consequence, will have need of him. Perhaps he's trying to harden him, trying to assure his success in life at whatever cost, as a kind of compensation for his own failure.

It makes me realize how alone he has been all his life, even the last twelve years, the way he reaches out for Steve's companionship, tries to shape him, put years on him, so that companionship will be possible. I find Steve bewildered by things too old for him. He reads too much, spends too much time in Philip's study. Just once I suggested he ought to be out with the other boys, getting fresh air and exercise, but Philip frowned, and said to wait until we get the horse.

In return, though, Steve seems to care little enough for Philip, accepts him with a casual, slightly condescending air. When he first came he was shy and diffident. To put him at his ease and win his confidence Philip was too indulgent; now Steve is responding with a touch of insolence. He understands already that he can play on Philip to his advantage. There was a kind of shrewdness and strategy in the way he mentioned the red-striped trousers at the table yesterday – in the way he says they laugh at him at school when he tells them he's going to have a horse next month. It isn't that he's sly or crafty – what boy wouldn't scheme a little for a horse? – it's that his scheming is too successful, is never seen through for what it really is. I'm afraid that what little respect he has for Philip now won't last much longer. And in a little while, when Philip and Paul and the horse have succeeded in teaching him to think, just what then will he think? When he sets up for comparison the man he knows in here with the one he sees in the pulpit every Sunday?

I'm sorry for Philip. He's trying hard, and his clumsy earnestness is only putting distance between him and Steve. Sorry for Philip, sorrier for myself. For Steve isn't the kind of boy you pick up every day. There's more to him than just good looks. He has mind and imagination. Enough, I'm afraid, to make Philip's marsh-fire chase a long one.

Wednesday Evening, June 7

Paul came this afternoon while I was in the garden, and squatting on his hunkers helped me clear away the dust that was drifted round my beans.

Did I know, he asked, that *garden* and *yard* and *court* were etymologically all related? That a king's pomp and retinue is descended from a peasant's chicken run? *Paling*, too, he said, with a nod toward the fence, there was another social climber: in actual possession of the palace now that once it guarded as a humble palisade.

But while words socially come up in the world, most of them morally go down. *Retaliate*, for instance: once you could retaliate a favor or a kindness – it simply meant to give again as much as had been given – but memories being short for benefits and long for grievances, its sense was gradually perverted, and its better nature lost.

You learn a lot from a philologist. Cupid, he says, has given us *cupidity*, Eros, *erotic*, Venus, *venereal*, and Aphrodite, *aphrodisiac*.

Thursday Evening, June 8

There was a tea this afternoon at Mrs. Nicholson's, the station agent's wife, but I sent my apologies with Steve at noon, and went for a walk with Judith up the railway track instead.

We came to a place where the dust was drifted so high we could walk right over the railway fence. We sat down for a while, and then stretched out and moved our arms up and down to make angels the way we used to do in the snow when we were children.

They weren't very good angels though, for the dust was drifted so hard and firm that when we got up and looked at them there were just behinds and wings. Judith used to do it with the neighbor boy who keeps asking her to marry him, and I used to do it with another neighbor boy called Percy Glenn. He had a squint, and red hair, and skinny knees, and started at seven every morning practicing his violin.

My family didn't like his violin, and his family didn't like my piano, and out of it we managed to become fairly good friends. Later we played duets together, and helped each other studying harmony and counterpoint. Once when he gave a recital I accompanied him, and for my part of the program played Debussy's *Gardens in the Rain*.

He went to England shortly afterwards, played for a year or two in a string quartet, then made a concert tour of South America. That was the last I heard of him. From Buenos Aires he answered a letter I'd written months before to tell him I was married to a preacher and living in a little prairie town and playing *Hymns with Variations* for the Ladies Aid. He said it seemed a pity, told me how many thousand had heard him play the night before. And I laughed, and worried Philip with amorous attentions in the middle of the afternoon, and didn't trouble to write again.

But busy with my retrospects, looking at Horizon and drawing up a balance sheet, I wasn't much company for Judith. She sauntered off presently, and gathering a handful of pebbles started aiming them at a pile of ties across the track. The wind blew back her hair, and pressed in her dress so close against her body that I could see the firm profile of her breasts. It surprised me a little. Somehow, so white and silent and shy, she had never occurred to me as a woman before. I left off my balancing and sat watching her, with a vague uneasy feeling of regret. For I've never got along with women very well. Till I met Philip I was always impatient of what seemed their little rivalries and infatuations; and ever since I've been afraid.

We had been there about an hour when two men on a handcar came along, on their way back to town after doing repair work farther up the track. They stopped when they saw us, and one of them called out did we want a ride. I looked at Judith, and dared her, and she said all right, we'd go.

They were grizzled, dirty-looking men, one dark and oily-skinned, the other broad-nosed and stolid like a Slav. They jumped off the car and pushed their tools and crowbars back so that there was room for us to sit with our legs hanging over the side. In elaborate broken English the dark one said he was a friend of Steve's. Steve has told him that I play the piano, and now he often comes in the evening to walk up and down in front of our house in the hopes of hearing me.

I counted to ten twice, and didn't extend an invitation. They started working the lever that makes the handcar go, and when I said it was better than walking, redoubled their efforts until we were clipping along at all of fifteen miles an hour. Approaching Horizon and the station though, I began to think about the tea at Mrs. Nicholson's. It was dangerous, but if I asked them to let us off before we reached town they would think we didn't want to be seen with them. I hadn't the heart for that, they looked so appreciative of our company, and besides they were friends of Steve's. So I steeled myself, hoping we might reach Main Street unobserved.

Vainly, though, for they stopped at the station and gallantly helped us off the handcar just as the tea deployed on the platform twelve or thirteen strong.

"You do get around," said Mrs. Pratt. "We thought you were indisposed. I don't think that even you, Mrs. Bird, could have thought up a cure like that."

Anyway it was bad – so bad I couldn't find my tongue and just stood helpless, not even trying to make an explanation. Judith, at the sight of Mrs. Wenderby, made a bolt for home to hurry with the supper, but I had to walk up Main Street between Miss Twill and Mrs. Pratt. I was grained with dust, I had my old slippers on, my hair was down in wisps around my eyes.

I described it at the supper table, but Philip frowned and said I shouldn't concern myself so much about the opinion of the town. He, though, as he said it, clenched his jaws again, and squared his shoulders belligerently.

Monday Evening, June 12

Philip had a letter today with a postal order in it for twenty-five dollars. It was from Tillsonborough, our church before this one, on account of arrears that we'd given up all hope of ever collecting. He was a little excited over it too, but for the sake of his adult dignity he pursed up his lips and kept his eyes away from me. When I seized his hands and tried to do a maypole dance he resisted me severely. "After all they owe us something like a thousand. We're surely entitled to twenty-five."

Then with a frown he thrust the postal order into my hand and slammed the study door behind him, shamming a fit of pique and sulks to cover his generosity. Twenty-five dollars, though, I decided, was license enough for a breach of even the strict emotional restraint for the last few weeks had been a law between us, and bursting in after him I put my arms around his middle before he could sit down and hung on tight. He tried to laugh, but the sound curled up on him the same way my sick little poppy and nasturtium leaves curl up against the blistered earth. And I could only retreat, saying feebly we must have something good for supper, something Steve likes, as a little celebration.

It was a good supper, but Philip hadn't much appetite. I kept watching him, and the efforts he was making to enter into Steve's mood pretty well took away mine too. I saw my mistake now. It was the same not so very long ago when the church board gave him forty dollars all at once. I ought to have been more unconcerned about it. I humiliated him by making an event of it, letting him see how seldom twenty-five dollars come our way. For we're poor people, and whatever his own standards of success may be, he's nevertheless part enough of life, even away out here in Horizon, to smart a little with a feeling of incompetence when up for measurement against the world's yardstick of salary check and bank account.

Or it may have been that the money shamed him a little, reminded him how he earned it, for he's the kind that keeps his hypocrisy beside him the way a guilty monk would keep his scourge.

After supper he sat for a while with Steve in the living-room. Busy clearing the table I watched and listened. He was trying to laugh, make his voice brisk and companionable, but Steve met him warily. There are too many years between them, dark, bitter ones. In a few minutes Steve came out to watch me put away what was left of the meal and to make suggestions for tomorrow. I told him I was busy and that he should go back and talk to Philip, but Philip already was in his study for the evening.

He's still there, haggard and white again. A while ago when I went in to see him he glanced at me shiftily and marked his place in a book that I think he hadn't been reading. There's almost no wind tonight. It's hot and stuffy, and the moths are fluttering thick around the lamps. As I stood beside him he trapped one in his hand, made a puckered face and squeezed it, and then with a quick, revolted gesture tossed it into the flame. We talked primly about the heat and drought, wondered would rain now save the crops. Next Sunday, he says, we're having special prayers for rain at Partridge Hill.

He had been drawing again, and under his papers I found a sketch of a little country schoolhouse. A trim, white, neat-gabled little schoolhouse, just like Partridge Hill. There's a stable at the back, and some buggies in the yard. It stands up lonely and defiant on a landscape like a desert. Almost a lunar desert, with queer, fantastic pits and drifts of sand encroaching right to the doorstep. You see it the way Paul sees it. The distorted, barren landscape makes you feel the meaning of its persistence there. As Paul put it last Sunday when we drove up, it's *Humanity in microcosm*. Faith, ideals, reason – all the things that really are humanity – like Paul you feel them there, their stand against the implacable blunderings of Nature – and suddenly like Paul you begin to think poetry, and strive to utter eloquence.

And it was just a few rough pencil strokes, and he had it buried among some notes he'd been making for next Sunday's sermon.

According to Philip it's form that's important in a picture, not the subject or the associations that the subject calls to mind; the pattern you see, not the literary emotion you feel; and it follows, therefore, that my enthusiasm for his little schoolhouse doesn't mean much from an artist's point of view. A picture worth its salt is supposed to make you experience something that he calls aesthetic excitement, not send you into dithyrambs about humanity in microcosm. I've heard it all – and still I believe in his little schoolhouse. In his schoolhouse and in him. He's bigger even than his six foot three. I've been sure right from the beginning – sure that there's some twisted, stumbling power locked up within him, so blind and helpless still it can't find outlet, so clenched with urgency it can't release itself.

But it will some day. All in their own time things like that work out.

Anyway, it's helped me decide how to spend the twenty-five dollars. We'd have got along all right if it hadn't come. This much at least is worth a try.

Ten dollars toward the horse – our little budget will have to stand it one way or another anyway, so I might as well start off with a flourish of magnanimity – and the other fifteen for paints.

Paints and brushes and canvases, enough to start him up again. It's a good nine years since he worked in oils. One after another his colors kept running out, and we were always too hard up to order more.

Tonight now he ought to be making the order up himself, but there's no use mentioning it. He'd only draw his lips in white, then look at me hurt as if I were mocking him. Some morning I'll have to arrange them in his study, slip out to the garden, and leave him alone with them a while. That way it will work. I've watched him handling tubes and brushes in a store, laying them down, picking them up again. To make sure he doesn't get them first I'm having them come addressed to Mrs. Bird.

I haven't a catalogue, and my memory for what is essential in brushes and colors doesn't serve me very well, so at last I've simply written a store where he used to go for his supplies. and asked them to spend the fifteen dollars for me. It's a pity, though, he isn't doing it himself, because he would like picking out the colors, seeing each one as he wrote it down ooze out of the tube and glisten on the palette. I used to like the names the colors had myself – *terre verte* and *sienna*, *gamboge*, *vermilion lake*, *ultramarine* – just as names they suggested so much that the colors themselves always fell a little flat. There was *burnt umber*, too – and Philip told me that *umber* meant shade, the same as an *umbrella* – because it was a dark color, I suppose, and good for putting in shadows with. Anyway it's one I must remember next time I see him to try on Mr. Paul.

Wednesday Evening, June 14

Steve brought home a dog today. A big, rawboned, houndish brute. with sad running eyes and a ratty tail. He's black except for a little fleck of white round his face and chin that gives him an ancient, monkey-look of grief and wisdom; but even though his back comes up to Philip's knee there's a gangling awkwardness about the way he brings his big feet down to show him up as an overgrown and still self-conscious pup.

He limps, and smells, and has fleas. While Steve and I held him Philip examined his foot, and finally cut out a pebble imbedded between the toes. Then we bathed his eyes with boracic acid, spent eighty cents on a bottle of mange cure, and topped it off with a thorough scouring in the washtub.

He was too frightened to struggle, and when it was over and he stood dripping and bony and drowned-looking Philip named him. El Greco – because El Greco was an artist who had a way of painting people long and lean as if they'd all been put on the rack and stretched considerably, and if he had ever painted a dog, Philip says, it would have been just such a one as ours.

He's ours, all right. While we were drying him Mrs. Finley came in about some business for the Ladies Aid, and sitting down on the edge of a chair said sweetly what Christians we were, taking in every stray that comes along.

Which promptly settled it. Philip turned his back on her, and picking up the towel again rubbed so hard that El Greco started to whimper. It made me remember another stray dog we once had, and an hour or two after Philip brought him home another caller. With crops so poor, she said, we were fortunate to be able to afford a pet. Most of the people in town found it hard enough to manage just for themselves. I remember how gray Philip looked, and the flat, half-frightened stillness in his eyes. The same afternoon he borrowed a rifle and shot the dog, then came home and was sick behind the house. I found him there, and for my lack of tact in showing up at such a moment incurred his masculine aloofness at its severest for a week. There were fleas in plenty that time too, and bites, according to her own reports around the town, for even our visitor. From the bottom of my heart I wish as much for Mrs. Finley.

Friday Evening, June 16

We had callers today from Randolph, the next town, fifteen miles from here. The Reverend and Mrs. Albert Downie, to extend a word of brotherly encouragement and cheer. A quaint, serene little pair – piety and its rib in a Ford more battle-scarred even than ours – the parson and his wife in caricature.

He is bald and thin, confident and kindly. Like a just-awakened Rip Van Winkle who was an earnest little Boy Scout when he fell asleep, a lecture still ringing in his ears on *The Abundant Life*. You couldn't imagine him ever racked by a doubt or conflict. He said a word of prayer for us, and finished radiant. I glanced at Philip, and for a minute wished that I were the artist, with a pad and pencil at my hand.

Mrs. Downie has white hair and blue eyes, and a voice like a teaspoon tinkling in a china cup. A frail, tiny woman, with a fussy, beribboned hat too big for her that she has likely salvaged from a mission barrel, and that makes mine in contrast seem quite modish. And supporting it so bravely, with such stalwart, meek assurance. Over the tea and sponge cake I had a few gaunt moments, looking down a corridor of years and Horizons, at the end of which was a mirror and my own reflection. They had heard I was a musician, and wondered would I render something. Perhaps they expected hymns. I played two Chopin waltzes, and they exclaimed politely that all music was sacred.

It's hot and still tonight, and there's a swarm of little moths again around the lamp. We've fixed up a bed for El Greco with some old mats and blankets in the woodshed, but he won't resign himself to it, and every few minutes keeps giving a mournful little howl. Faithfully he kept Mrs. Ellingson's chickens out of the garden all morning, and then this afternoon dug a bed for himself in the middle of my poppies. There are ten left, and four nasturtiums. More and more I go walking on the railroad.

Steve made a very bad drawing of El Greco this evening, and then one of the Leaning Tower with me just coming out. Philip's jubilant, and says we must be careful to encourage Steve. He started off with twenty-five cents, at which rate of encouragement, I told him sourly, he could count on a sufficient supply of Pisas by fall to re-privy every Main Street in the Middle West.

Sunday Evening, June 18

This was the day out at Partridge Hill we prayed for rain. Sitting at the organ I could see the bare dry fields through the open window, quivering and blurred with a tremble of summer heat. The heat and hush was in the schoolhouse, too. One minute the faces in front of me were close, distinct. I could see the sunburn, the still flattened eyes, the red triangles of neck. The next they ran together, dimmed – and then were solid and still again.

It was dense, rigid heat. The schoolhouse seemed dark with it. On one side, coming through the windows. there were bright, clean-cornered planks of sunlight, but they went no farther than their corners, held in a cast by the breathless gloom of heat.

Joe Lawson, who looks like Philip, was there. More like him even than usual, for his face was haggard as Philip's often is, and there were tight little wincing lines around his eyes.

It's his crippled son Peter, who still has to keep his bed, and who Dr. Bird says should have a city specialist. Through the long prayers for rain he sat with his eyes fixed straight in front of him. My own went out again to the still expanse of prairie, the deadly sun glare over it; and for the first time I wished that Philip could mean his prayers, reach out and comfort a little.

A baby cried, and the mother carried it outside. I followed her, found a little tepid water in the porch that she dipped her handkerchief in to wipe off its forehead with, and then while it quietened sat with her on the steps.

She was a thin, hatched-faced woman, embarrassed at first because I had come out and was sitting with her, her hands nervous, tidying her dress and hair. Unless it rains, she says, this will be the fifth year they haven't harvested a crop. Through the open window we could hear the slow, heavy rhythm of Philip's prayer and motioning with her head in his direction she said, "We have a service for rain about this time every year."

And tonight again the sun went down through a clear, brassy sky. Surely it must be a very great faith that such indifference on the part of its deity cannot weaken – a very great faith, or a very foolish one. Paul and I are tied on it.

Monday Evening, June 19

El Greco took a mouthful of feathers out of one of Mrs. Ellingson's hens today, and in high dudgeon Mrs. Ellingson came over to tell us we'll get no more eggs from her.

Steve's jubilant – he's El Greco's trainer – and El Greco himself, I notice, has a smug and somewhat jaunty look. He goes padding through the house in complete possession now, his ears at a cock, his hindquarters fairly resolute. His appetite is so good that Steve tonight suggested going round the neighbors getting scraps for him, but Philip darkened like a thundercloud, and said we would feed our dog ourselves.

Paul dropped in this evening with a basket of strawberries from the restaurant. The bit of cream, though, that I save from the top of the milk had soured on account of the heat, and we had to eat them just with sugar. We left the stems on, and dipped them into saucers of sugar that I set in front of us. But Philip couldn't relax enough for such an informal way, and I noticed he dipped and took his bites self-consciously.

Paul was somewhat ill at ease too, and when we finished, and Steve had taken El Greco out to the woodshed, he asked did we ever wonder why he went so regularly to church.

"Why then?" I said, but instead of answering he only made out a case for staying away.

"I don't like to give a false impression," he insisted. "I don't like sailing under false colors. I'm a rationalist – and yesterday, you see, the prayers for rain – well, after I left you, I started wondering if you suspected what I really thought –"

"You won't be coming then any more –"

"I didn't mean that – quite the contrary – I just wanted to be sure you understood why I keep on coming. The first time, you remember, it was only to show you the way to Partridge Hill."

There was nothing to do but nod and leave it there. He started pressing his finger tips into the sugar that was left in his saucer, and taking absent-minded little licks at his fingers. We went on talking about the vacation we're going to spend on his brother's ranch next month, then about a horse for Steve, then about Steve himself. He likes Steve, and as we talked I saw Philip's mouth set a little contentious. He never unbends to Paul completely anyway. I detect just the faintest air of condescension when they're together, the natural conviction of superiority that it seems a man six foot three can't help feeling over one just five foot seven and a half.

And Paul keeps on trying so hard to be friends with Philip. He's a born scholar – with the enthusiasm and humility for it anyway, even if not the background – and primed as he always is with learning and ideas he needs someone like Philip to work himself out on – just as El Greco needs my flower beds for rolling in to work out his exuberance and itch. It's the real reason he comes to church so regularly, only Philip knowing that he is rational-minded, at the same time smarting with a sense of his own hypocrisy, can't give him much of a welcome. Philip is actually a little envious. He's the kind, too, that doesn't like sailing under false colors.

I don't know what the solution is. Surely there's more than one way for a man like Philip to earn his living. Surely something can be done to make him realize it. Because you're a hypocrite you lose your self-respect, because you lose your self-respect you lose your initiative and self-belief – it's the same vicious circle, every year closing in a little tighter. Already it's making him morose and cynical – smaller than he ought to be. I can't help wondering what he'll be like ten years from now.

Wednesday Evening, June 21

There was a letter today from another town where we used to be, Kelby, and another check for twenty-five dollars. Philip tried to look unconcerned, but as soon as I met his eyes he flinched and turned away. Something about his shoulders as he started for his study told me what he had done.

I took his arm and pressed close to him, trying to tell him I understood, saying wasn't it high time we did ask for our money; but he stood erect and grim, and bit off his words as if determined not to let me spare him.

"I wrote to them all – said we had to have money on account of Steve. This letter says they're going to send fifteen dollars every month. There was another I didn't show you promising a hundred after harvest. I went to the church board here, too. They'll try to have the arrears paid up by the end of next month."

He drew away from me then, and closed the study door. All afternoon there wasn't a sound. He sat white and silent at the supper table, and escaped again as soon as the meal was finished. Steve went outside with El Greco. For a few minutes I sat quiet, clamped by the dry hot stillness, and then a little desperately I broke in on him.

I was bitter. He had never asked for money for me. He had let me skimp and deny myself, and wear shabby, humiliating old clothes. I thought of the way I had borne it, pitying him, admiring him. It was because he was sensitive, fine-grained, I always said, because the hypocrisy hurt him, because beneath it all he was a genuine man. And I threw it all at him. I told him that when I married him I didn't know it was to be a four-roomed shack in Horizon. I called him a hypocrite again, and a poor contemptible coward.

And then as I stood spitting it at him he turned in his chair and looked up at me, his lips drawn, the hurt flatness in his eyes again; and all at once ashamed I dropped beside him, and put my arms around his knees and buried my face.

I tried to tell him I hadn't meant it. I wanted to comfort him now, to ease the hurt look. I wanted him to know it was really because I cared so much that I had said it all. The way we lived – the door between us – couldn't he understand it was because I was hurt too?

I sobbed it all foolishly, clinging to him, trying to make him look at me, but he helped me to my feet and said I had better lie down for a while. A few minutes later he went out. From the window I saw Steve and El Greco run up to him, then all three of them go off somewhere together.

He hadn't been gone long when Mrs. Bird came. I lit the lamp and she saw I had been crying. She drew her chair close, gave my knee a confidential pat. "I know, my dear. Clever men are always hard to live with. I have a clever husband too. But you shouldn't distress him this way, letting him see you cry. He'll never forgive you for it."

I sat biting my lip. She went on, "The doctor and I have written several papers on the subject – you'll read them some day. In his own way he's an authority – and I lend the human touch. Always let a man think how fine and tolerant he is to put up with you. That's the formula for marital success. I follow it myself and know it works. The doctor – why on some of his condescending days he's absolutely insufferable."

While we talked, Philip and Steve returned. She winked me out to the kitchen to bathe my eyes, and when I returned was reciting a hymn that she has written for next Sunday's service. "You've had prayers for rain out at Partridge Hill already," she said. "It's up to us now to try in town. I thought it would be nice for a change to have a hymn."

There's a blur after that. I went to the piano to help her fit the words to *Rock of Ages*. Steve lifted El Greco's forefeet onto his shoulders to show him off, and El Greco, thinking it was to be a game or romp, knocked a chair over and began to bark. Philip told Steve to take him out to the shed and lock him up for the night. Mrs. Bird was singing sturdily,

Let us labor not in vain,
Hear us Father, send us rain.

I don't remember clearly till it was quiet again, Philip in his study, Steve asleep. There was the dense, sickly heat, the yellow lamp flame, the patter of moth wings on the glass. I made up little speeches that I thought might help Philip and me to understand each other. I went as far as the study door once, and without opening it came back to my chair. I tried to pretend again that I despised him. I tried to laugh, saying what a fool I was, not to have seen through him long ago. I thought of Steve and tried to set myself against him, too. I tried to cry, to ease a little the ache inside me that was getting quicker, tighter, every minute. I tried a lot of things and didn't do any of them. Instead, I just sat staring at the lamp flame, my mind somehow like it, clear, burning, blank.

Then El Greco started to howl, sending a little shiver through the night, and at last, by way of the front door, I went out to quiet him. He sprang up from the darkness when I opened the door, whining happily. His feet scratched my arm; he reached my face with his slavering tongue. I sat down on the bed of old blankets Steve has made for him, and let him lie close to me with his nose in my lap. The shed was dark like the bottom of a well. I stroked him a while, then bent down with my head against his ribs and had my cry. I talked too. He must wonder at us, now that he has heard it all.

The lamp is burning dry. There's only a little globe of light left, hollowed out of the darkness like a cage for the gray-winged moths. It might be a wind tossing snow or chaff, so ceaselessly they whirl. Philip's lamp has a smaller bowl than this one; it must be burned dry too. My mind is still wide awake and clear, but I'd better go to bed so that he can follow. The last few weeks he's been careful to wait an hour or more, to be sure when he comes I'll be asleep.

Thursday Evening, June 22

The paints came today. Mrs. Bird brought them about three o'clock, just after Philip had gone up to the barber's to have his hair cut. I told her yesterday that when some parcels arrived she wasn't expecting they would be for me, some stationery and other things I had had to order for Philip.

It hadn't occurred to me, though, to ask for plain wrapping, and both packages, one of canvases and brushes, one of paints, had labels on showing they were from dealers in artists' materials. I took them from her casually, excused myself a minute to stow them away out of sight underneath Steve's bed, but when I returned she looked so mystified and curious there was nothing for it but to take her into my confidence and explain.

She listened, however, with such an indulgent, skeptical expression that on a sudden impulse to defend him, to prove he really was an artist, I led the way to the study and brought out a pile of drawings. Time went quickly for the next few minutes. She was excited and amazed and astounded to my heart's content. I drank it in deeply. I kept bringing out more and more drawings. I boasted a little, said she should have seen the things he used to do. And then at the height of it Philip came.

He has a dark look anyway at times, and a way of using it to clear a room. He used it that way this afternoon. Without a word we left the litter of drawings just as they were, and vanished to the kitchen. I made her tea out there, while she burbled how Michelangelo once dropped a hammer, from the trestle where he was working, on an unwanted visitor. It was kind of her. In return I brewed her tea strong and gave her little frosted cakes, and for reasons of my own kept her talking there till Steve came home from school.

But it was Steve's afternoon for riding Harlequin, and I found myself alone with Philip anyway. To get it over with I went in to him at once. There was such a dark, threatening silence for a moment as I closed the study door behind him that I nearly told him about the paints. But then I thought of the scene yesterday over the second twenty-five dollars, and for fear of making it even harder for him managed to restrain myself.

He glanced up irritably. I took a quick step to his chair and put a hand on his shoulder; then as I felt the bone and muscles click up hard together said humbly that I didn't know what could have come over me, that I'd never done anything like that before.

But without looking up he said bitterly, "I know all right what came over you. I don't speak well enough for myself. That's it, isn't it? You have to put in a word for me – impress them – let them see that your small-town preacher husband has more to him than they can see on the surface –"

"As if I couldn't be proud too," I said, bending down, putting my lips restrained and dry on his cheek. "Big overgrown fool. If I could draw like that would you never want to show me off?"

He didn't answer. His shoulder under my hand was like a lump of stone. I slipped away to the kitchen again, and started getting supper.

Steve was late, and I waited the meal an hour for him, dreading it alone with Philip. Steve's useful that way. On trying days like this I've known it to be an ordeal with just the two of us. Philip's a silent man anyway, and even without an atmosphere of tension between us it's sometimes hard enough, his rule to maintain silence unless there's something to say. But Steve's a chatterer. He doesn't know that the obvious is forbidden ground. He comments on the food, gossips about Paul and the classroom, gives the highlights of his lessons, even draws Philip sometimes into an argument. It was Harlequin tonight again, and his own horse just two weeks away.

It's been a good day, one of the best. There has to be a hard half-hour or two like this afternoon to make it so. After Steve was asleep Philip went out for a book that I had put on the shelf out there, and leaning over the cot he touched his foot against the paints and canvases.

I was sitting here pretending to read when he brought them in. I turned my page and read hard a minute, going all gooseflesh as I felt him looking at me. Then I stood up and took the parcels from him, and without speaking went to my sewing basket for the scissors.

"They're addressed to Mrs. Bird," he said. "What are we doing with them here?"

I nodded, didn't answer. I opened the paints first, and one by one as I took the tubes out of the corrugated cardboard they were packed in laid them out on the table. And he came over to the table where I stood, and one by one picked them up again. I didn't look at him, but I could see his hands, the way his fingers turned and felt each tube a moment, then put it down reluctantly to take the next. Still without a word I went on and opened the canvases and brushes, and busy tidying the string and paper watched him take the brushes up again to try them, the hog's hair with his finger tip against the bristly ends, the camel's hair in even strokes across his palm.

Then I saw him lay the last one down, and his hand against the darkness gather, hesitate. It was good to stand there waiting for it, blind and choked, knowing it would come. "You're a fool too," he said at last, and let me snuggle close to him. "You'd have spent the money better on a dress. These are only wasted, you know, on me."

I snuggled closer, as the best way of letting him know I didn't think so, and he took my chin in his fingers and made me look up at him, and with a twisted, grateful little smile said he was sorry about this afternoon.

It was all good, even the shy, half-frightened way he looked at me, and the hint of promise as his hand grew tight on mine.

Maybe I oughtn't to. Maybe I ought to have more pride, think of the other nights, and remember that this time it's only because I bought him canvases and paints. Maybe I oughtn't to, but I will. That's the kind he is – and the kind I am. Better for paints and canvases than not at all – than his shoulder hard against me like a wall.

Monday Evening, June 26

We leave on our holidays a week from today. The thought of it now makes the town unbearable. The wind has blown itself out. The heat when you step outside is dry and deadly like a drill. I walk up Main Street furtively, an alien in its blistered lifelessness. Back here the doors are closed, the blinds all drawn against the sun. The air is thick and heavy; a twitch comes to my hands to thresh out against it, keep from smothering. I go outside again, but the garden is bare, inert, impaled by the rays of sun and left to die.

It dies slowly – and the twitch returns to my hands. I could tear out and slash the yellow stalks that shrivel and droop, yet cling so stubbornly to life. My fuchsias, too, seem losing heart, and all the six geraniums. Steve says it's because I got them from Mrs. Ellingson, and she still isn't speaking to us on account of El Greco and her hens. I look across at her hip-roofed house, at the blistered street again, and wonder how I'd ever stand it if I didn't know we were going to get away.

Paul says we'll be welcome at the ranch, and has written already that we are coming. Laura, he tells us, his sister-in-law, used to ride with a traveling rodeo. She chafes now a little at the monotony of the ranch, and will be grateful even for a parson and his wife.

Philip, however, is planning the privacy of our own tent. Partly because he doesn't like being under an obligation to anyone – partly because he fancies a campfire and the open night. He let it slip to Steve yesterday, and Steve let it slip to me.

He did a little prairie scene in oils this afternoon – on cardboard, because he wants to save the canvases till he's found himself in paints again – and when I called Paul in after school to look at it he screwed his face up hard to keep me from suspecting he was pleased. He was pleased even more though when Paul stood quite still in front of it a minute; so pleased that relaxing a little he asked him to stay for supper with us, and was nicer to him than he's ever been.

We had canned salmon with lettuce from the store and hard-boiled eggs around it, and stewed dried apricots and cake and tea. When Steve's plate was clean I tried to catch his eye so that he wouldn't ask for more till Paul had had a second helping, but Paul noticed and understood, and with the best of intentions said he got canned salmon twice a week where he boarded, and that he never ate it except when he had to anyway.

Later he wondered bluntly how any man would rather preach than paint, and went in again to admire Philip's picture. He's looking forward to getting away from Horizon too. There was another note from Mrs. Wenderby at noon today, warning him that if he insists on saying *sweat* in the classroom instead of *perspiration* she'll use her influence to have the school board ask him to resign. He thinks maybe he belongs in the country anyway.

Saturday Evening, July 1

Judith was here today. After supper we walked up the railroad track again as far as the ravine where Philip and I sat last April in a snowstorm. We came home slowly, watching the straggle of town slip into the prairie, and the little lights grow strong against the dusk. There was a strange wariness in her eyes. I asked her to sing, and her voice was the same, not strong and full as usual, but constrained, lifeless. We tried a while, but couldn't find much to talk about. I admitted to myself at last that the trouble is Philip.

She doesn't know yet. I wish I could spare her the day she must find out. For behind the white face and timid eyes there's something fearless, a press of strong, untried womanhood. It's just like the day Philip and I sat in the snowstorm watching the water rush through the stones so swift that sometimes, as we watched, it seemed still, solid like glass. I've looked at her sometimes, slight, self-conscious, irresolute, and wondered at the will and strength it must have taken to resist her family and leave the farm. Philip was away with Steve in the car again this afternoon. Hidden behind the curtain I stood watching them drive off, trying not to mind, to resign myself. That's why I wish I could spare her – because I've gone through it, know how much it costs. She's going to find there are harder things than driving a grain team or stooking in the harvest field.

Wednesday Evening, July 5

We arrived Monday afternoon. Just as Paul promised there are the hills and river and horses all right, but the trees turn out to be scraggly little willow bushes that Philip describes contemptuously as "brush."

With his artist's eye for character he says the best ones are the driftwood logs, come all the way from the mountains likely, four or five hundred miles west. They lie gnarled and blackened on the white sand like writhing, petrified serpents. It was Paul's fancy, one of his boyhood's. Pointing to a big, somber-looking hill across the river he said, "We still call it the Gorgon."

You leave the farms and wheat land fifty miles away, and drive through white dry grass that throws back the glare of the sun and burns your eyes like sand. There's a slow incline to the prairie, and ahead you think you see a range of hills. But their crests retreat as you advance. The trail keeps nosing on and up.

The trail forks sometimes. It's such a long way you begin to wonder is Paul as sure of the turns to take as he insists. There are scattered herds of cattle grazing, and broncos that wheel off a little way to snort disdainfully at the advent of a Ford, and then with a toss of their manes go streaking across the prairie to show what they can do. And there's a cowboy once who waves as we pass, and whose solitary figure against the horizon gives the landscape for a moment vastness that we hadn't felt before.

Then suddenly the climbing prairie draws up short, and spread out before us are the valley and the river. The river flows indolently through a mile-wide, sandy flat. Sand bars in places split it up into six and seven channels, and so far below us, reflecting the afternoon sun, it looks like a piece of shining filigree. Beyond there are the hills, rising steep and buttresslike to our own level, their smooth, rounded contours white with sun and sand. Like skulls, suggests Paul – skulls that once were mountains.

The way down is slow and tortuous, and we reach the flat more than a mile from where the road drops off the prairie.

Laura is away riding when we arrive. A neat half-breed girl called Annie takes us inside, and as a stay till suppertime sets us down to bread and sirup, and weak green tea served in enamel cups. After a sip or two Steve says he doesn't like the tea, and hopes he isn't going to have to drink it for the next two weeks. She glares with her beady eyes a moment, then tells him he'll get coffee for breakfast. Three half-naked little girls file in and stand watching us eat, and the moment we leave the table make a rush for the sirup jug. The eldest is seven, the youngest two. They look so dirty and neglected I volunteer to wash them and get their hair combed before supper. "Suit yourself," Annie says shortly. "I do the cooking here."

It turns out I've given myself practically a full-time job. For Laura is a thorough ranch woman, with a disdainful shrug for all such domestic ties. There's a mannish verve about her that somehow is what you expect, that fits into a background of range and broncos, and at the same time a kind of glamour, to confirm all you've ever imagined about an older, more colorful West.

She wears a bright red bandeau over her hair, a man's shirt and trousers, and for riding fine leather chaps studded with silver nails. She breaks broncos and punches cattle a match for any cowboy. They call her familiarly by name, give her backside every now and then a companionable cuff, and saddle her little buckskin stallion with the bunkhouse counterpart of gallantry.

She's slim and supple like a girl still, but when near her you see the lines and crow's-feet. Forty-five anyway, says Paul. She was a star attraction in rodeos fifteen years before Stanley married her.

She's good to Steve and me, but has taken an unaccountable dislike to Philip. This morning when he went off to sketch she told me bluntly he wasn't the right kind of man to bring up Steve. I asked why, and, her voice pitched incredulous she said, "And have him go round drawing little pictures too?"

I must admit that Philip isn't showing up to advantage here. He can't make the cowboys forget he's a preacher, and at mealtimes they all look awkward and uncomfortable. For so many years he's spoken only when he's had something to say that his attempts now to be conversational make him sound like a priggish young evangelist. I find myself a little the same way too at times. I speak or laugh, and suddenly in my voice catch a hint of the benediction. It just means, I suppose, that all these years the Horizons have been working their will on me. My heresy, perhaps, is less than I sometimes think.

And seeing him as likely all the others do, I'm afraid that Steve's going to stand some careful watching too. At home he never stops his chatter, but here he sits through a meal in superior silence. Every now and then there's a little twitch to his nostrils, as if he were sniffing. This morning he came to me in a pout because Annie ordered him out of the kitchen. No halfbreed, he says, is going to talk like that to him.

He's an attractive boy, fearless with a horse, and the cowboys are willing to accept him. One of them even says he's going to make him leather chaps out of an old pair of his own, studding them like Laura's except that the nails will be brass instead of silver. But Steve stands aloof, meets their banter with the same little twitching of his nostrils, takes no pains to conceal that their company isn't to his taste.

Even Paul screws up his face, wondering what's come over the boy. "Shyness," I suggest, "I used to be like that with strangers too." But Paul goes off looking dubious.

It's really Philip who's to blame, and whether I like the

prospect or not we must soon have a stiff half-hour and thresh it out. Philip himself is an artist, sensitive and impressionable, wary of life because he's expected too much of it, and now to spare Steve his own disappointments he encourages him to stand aloof and distrustful of it too. He cares deeply for Steve. He found him with the town against him, just as another town was once against himself. It will be easier, he thinks, if he helps him to a disillusioned, unexpectant self-sufficiency. But a man's tragedy is himself, not the events that overtake him, and the same Main Street slight and condescension that put a cloud over Philip for life, Steve is emerging from already and shaking off.

Life has proved bitter and deceptive to Philip because of the artist in him, because he has kept seeking a beauty and significance that isn't life's to give; but Steve is a shrewd little realist, who, given opportunity to meet life on its own terms, ought to make a fair success of it.

He's so wrapped up in Steve, so jealously devoted to him, yet when Steve wants companionship or affection it's always to me he comes. "A horse," Paul said. "Give him a horse – keep him out of the herd –" and now he turns on Philip and insists, "Let him ride with the men – or alone. He sees enough of you. His horse will bring him home all right. You come with me or Stanley."

And Philip watches him ride off, paces round the corral a few times, then takes his sketch pad and spends a poky afternoon along the river bank.

As to the horse itself that Steve's to have, there's disagreement. Steve has his heart set on a sorrel three-year-old that Paul says is too wild and nervous for him. Philip agrees – is afraid for Steve – yet finds the spirited sorrel and the dashing way Steve rides him hard to resist. Laura suggests a rangy bay she sometimes rides herself, fast, but ten years old. Paul argues for another three-year-old that's shaping up well and has steady blood behind him. Stanley talks quietly about a dark brown mare called Minnie, fast enough, and thoroughly dependable.

Stanley has less to say than Paul, is a year or two older. Yesterday he saddled a quiet old horse and took me riding. We followed a cattle path up to the level of the prairie, then, so I wouldn't get too stiff the first time out, dismounted and sat down a while like a pair of flies on an upturned mixing bowl. Annie, he told me after a silence, plans shortly to marry one of his cowboys, and they're wondering if they mightn't hurry things up now, and take advantage of Philip. I said I was quite sure he would be pleased to oblige them, but suggested they mention it to him themselves. I don't want to be accused of making a good fellow of myself at his expense.

I see Stanley seldom, though: he avoids Laura, and Laura spends most of her time with me. Paul blames a cowboy a few summers ago who left her the silver-studded chaps and buckskin stallion. "A big handsome fellow," he says resignedly. "I suppose it wasn't altogether her fault. We Kirbys were never much to look at."

There are times when I wish Laura wasn't quite so attentive. She has a bitter way of questioning and ridiculing me. She laughs at Philip, wonders how I ever came to marry a preacher. In front of the cowboys at noon today she mimicked me at a Ladies Aid meeting leading in prayer. Some of them in Horizon are just as critical and venomous, but they work with more finesse. The needle's in before you know it. It's easier to maintain face.

We've brought a tent, but she insists I sleep in Annie's room. It's small and stuffy, with pictures on the walls of purebred bulls and stallions, and there's always the thought of the dispossessed Annie sleeping in the kitchen on a makeshift mattress. Steve and Philip and Paul have the tent, and for atmosphere, I suppose, they've built a fire tonight down by the river. A while ago it was so hot and close in here I slipped out of the house to join them; but after watching a few minutes from the darkness I went on again, and walked along the river bank alone.

When I rounded a point and looked back and couldn't see the fire I was afraid for a minute. The close black hills, the stealthy slipping sound the river made – it was as if I were entering dead, forbidden country, approaching the lair of the terror that destroyed the hills, that was lurking there still among the skulls. For like draws to like, they say, which makes it reasonable to suppose that, when you've just walked away from a man because you feel he doesn't want to be bothered with you, you're capable of attracting a few ghouls and demons anyway. I stood rooted a moment, imagining shapes in the darkness closing in on me, and then with a whole witches' Sabbath at my heels turned and made a bolt for the house. And now, an hour later, it's still a relief to look up and see the fleshy, moon-faced Hereford above my bed.

Sunday Evening, July 9

About twenty miles from here there's a booming little town that started up just a year ago. We went there last night, Philip, Laura, Steve and Paul and I, slept in a Chinese restaurant, and reached home this morning a little after ten.

A cowboy rode over yesterday from one of the neighboring ranches with word that there was to be a dance in the new poolroom. Laura wanted to go, and Stanley wouldn't. I whispered to Philip it was a chance to repay her a little for her hospitality. He had promised Steve a sombrero anyway, Paul had another book to order on philology, and I thought I'd like to see a Main Street in the making.

Between them Laura and Annie found some clothes for me not quite so staid and prosy as my own, while the cowboys took Philip to the bunkhouse and fitted him out in a dark blue shirt, ten-gallon hat and a red silk handkerchief. Laura looked him over critically a minute, and as we were gettiag into the car said it was a pity he couldn't dance.

I wish Horizon could have seen us. As we strode up Main Street, into the crowded poolroom, past the busy barber chairs, I was thinking of Mrs. Pratt and Mrs. Finley. They were dancing to an orchestra of piano, saxophone, and two guitars. Farmers mostly, with awkward sunburned girls who laughed too much and couldn't forget their clothes; cowboys here and there in chaps and gaudy shirts and handkerchiefs, sombreroed some of them even while they danced, all swaggering a little to maintain the dashing, picturesque traditions of a West that they had read about in magazines.

But for a long time I sat out of it, more Horizon-minded, I suppose, than sometimes I admit. Like an old philosopher I found myself wondering had Horizon ever been like this, with prophetic satisfaction seeing the day when here, too, it would all be weather-beaten and subdued, the poolroom with a placard up like Horizon's, THE LANGUAGE THAT YOUR MOTHER USED IS GOOD ENOUGH FOR HERE.

They're sad little towns when a philosopher looks at them. Brave little mushroom heyday – new town, new world – false fronts and future, the way all Main Streets grow – and then prolonged senility.

I whispered it to Paul, and he whispered back, "Grasshopper towns."

For there's a story that a goddess once, enamored of a mortal, sought for him from the other gods the gift of immortality. But not of youth. The years went on, and her handsome lover grew bald and bleary-eyed. Young and beautiful herself she begged the gods again either to grant him youth or let him die like other men, but this time they were obdurate. And she hardened at last, and found another lover, and to escape the first one changed him into a grasshopper.

They're poor, tumbledown, shabby little towns, but they persist. Even the dry years yield a little wheat; even the little means livelihood for some. I know a town where once it rained all June, and that fall the grain lay in piles outside full granaries. It's an old town now, shabby and decrepit like the others, but it, too, persists. It knows only two years: the year it rained all June, and next year.

But while I sat philosophizing the heyday, mushroom town was there; and gradually the Horizon matron slipped away from me, and before I knew it my foot had started tapping with the music too.

Philip and Steve went off to find a store that sold sombreros. Paul danced with Laura, then with me. And after fifteen years it was good again, even though I only shuffled round the floor, and all the time kept wishing it were Philip instead of Paul.

Laura had used the tongs on my hair and given it a little wave, and Paul said gallantly that I didn't look so old that way. His dancing was about like mine. "I've tried," he said seriously, "but I can't quite catch on. Maybe it was so much riding when I was a boy."

Then it was Laura's turn again, and as they started off a shy young cowboy came and asked me would I dance with him. He was as tall as Philip, but gangling and stooped and narrow-shouldered, with a big loose mouth and light-brown speckled eyes. He looked frightened, and spoke like a boy with a message to deliver. We went round the floor once or twice in silence, then he said his name was Sam, and I said "Glad to know you, Sam. You sure dance swell."

It was a long, labored dance, both of us a little dubious of the other, but rallying suddenly as the music finished he took my arm and said we were going into the restaurant now for supper. "Those fellows you see looking at us," he explained with a nod towards two cowboys by the door, "they bet a dollar you wouldn't dance with me, and we're going out now to spend it."

I went, hoping absurdly Philip might see me. In the restaurant, facing me across a little table, he proved younger even than I had thought. To help him believe in his success as a worldly-wise young blade I finished my coffee and asked for pop, had a ham sandwich, pickles, and raisin pie. There were fifteen cents left when we finished, which he spent on candy for his horse.

Then we went for a walk, up one side of Main Street and down the other, stopping outside the stores to marvel at the Saturday night crowds, admiring the new, unpainted buildings with their false fronts going up, predicting great things for the future.

We ended up at a hitching rail on the outskirts of the town, feeding his horse the candy. Smoke, he called him, a little ghost-horse in the stray flickers of light from the street, a light mottled gray, with pure white mane and tail.

We took turns feeding him the candy. Sam bragged a little, talked of a race and a fifty-dollar bet he'd won only the week before. I admitted laconically that Smoke was built for speed all right, and slapped his hips and belly like an expert.

When we reached the poolroom again he asked me for another dance. Philip and Steve were back, sprawling on one of the benches along the wall. Steve was asleep, Philip's arm supporting his shoulder to keep him from slipping forward. Philip nodded good-humoredly each time we danced past, a faint twist to his lips, as if he thought my stripling cowboy funny. I hoped he would resent him, but he didn't.

When the dance finished Paul was waiting for the next one. A puritanical corner of his modern young mind in ascendancy for the moment, he told me roundly I should have had more sense. After a long, celibate week on the range just what did I think brought the cowboys to town on Saturday night? It was especially bad being asked to go and see a horse.

Laura meanwhile had found some acquaintances among the cowboys; it was one o'clock before she was ready to leave the poolroom.

Then when finally we did reach the car Philip couldn't get it to start. For all the old ones he's had to drive he's still quite useless when anything goes wrong. He tinkered sleepily a while, Steve and Paul looking on and giving instructions, then went to the garage and found it closed for the night. There was no hotel; the best we could do was the Chinese restaurant. After a lot of haranguing they yielded two little rooms to us, hot and dusty, thick with a reek of the kitchen and the Orient.

We were too tired, though, to be fastidious, and slept right through till Philip wakened us at eight o'clock. He and Paul and Steve had been up since six. The car was running again, and they had a surly Chinaman out of bed to make us coffee.

It had been a big night for the town. On the floor there were maybe a dozen men stretched out asleep, huddled and sodden as if they had lain down sick for a while and had had to stay that way. Like a minister's wife I hurried over them and didn't look too close, but out on the street Paul insisted that he had seen my cowboy friend.

Anyway it was good to escape the Horizon matrons for a while, and good to get home to the ranch again, and stretch out in bed for a second sleep beneath my guardian Hereford. I looked at him closer when I got up today, and found that his name was Gallant Lad the Third. His son, Annie tells me, is here now on the ranch and carrying on. As a calf, though, he belonged to Paul, and instead of Gallant Lad the Fourth he's Priapus the First.

Monday Evening, July 10

The arguments about the proper horse for Steve keep on. I for the most part stay discreetly out, and only wonder what the price will be. Steve is still determined to have the sorrel three-year-old, and he sits him so well, and looks so trim and competent, that Philip stands looking on in a trance of admiration, and hasn't the heart to say a prudent no.

Philip has been working in oils today, but he didn't finish his picture and refuses to let me look. Laura, I see, still thinks that it's a pity.

Tuesday Evening, July 11

It's not going to be the sorrel three-year-old. He threw Steve in front of the stable this afternoon, and Philip has agreed to the brown mare Minnie. Steve sulks and declares he won't have her, but it's just to save his face. She's a graceful, friendly little thing, a dark sleek brown that dapples down her hips to solid black. Paul found them after supper getting acquainted out in the corral, and wisely slipped away to let things take their course. Steve won't admit it, but I think his tumble has left him pretty sore in spots.

He's beginning now to find the days heavy on his hands. He wondered at breakfast time if El Greco's getting enough to eat with Mrs. Bird. I hear him arguing with Philip whether they should put Minnie's stall in the woodshed or the garage. The novelty is over now. Like Philip and me he's getting tired.

We've all lived in a little town too long. The wilderness here makes us uneasy. I felt it first the night I walked alone along the river bank – a queer sense of something cold and fearful, something inanimate, yet aware of us. A Main Street is such a self-sufficient little pocket of existence, so smug, compact, that here we feel abashed somehow before the hills, their passiveness, the unheeding way they sleep. We climb them, but they withstand us, remain as serene and unrevealed as ever. The river slips past, unperturbed by our coming and going, stealthily confident. We shrink from our insignificance. The stillness and solitude – we think a force or presence into it – even a hostile presence, deliberate, aligned against us – for we dare not admit an indifferent wilderness, where we may have no meaning at all.

Paul this morning persuaded me to go riding with him, and for an hour or more while the horses cropped we sat on the smooth round dome of one of the hills just above the river, talking for a while, then just thinking, then just sitting there, somehow stripped of ourselves, as if while we looked at them the hills had spread round us, drawn us into their passionless, sky-worn reality.

I said they were old hills, that for a long time the river must have glittered there. Paul tried to make me understand how old, how long. In the banks of this very river, he said, only a hundred or so miles away, there are fossil remains of the prehistoric lizards. They lived eighty, maybe a hundred million years ago. With his forehead wrinkled he tried to stretch the span of my mind that I might understand him when he said a million years. Like a solemn young professor in geology he went still farther back, millions and more millions of years, all the ages of the earth set up for me to wonder at in orderly perspective, till at last there were only dust and nebula, and a whirlwind out of space.

And then like a virtuoso he sped forward: mountains to hills this time – hills to the stretch of sandy flat along the river – strange other fossils in it that were men and women once like us.

Eternity, though, was too big for me, and even while we sat there, looking at the hills, I slipped away from them to think of us.

I went back to the first pulpit, the first Main Street; then still farther back, to his first Main Street. I thought of the restaurant, the bell he used to ring at train time – the empty little town, the first faint stirrings of belief and will.

I went forward, too, the next pulpit and the next, the next Main Street and the next. I saw Steve grown, straining away from us, life of his own to live – and an old, unwanted Philip straining after him. I saw the last church, the last town.

Philip meanwhile had been going through it too. At least so his sketches said tonight. There were half a dozen that he grumbled at and crumpled up and then smoothed out again. Just the hills, the driftwood logs, and stunted trees – but brooding over and pervading everything the same conviction of approaching dissolution that made it cold sometimes this morning out in the blazing sun.

As always with his drawings it's what you feel, not what you see. Paul and Stanley came over to the tent while I was there, looked at the sketches over my shoulder, and then went off again. I followed them, feeling that Philip would rather be alone. It didn't hurt tonight, though, because only a moment before he had ordered Steve out of the tent. Steve came into the kitchen later, and while Annie spread him bread and sirup said that Philip told him he's going to work tomorrow in oils. With his mouth full he hoped things would go better than they did today.

Wednesday Evening, July 12

They didn't though. It's been one of Philip's hard days, when the artist in him gets the upper hand. Reality as the rest of us know it disappears from him. It isn't that he sits daydreaming or lost in the clouds – at such times there's actually a vitality about him that you're relieved to get away from – but rather as if he pierces this workaday reality of ours, half scales it off, sees hidden behind it another. ·More important, more significant than ours, but that he understands only vaguely. He tries to solve it, give it expression, and doesn't quite succeed. His nerves wear thin, let fly if you happen to intrude. He slips off limp to bed at last, and sleeps as if drugged till the next day, sometimes as late as noon.

Such days are seldom now. That's why, perhaps, because he had so long to gather for it, today was harder even than usual. Just before noon Laura came in and said he was sitting out in the sun near the river without a hat. I said it might be better to leave him alone, but she insisted on taking him out one of Stanley's sombreros. Knowing how they irritate each other at the best of times I went along.

He glared at us, and kept on painting. Laura said she had brought a hat for him, and he snapped back he didn't want it. I suggested meekly he could wait and paint when we got back to town. For answer he gave such a squeeze to a tube of paint that it squirted across the palette and down his leg.

I motioned Laura to come away, but instead she went behind him and tried to crush the hat down over his head. He sprang to his feet and spun round on her, such a quick hot look in his eyes that she sidled back and stood close to me. He glared like that maybe half a minute, then took the sombrero off, and with the same vicious kind of energy as when he squeezed the paint, sent it spinning across the bank and into the river.

It was a good sombrero, worth maybe fifteen dollars. I ran after it about a mile, then waded out up past my middle, and caught it on a sand bar.

Laura came to meet me, and for the rest of the way back to the house took my arm, determined to be sympathetic. At the table when Paul asked where Philip was she told them what had happened. "Just like a lunatic he stood there. You never saw such eyes – and him a preacher too. I wish I had the handling of him for a day or two."

But all that's over now, doesn't matter much. The really hard part is the picture he turned out. The hills and river and driftwood logs again – not so deft or finished as the pencil sketches yesterday; you can see he's a little clumsy still in oils – but with the same strength and fatalism, the same unflinching insight.

Anyway they were words something like that that Paul used. He went into the tent after supper and found Philip asleep, then came for me to see it too.

It was all he said. He brought the canvas out of the tent and stood holding it in front of me a minute, then put it back and went off to the stables.

When he was gone I went inside to Philip. I took off his shoes and unbuttoned his shirt at the throat, but he was sleeping sound and didn't stir. They have an old chair in the tent for holding the lantern and their shaving things. I cleared it off and sat with him till Paul and Steve came in at nine o'clock.

It was simple enough. There was no hard thinking to do, nothing tangled to get straight. He's an artist, that's all, and he's going to waste. It wasn't just temper or a fit of pique today. He's as big a coward as the next one when it comes to appearing ridiculous or making a scene. Paul lit the lantern when he came in, and I looked at the canvas again. He came over to it too, and Steve held the lantern up to let us see. We stood like that till Steve's arm was tired; then Paul said he'd better waken Philip and help him off with his clothes.

It's late now, but I can't sleep. It's always been my way to comfort myself thinking that water finds its own level, that if there's anything great or good in a man it will eventually find its way out. But I've never taken hold of the thought and analyzed it before, never seen how false it really is. Water gets dammed sometimes; and sometimes, seeking its level, it seeps away in dry, barren earth. Just as he's seeping away among the false fronts of these little towns.

Perhaps it's been his own sermons Sunday after Sunday, the accepted, orthodox way he'd had to talk about a watchful Almighty who plans for and leads us and lets nothing go astray. Perhaps, all unknown to myself, the repetition has made me half-believe it. Or perhaps it's because years ago, trying to measure up intellectually to Philip, I read Carlyle too impressionably, his thunder that a great man is part of a universal plan, that he can't be pushed aside or lost. Anyway I kept on. It was easier that way.

It was in the tent tonight while he was asleep that I thought things out. Perhaps had he been stronger he might not have let me stop him. He might have shouldered me, gone his own way too. But there was a hardness lacking. His grain was too fine. It doesn't follow that the sensitive qualities that make an artist are accompanied by the unflinching, stubborn ones that make a man of action and success.

I've comforted myself, too, trying to be a good wife, seeing religiously that his socks were always darned, his books in order, his dinner hot. But it was all wrong. Comfort and routine were the last things he needed. Instead he ought to have been out mingling with his own kind. He ought to have whetted himself against them, then gone off to fight it out alone. He ought to have had the opportunity to live, to be reckless, spendthrift, bawdy, anything but what he is, what I've made him.

It seems that tonight for the first time in my life I'm really mature. Other times, even when trying to be honest with myself, I've always contrived to think that at least we had each other, that what was between us was strong and genuine enough to compensate for all the rest. But tonight I'm doubtful. All I see is the futility of it. It destroyed him; it leaves me alone outside his study door. I'm not bitter, just tired, whipped. I see things clearly. The next town – the next and the next. There doesn't seem much meaning to our going on.

Friday Evening, July 14

Annie and her cowboy are to be married tomorrow morning at ten o'clock, just before we start for home. "Why did you put it off till the last minute?" I asked her today, and she explained, "Well, George you see sleeps in the bunkhouse with the other boys. We had to wait till you were through with my room. Later on maybe we're going to fix up a shack of our own."

I told her I was sorry, but with a shrug she said it didn't make much difference – she and George had been keeping company quite a while now anyway.

She's been put to a lot of extra work on our account, and I'm hoping when we get back to Horizon there'll be another check waiting for us so that I can stretch my budget to allow for a little wedding gift.

Speaking of gifts, though, it's Philip who has excelled himself. Unknown to any of us he's been working the last two days on a painting of Laura's buckskin stallion, and at suppertime, when Paul and Stanley and all the cowboys were there, he brought it in and asked if it was a good likeness.

It was – for once, he had stooped to copy – and while the cowboys stared, Laura took it from him with a strange, soft look in her eyes, and said it was the nicest thing that anybody had ever given her.

It was something of a revelation to me, too – not the picture, but Philip. He's always been so disillusioned and unexpectant about his drawings – it never occurred to me that underneath such a front of resignation there might be a little pride in what he could do, and a secret little hankering for recognition. The way he brought the picture in when we were all at the table, the steeled, dubious expression on his face as he waited for us to speak, the little flush that crept up anyway, no matter how he set his lips to keep it out – it was there before me plain enough today. He's not entirely disillusioned yet. I've taken him too literally, all the times he's growled and said he wouldn't stand for a lot of silly women looking on and simpering "How nice."

Back to the gifts, though, there was one for him too. "I thought it might come in handy," Paul fidgeted. "Not very fancy, but it's strong. You can stain it yourself when you get back to town. It's the first time I ever tried to make one, and the only wood I had was pine."

It was an easel that he must have spent all last week on, a little on the big side, but neat and well-finished, with hinges on the arms and legs so that it can be folded and packed away. "It's a Dutch word," he intercepted me, just as I was about to be demonstrative for Philip. "Means a little ass. You know – just like we say clothes-horse."

He starts for Horizon too in the morning, at four o'clock, so that during the worst heat of the day he can stop somewhere and let Minnie rest. He expects to arrive Monday, and then in a day or two will come back on Harlequin. I protest against such a ride, suggest we drive slowly and lead Minnie, stopping frequently to give her a breather, but with a nod in the general direction of my abrasions he tells me not to judge other people's susceptibility to saddle leather by my own.

Steve remains unconcerned about it all, has a chilling way of taking everything as if it were his due. His only elation seems to be at the prospect of showing off in front of Horizon and settling some of his old scores. Philip is paying a hundred dollars for Minnie, but Stanley has thrown in a saddle and bridle that themselves must be worth nearly fifty. First it was a good, plain, everyday bridle; then a few hours later an expensive one of finely-braided leather all tricked out in brass. Steve sulked and insisted he didn't ask for it. Stanley evaded me, saying it was the right one to go with the brass-studded chaps.

As to the chaps, I doubt whether Steve has taken the trouble to thank the old cowboy who made them for him. At least he hasn't condescended to be more familiar. When I complained about it last night Philip said loftily, "You women don't understand. A man can be grateful without splurging all over the place about it."

Wednesday Evening, July 19

It's Horizon again. We're back to routine.

We've told everybody already how much we enjoyed our vacation, how it's heartened and refreshed us, with what renewed enthusiasm we take up our task again of working for the Lord.

"*Enthusiasm*," says Paul dryly, suspecting more already than we've told him, "that's what it means, you know, the *god within*."

I took a rake yesterday and went round the garden, gathering the last few withered stalks and leaves. There was a single poppy that flowered while we were away. I snapped the pod off yesterday, shook the seeds into my palm and scattered them. "Casting the ashes to the wind," an unexpected and unfeeling Philip asked, and I answered, "Obsequies."

We're still marveling that in a bare two weeks El Greco should have become a handsome dog, in his quieter moments almost a graceful one. His whilom ratty tail goes waving like a plume, and with his head and ears cocked pert you scarcely see the ancient monkey-sorrow of his face. The change, I suppose, was taking place before we went, but always remembering the hungry brute he was when Steve first brought him home, we failed to notice the improvement. Yesterday morning when I went uptown to the butcher shop he stalked beside me like a blue blood to the manner born, such a courtly, old-world elegance about him that I've been wondering since if we shouldn't call him Romney now, or Gainsborough.

Mrs. Bird was over to tell us that he howled the first two nights we were away, and that then the doctor mixed him a sleeping draught. "Resourceful man – I will admit the dose was just a little strong – your Greco dog was three days coming out of it – but such a sleep we had."

Mrs. Ellingson came over too today to clap him and say what a fine big dog he was, and to hope, now that the garden's done with for the year, that we won't be sicking him on her chickens any more. As a peace offering she brought three eggs and a white geranium, said we were to keep Steve's cot as long as we need it, and invited me to come over tomorrow to a tea.

Thanks to Paul we've the woodshed converted into a stable already, a comfortable, roomy stall on one side, a neat oatbin and a place for hay on the other. Minnie's an obliging, patient little beast, who for all her self-effacing gentleness is capable of a gallop that even Steve begins to boast could outstrip the sorrel three-year-old.

"We couldn't have picked a better horse for him," I said to Philip this morning as we watched him ride out to show himself to Horizon. But Philip only nodded, unconvinced. Minnie was cantering brisk and dainty-footed, ears pricked up as if in amused consternation at the spectacle of such a town; but still she was just a middle-aged mare, a pot to her belly from too many foals, and none of the other horse's dash or devil-blood to seize a man and strike sparks from his imagination. Philip hasn't even given her another name. In an hour or two the sorrel would have been Sleipnir or Pegasus anyway, but for a mere mare plain Minnie has to do.

And we've had a visit from Mrs. Finley to let us know that she thinks making a boy the talk of the town by decking him out in red handkerchiefs and cowboy hats is a poor way to bring him up. Her boys, too, now want a horse, and by the time the Finleys pay their debts, keep themselves decent and respectable and support the Church, they've nothing left for making broncobusters out of their children.

It's Horizon again. We're in the thick of it.

Friday Evening, July 21

We've sent the hundred dollars for Minnie back with Paul, settled the store accounts, paid next month's installment on the car, and still have a little over. If the other churches keep sending their checks along there's no reason why we shouldn't be able to put something by. I've been doing arithmetic today, and allowing for the payments already made this summer, they still owe us twenty-eight hundred dollars.

In a lump sum we could do a lot with it. Even in a year, if we were careful and saved, we might be able to go into a city or big town and start a book and music store. Years ago I used to think of it, then gave it up as hopeless. Philip likes books, and I like music. It would be better than this, even if we were just as hard up. Now and then he might be able to sell a picture.

I feel determined about it tonight. At least it's worth a try. I'll wait, though, till we have a thousand dollars before mentioning it. Then it won't sound too fantastic. He won't just look at me and walk off to his study. We'll live on what they pay us here in Horizon, and put everything else away. I'll say, maybe, that it's for Steve's education, or a trip to Europe. I'll even go to Dr. Bird for a tonic, and come back and tell Philip there's an operation coming up. There's to be no new hat or coat this fall, no new curtains, no new rug. Steve's going to keep on sleeping on Mrs. Ellingson's cot. What Horizon thinks or says – none of it's going to matter. This is to be our last year. It's got to be.

Things haven't been the same since our two weeks on the ranch. Horizon was always bad enough. Now it's simply out of the question.

Without knowing it we relaxed a little out there, looked back and saw ourselves. Maybe Laura helped us. We didn't like it when she sneered, but she was right. We said to ourselves she was just loud and common, but she saw us pretty well for what we are. She was honest when she looked at Philip and said it seemed a pity.

And at that he was different out there. Bigger somehow, freer – even though most of the time he was off with his paints and sketch pad just as usual. I didn't realize till I saw him back here again, his shoulders hunched a little as if the ceilings were holding him down. Another time I'd likely just have said it's because he's so tanned and sunburned, because a white collar makes him look like a farmer dressed up to go to town, but this time I'm admitting no such easy answers. I'm remembering instead the day he sat bareheaded in the sun up against the problem of putting eternity into his hills – and that same night when I sat alone beside him in the tent.

That's why I must start saving, have an iron *no* at hand for every little wish and vanity. For these last twelve years I've kept him in the Church – no one else. The least I can do now is help get him out again.

From here a thousand dollars looks a long way off, but I must screw myself up to it. It will be good discipline anyway. As it is I'm making far too much fuss about it. It warns me that I'm getting old.

Because once I set myself a goal five years away, and had no great difficulty remembering or keeping faith with it. I was twelve, and had just heard the *Appassionata* Sonata and Chopin's *Polonaise* in A Flat Major. And in a cool, simple way I resolved then and there that I would learn to play them too. That same night I lay in bed and took stock of myself. Five years seemed in reason. It was just about as far away from Czerny exercises and the C Sharp Minor waltz as a thousand dollars is from the twenty-five I'm starting with tonight. I didn't think, though, that it was too far. I didn't have to screw myself up to it. I said five, and I took seven. I gave a recital when I was nineteen, and played them both. I look back now and think they were maybe a little premature, but it didn't matter. Philip was there that night. A friend brought him round to meet me afterwards, and from then on I had another goal.

Saturday Evening, July 22

I've slipped already. Judith was here this afternoon and stayed for supper. There was enough of our ordinary fare, but I forgot and sent Steve to the store for some little extras. I like Judith, and I like playing the hostess. We've been skimped so long that a few spare dollars puts an itch in my fingers to spend. I didn't know before, but I discover in myself something like a social bent, an instinct for expansive living. It means I must screw myself up just that much tighter, keep primed to let fly my iron *no*. There's a time for nearness, even when it isn't strictly necessary.

Judith says so too. She's still saving out of her twenty-five dollars a month, and maybe in a year can try the city again. She was wearing a new blue and white print dress today that she made herself for a dollar and a half. It was becoming, though, and I rather think she had it on for Philip's benefit.

She still doesn't know. If she did she wouldn't have come here today and sat looking at him so admiringly right in front of me. It's small-town manners for the guest to help her hostess with the dishes, but deciding apparently that she was going to be the lady for once in her life, she demurely sat down again when we left the table and did her best to talk to him. He stood it for about ten minutes, then said he had to go out and get the car ready for tomorrow. His expression as he passed me in the kitchen made me realize what a good job I once did.

Tuesday Evening, July 25

Joe Lawson's boy died Sunday morning, and they had the funeral today at Partridge Hill schoolhouse. For the second time as I sat looking down at him from the organ, Lawson made me wish that Philip could preach a sermon with more comfort and conviction in it. I think Philip wished it himself today. There was something different in his voice; it lacked the churchly unction that usually he hides behind. It seemed groping instead, and humbler. He kept clearing his throat, and was a long time getting started.

The cemetery is just a fenced-in acre or two on the prairie. There are dry, stalky weeds on the graves, and you can see where gophers and badgers have been burrowing. When the service was over and the others had gone Mrs. Lawson started crying again that she didn't want anyone belonging to her left in such a place. Lawson told her he would go to town tomorrow for chicken wire, and sink a fence of it all round the grave to the depth of the coffin. Philip led her back to the car then, and I waited a few minutes longer with Lawson. He stood staring across the hot burned fields, his lips pinched tight and the veins on his forehead standing out as he tried to steady himself. At last, almost bitterly, he said, "We aren't going to get even our seed this year. Maybe he's not missing such a lot."

We drove them home then, and brisk and talkative suddenly Mrs. Lawson insisted we wait while they killed and dressed a chicken for us. I didn't want to take it, thinking guiltily of their burned-up crop and the money that's been coming this summer from the other churches, but Philip saw it was helping them forget for a while, and he came close to me and whispered we could make it up to them some other time. Half a mile down the road I glanced back, and as if afraid to go in they were still at the gate looking after us.

Friday Evening, July 28

I met Judith this afternoon when I was up in the store for groceries, and invited her to have supper with us again. First she had to go home to see Mrs. Wenderby and make sure it would be all right. When she came back she had put a little make-up on, and was changed into her new blue and white print dress.

"Mrs. Wenderby told me to do it," she explained the rouge. "I'm always so white – she says people will think I don't get enough to eat."

Philip excused himself again as soon as supper was over and disappeared with Steve. I think that was maybe why I asked her – to watch her eyes follow him, her breathing quicken a little – to look then at him, and know how completely it was wasted. My possession now is little more than nominal, but still it's more than hers; and perhaps, valuing it even more as it wears thin and crumbles, I'm not above gloating over the shadow of it that is left.

Yet I'm sorry too, and would like to tell her. I don't because it would let her know how small is my own place in his life. And that's too much. Sweet and innocent and all the rest, she's nevertheless another woman.

It's only since we've had Steve with us that I've realized how much of himself a man has to give before he's really possessed. I used to think it was possession because we lived together as man and wife. I didn't know how little it can amount to wanting a woman at night, putting up with her in the daytime.

Steve possesses him – has even made him forget his hypocrisy. It used to humiliate him to ask for enough money to buy food and clothes. Now he writes a curt note to one of the churches that has fallen down on its payment this month, talks about a bedroom this fall for Steve. His plan is to provide whatever lumber and material are necessary for a lean-to, and to suggest to the church board that they call for volunteers from the congregation to do the work. Then they can deduct the worth of it from his salary still in arrears.

He's right. I don't grudge Steve a proper bedroom. The cold weather's coming, and the back shed won't do. But I can't help thinking of the clothes I've had to wear all these years, the way we've hung coats and blankets round the doors in winter because we were trying to save a little fuel.

I went into the study yesterday and found Philip writing. Without looking up he said tersely that it wasn't his sermon, but an article for a missionary magazine. A little while before I had suggested we ought to get along without the bedroom and put everything we could away for Steve. Now he ground his pen into the paper to make a period, and said, "There's no harm anyway in keeping my name in front of them. It may mean a better church in a year or two, and a better salary. Somebody gets the good appointments. And that will go farther towards Steve's education than the few dollars we can save out of what we're getting now."

I didn't say anything. I just went out to the stable to Minnie for a while, then walked round the garden with a queer, numb feeling in my stomach as if I had been hit there with a cold lead ball.

Later, when he was away somewhere with Steve, I read his article: a sober discussion of a minister's problems in a district that has suffered drought and dust storms for five years – well written, all his sentences and paragraphs rounded out sonorously with the puffy, imageless language that gives dignity to church literature, a few well-placed quotations from scripture, and for peroration unbounded faith in the Lord's watchfulness over flocks and shepherds alike.

I don't blame him. If I were a minister and could do something for *his* future writing such stuff I'd turn it out by the bookful. I don't blame him. I just can't help thinking that he never did it for me.

And yet it's always to me Steve comes – to me, who, instead of Philip's solemn, almost selfless devotion, can give him only a twisted, hybrid love.

Half love, half bitterness. Love because at times he seems like the son of my own I've never had. Bitterness because he's taken Philip from me – or if not that much, if Philip was gone anyway, then at least made me realize my loss.

He's proving a hard boy to bring up, and we're not the easiest of parents. By nature he's a little quick and overbearing anyway. The encouragement he gets from Philip to think himself better than anyone else in the town is making him a selfish little upstart. Instead of riding into the country as we expected he would, he gallops up and down the streets in his cowboy outfit to show himself off. Last Saturday morning he rented out Minnie at five cents a ten-minute ride, and when he came home with his earnings and I said he must return them right away, there was a scene. Giving back the money wasn't what hurt – trust him to wheedle a dime every time he wants it out of Philip – but the comedown for a dashing young cock of the walk to make a deflated reappearance as a small boy reprimanded for his precocious business enterprise. I called Philip, but frowning, he only said that since Steve had sold the rides without realizing it wasn't the right thing to do, it wasn't fair to humiliate him for it now. I agreed and to forestall a scandal over the minister's son going into the livery business, got the names from Steve and took the money back myself.

And that's roughly the kind of solution we find for all the problems that come up. This is a fundamentalist town. To the letter it believes in the Old Testament stories that we, wisely or presumptuously, choose to accept only as tales and allegories. Sunday after church Mrs. Rawlins, the blacksmith's wife, questioned me sharply about the kind of religious instruction we're giving Steve. It seems that a few days ago in a street corner discussion of the Sunday School lesson he succeeded in completely disproving the *with God all things are possible* explanation, and in sending her hitherto orthodox son home with grave doubts implanted in his mind as to the likelihood of a Noah's Ark capable of the cargo credited to it by scripture. I said lamely he must have overheard Philip and me discussing the moderns and not understood that their views weren't our own; but she was only half-appeased, and stumped off hoping that in future we would try to be more careful.

How be more careful, though, when it's either impose the Bible on Steve literally, or take him into our confidence and tell him he's not supposed to believe everything Philip preaches but for the sake of our bread and butter just to hold his tongue and pretend he does.

Philip won't do the first, because in his own words it means committing the boy to bigotry, and he can't do the second because it means revealing himself to Steve as a hypocrite. My solution is a thousand dollars and a little store somewhere. Philip's is another church and a bigger salary.

Steve meanwhile remains a good Roman Catholic. We buy him a horse, teach him to think, explain the Old Testament to him so well that in turn he explains it to Horizon – and all the time in his own faith he never falters. I took his crucifix down the other day, thinking he wouldn't notice now, and half an hour later he was firm and reproachful in front of me, asking for it back. Then I suggested some horses I found in a magazine instead of the Sacred Heart picture of the Virgin, but he looked up uneasily, said he was afraid that it wouldn't be right.

He doesn't feel his religion in any sense a duty; so far as we can see he has set himself no observances or prayers; but the religion itself, the emotional, instinctive part of it, it possesses him at times so completely that we and this fine young mind we're trying to help him build simply don't exist.

And Philip approves, looks rather satisfied. "Religion and art," he says, "are almost the same thing anyway. Just different ways of taking a man out of himself, bringing him to the emotional pitch that we call ecstasy or rapture. They're both a rejection of the material, common-sense world for one that's illusory, yet somehow more important. Now it's always when a man turns away from this common-sense world around him that he begins to create, when he looks into a void, and has to give it life and form. Steve, you see – if he can lose himself in religion, he can lose himself just as easily in art."

For there's a strange arrogance in his devotion to Steve, an unconscious determination to mold him in his own image, even though it's an image in which he himself must find little satisfaction; and stubborn still he keeps on trying to make an artist of the boy, puffing himself out for every Leaning Tower of Pisa as if he were fostering a prodigy.

And Steve's turning out to be after all just an ordinary boy. Fond of his bed, his stomach, and his own way. Clever and imaginative enough, but not to an exceptional degree. Too astute and calculating ever to make an artist. The best thing he does is whistle, everything he hears me play, from Handel to Debussy, but for Philip's sake I don't encourage him when he joins me at the piano, convinced that it isn't in him to make a genuine musician anyway.

The little moths are thick again tonight, fluttering and whirling round the lamp as if it were a hypnotist. To them, I dare say, its feeble light is just as fierce and compelling as the passions we live by. Philip is in his study drawing again a woman with a hoe in a potato patch this time – pretending anyway to draw, for his touch is sure and he had the last strokes in an hour ago – waiting for me to go to bed and be asleep before he comes.

It's hard to sleep these nights, the heat so dense and sickly, and never a breath of wind. Sometimes we both lie awake for hours, cramped up and still, trying not to let the other know. I have a feeling all the time that rain would help.

Sunday Evening, July 30

After service this morning at Partridge Hill a woman came up to us and said it was well to be a preacher, money to spend, not much to do, a car to drive round the country in. They won't thresh a bushel this fall. They won't have potatoes even, or feed for their chickens and pigs. It's going to be a chance, she says, for the Lord to show some of the compassion that Philip's forever talking about in his sermons. She has five children. This winter they're going to need shoes and underwear.

She was a stooped, shriveled little woman. Her voice was coarse and strident. There was a look of worry and exasperation in her eyes. Some loose wisps of hair hung over her forehead, adding hopelessness.

Philip's been changing of late, growing harder, more self-assertive, but today again he winced. He couldn't answer her. He just stood wetting his lips till she saw how it was with him and said, "You never mind – I'd no right saying such things anyway." Then she put her hand on his sleeve as if he were a boy in trouble, and without looking up again hurried off to her democrat.

A minute later I heard him discussing the price of horse feed. It's going to be high this fall. A few showers now would freshen up the pastures, but there'll be no hay or oats. The man he was talking to glanced at Steve and said, "What did you want to get him a horse for anyway? You're not going to make him a farmer, are you?"

Philip didn't answer for a minute. Instead he turned sidewise a little and put his hands on Steve's shoulders, bearing down, pushing his own shoulders up and back, as if he were trying to straighten out his arms. Then he said bluntly, "We'll let him decide for himself. When he's old enough."

The man moved away, others of the congregation came to talk with us, and still, until they were all gone, Philip stood there holding Steve's shoulders as if he had forgotten himself, heedless of the way Steve was fidgeting to be free.

They've both been hard to live with since. After church this evening, to keep Philip out of his study, I suggested we take a walk up the railroad track. But he made excuses, put it off for an hour or more, and then instead of me asked Steve to go with him. Steve, however, was in the sulks because he hadn't been able to take his ride on Minnie – Sundays we have to forbid it – and slamming out with El Greco he flung back an insolent refusal. Philip slipped off alone somewhere, and came back just a little while ago.

There's been a tension between them all week. Philip is nervous and unsettled. He can't bear Steve to be alone with me. He watches to see whether he rides out to the country or stops in town. He doesn't say anything, does his best not to let either of us see, but his silence is an alert, vigilant one that Steve resents. They're both on edge. Each meal is a little harder than the one before it.

There's the same tension in the heat tonight. It's been gathering and tightening now for weeks, and this has been the hottest, stillest day of all. It's like watching an inflated, ever-distending balloon, waiting with bated breath for it to burst. Even the thud of moth wings on the lamp – through the dense, clotted heat tonight it's like a drum.

Tuesday Evening, August 1

Mrs. Finley called this afternoon about some Ladies Aid work. The twins came with her, and while she was having her tea and sponge cake they got into a fight out in the back yard with Steve. According to Steve they picked the quarrel, and when he wasn't expecting it jumped on him together. A good and prompt fighter, he bloodied Stanley's nose and sent him screaming in to us, then got George down and started to pommel him.

Philip was cleaning the car when the scuffle started. When we got there he was leaning against the woodshed, coolly looking on.

Steve saw Mrs. Finley coming, took a final punch at George, and disappeared down the back alley. She stopped to help George up and brush his clothes, then turned on Philip. For a full minute she stood in front of him, small and contracted like a cat. I seemed to know what was going to happen, as if I had seen it rehearsed, but I couldn't bring myself to speak or move. She had snatched up her purse when the screaming started, and now as she glared at him it was her only movement, the way she worked and squeezed it with her fingers, her knuckles as clenched and bloodless as his face.

He seemed to know too what was coming. It might have been a face drawn in chalk, pressed so close and still against the woodshed wall – a face he might have drawn himself. She asked him at last why he had stood there letting the fight go on. He said it had been a fair fight, that George had only got what was coming to him. I shut my eyes then, and heard the swipe of her purse across his face three times.

When I looked again his head was down, and he had a hand across his eyes. There was a small trickle of blood from his mouth, but it may have been from biting his lip to keep himself controlled. I got a glimpse of Mrs. Finley walking out the gate with the twins at her skirt. He ignored me when I turned to him, and afraid I was going to say something sympathetic went over to the car and started in cleaning it again.

There's not much you can do with a woman like that, but at least it's made me more determined than ever to get a thousand dollars saved. Another check came in the mail today, and I went in tonight and asked him for it. He frowned a minute, then wanted to know what I was doing with it all. I didn't intend to tell him yet, but he stung me a little and made me forget myself. I lit into him in earnest, let him know what I thought of his scheming to get another church and a bigger salary. All the time I was talking he met my eyes squarely. Then he smiled dubiously, took the check out of his pocket, and said, "Good luck."

Saturday Evening, August 5

They've taken Steve away. Someone went to the trouble of sending word to an official of the Roman Catholic Church that he was living in a Protestant home. Two priests came for him Thursday.

They were tactful, kindly enough men. They thanked us for everything we had done for Steve – in a sentence or two let us know we had no claim on him. Philip didn't argue or protest. Going into a storm about it would have helped him through the first few minutes, but he just said, "It doesn't seem right Steve in an orphanage –" and then walked over to the window where we couldn't see his face.

He had a still, bled look when he turned again. Mechanically, as if the gesture were helping him steady himself, he asked the priests to have dinner with us, and said they could likely get rooms for the night at Mrs. Ellingson's. Then he went out to the stable to tell Steve, who had just ridden up on Minnie. I expected they would be alone out there a long time, but it was only a minute or two till Steve burst in to me. He had never been on a train before, and the prospect of a two days' journey was for the moment completely absorbing him. As he talked I heard Philip coming up the steps, and hurried him in to meet the priests.

Back in the kitchen I watched Philip a minute or two in uneasy silence. Then, both of us wanting to speak, both feeling that we could were it not for the restraint of the house, we went outside and stood together in the yard.

But still we were silent, and I could feel the strain with which he maintained his white-lipped composure. At last I started along the walk towards the stable, slowly, so that he could follow. El Greco loped after us. We both stopped to clap and speak to him, then went on toward the stable as if there were a purpose in our going there.

But inside we were trapped. All we could do was talk to Minnie, scold at the way she slobbered on our sleeves, tell her she shouldn't push her hay out of the manger and trample it underfoot. Then we came out, let a little distance grow between us as we walked up the path, went inside again.

It seemed a long time till dinner was over and the priests gone for the night. After Steve was asleep I washed and ironed dry the socks and shirt he was wearing so that he would have everything clean to take away with him. Philip stayed up still later, getting out an old suitcase, and mending the straps and clasps.

When at last he came into the bedroom I pretended to be asleep. For a long time after he had undressed and blown out the lamp he sat on the edge of the bed. I could see his profile, motionless as if it were painted there, against the lighter rectangle of the window. We both lay awake most of the night. I could feel the strain of his rigid, aching muscles. Once I pressed closer to him, as if I were stirring in my sleep, but when I put my hand on his arm there was a sharp little contraction against my touch, and after a minute I shifted again, and went back to my own pillow.

He was up at daybreak. I heard him steal outside, the faint careful click of the door after him. Steve and I were having breakfast when he came back. His eyes were heavy, but he spoke cheerfully enough. He spent a long time over his coffee, and I could see the pains he was taking with his cup and spoon.

Word that Steve was leaving had already spread round the town, and at the station there was a little crowd gathered to say good-by to him. It's the way of a Main Street. We could scarcely get near him to say good-by ourselves. There were three or four little gifts for him. Even Mrs. Finley was there. She asked God to bless him, and knew he was going to be a better boy. Self-assured, almost as if to make the most of the situation, he sauntered up and down the platform, shaking hands, youngster-fashion telling the other boys about the fine big school where he would be living. When the train came in I couldn't get near him. Philip held him tight by the shoulders a minute. Then we were standing there alone, the crowd round us thinning away.

We seemed to take a long time getting home. It seemed all the way that people were watching us – yet that it was the hottest, emptiest street we had ever walked in – emptier than even Horizon's streets.

Philip stayed in his study all afternoon. The heat was heavy and suffocating. We seemed imbedded in it, like insects in a fluid that has congealed. El Greco nosed in and out from the kitchen to the front door, sniffing at the furniture and panting wheezily. Once he scratched at the study door, but I clicked him back to the kitchen. Late in the afternoon when it was time to think of supper I went up to the store for some things to tempt Philip's appetite. The sun by this time seemed to have dissolved into a brassy mist that towards the west was darkening to a heavy, purplish haze. I noticed as I walked that my shadow on the sidewalk was a little blurred. I met no one, coming or going. El Greco followed me out of the house, but after a few steps dropped on his belly, and lay there panting till I returned.

To give Philip something to do I called in to him that it was so hot I thought he should water Minnie while I was getting the supper. He came out at once, saying in a strangely compliant voice that he had forgotten her. Unseen behind the curtains

I watched him lead her out of the stable. Tentatively she made a playful snap at his sleeve. He stopped, stroked her, put his face against her nose a minute. Then El Greco joined them, and they all set off staidly for the pump at the other side of town.

It was long after I had put away an uneaten supper, nine o'clock, and quite dark, that the storm broke. A wind sprang up first, whirling the curtains and rocking the pictures till I could run and shut the windows. Then there was such an ear-splitting clap of thunder that it seemed for a minute the roof was coming down, and in a fright I burst into Philip's study.

He let me huddle against him a minute, then gave a shaky laugh and said that rain was such an event we had better go and watch it.

The eaves already were running over. We stood in the doorway with some of the splash in our faces. When there was lightning the town looked white, half-hidden in a mist. It was like foam in the street, the way the rain whipped down, then hissed and spattered up again.

There was a safe, peaceful swish on the windows when we came inside. We left the door open for the wet fresh smell of earth, just like it is in spring. The roof was leaking already, and when I put out a pail to catch the drip it made a clear glassy clink against the drone of rain. The walls seemed to press closer, driven in by the night and wetness. He didn't speak, but I think he was glad of me again. He slept soon, and I lay a long time listening to the rain. It was good to have him to myself again.

Monday Evening, August 7

It's still raining. The roof's leaking. There's that old, musty smell again.

Philip is hard put to let me see how unconcerned he is. Just to prove that he's not sitting in the study eating out his heart he goes uptown, tinkers with the car, rides Minnie, even talks to me.

"You like walking in a drizzle, don't you?" he said this afternoon, and we got our old raincoats on, and went up the railroad track.

At the ravine the rain was coming harder. We slipped and crawled down the muddy bank, and huddled for shelter in the channel-bed, with a little turf-cliff beetling over us. He picked up a handful of pebbles, and started throwing them at a small white rock on the far side of the ravine. He took careful aim, made a little clicking sound with his lips for every hit. Most of them were hits. If you hadn't known him you'd have said that pebbles were his favorite sport.

He kept it up a good ten minutes, then brushed his hands and said, "What about Minnie? It's going to be expensive feeding her. She's too small for me – I felt a sight this moming, my legs nearly to the ground."

His voice had a dry, papery sound. I suggested, "Sell her back to Kirby. He told me we could if Steve got tired of her. A hundred dollars – besides the feed that we'll save – it will go a long way toward our thousand."

He threw another pebble. "El Greco's getting to be worth something too."

I thought for a moment it was sarcasm, but it wasn't, just his best to let me see he didn't care. "He's a wolfhound. Town's no place for him, making a fool of himself with a lot of youngsters. They tell me some of the farmers up in the hills north of town keep them for running down coyotes. It might be worth our while."

I went back to the thousand dollars, talked of getting out of the Church and starting up in a little store somewhere –

said hopefully that maybe he'd be able to study and paint again. "After all, you're not so old at thirty-six."

He laughed then a laugh like all his little pebbles clicking quick and hard one after the other on the rock across the ravine, a dead, vacant laugh that he intended to be reckless.

"That's over now. It's just that I've been a long time growing up. How hard life is, you know, pretty well depends on yourself – whether you want to keep keyed up for something beyond yourself all the time, or whether you're willing to accept things at their face value. Steve's been good for me. The last few days I've been really down to earth, looking myself over. The way he dropped out on me – the unimportance of it to everyone else – it made me realize you're a fool not to be just as casual with life as life is with you. Take things as they come – get what you can out of them. Don't want or care too much for anything."

It's never been his way to pile words on top of one another like that. Maybe because I meant it, maybe because I wanted to hear him laugh and tell me not to be such a fool, I said I was sorry I had hindered him. But it didn't seem to strike him as a new or very foolish thought. He sat a minute tossing pebbles at the stone again, then without looking at me said, "If a man's a victim of circumstances he deserves to be."

He must have said it to himself a great many times, the words slipped out so neat and well prepared. On the way home I asked him what he would like for supper on such a chilly night, and he thought pancakes would be good. But he ate only one – El Greco and I had the rest between us. When I plied him with more he remembered that the last time they gave him indigestion.

It's going to be all right, though. He'll find himself again. In the meantime I can be thankful that Horizon isn't much of a town to be reckless in, offers only limited scope for the beginner.

I wish, though, that Steve had gone differently, not quite so soon. Because in a little while Philip would have found him out, seen him plain, and then given me my turn again.

That's how it has happened other times. An idol turned clay can make even an earthly woman desirable. But this time I'm afraid it's going to be different. Steve's away now, still firm on the pinnacle where Philip set him. He wasn't found out; he wasn't seen plain. Now he never will be. He's one idol tarnish-proof. Philip will forget the real Steve before long, and behind his cold locked lips mourn another of his own creating. I know him. I know as a creator what he's capable of. I know too, I'm afraid, the kind of showing I'm going to make set up alongside this other Steve. After twelve years there's not much glamour left. In your middle thirties it's hard to look alluring in a hat that cost a dollar forty-five.

Tuesday Evening, August 8

The sun came out for a while this afternoon, but tonight it's cloudy again, and feels like rain. The house smells damp and moldy, and after our walk yesterday up the railroad track I've got a cold. The kind that gives you bleary eyes and sniffles. Philip can't help an occasional glance of lofty disapproval, though he tries his hardest to be kind. He brought me home lemons this afternoon for hot lemonade, and aspirin and cough candies from the drugstore. I was so tired after supper blowing my nose on inadequate little handkerchiefs that I tore the back out of one of my old striped winter nightgowns. He watched me blow just once, then went back to the drugstore for a box of sanitary tissue. The motive was aesthetic this time, though, not humanitarian.

I see an unflaring, leaden look in his eyes. It was recklessness at first – the best anyway he could do – now it's resignation. And I don't know whether to regret it or be glad. It will be easier if it's really resignation, if the dreams have run themselves out, if he submits at last to the inevitable, to me; only now, queerly, I start wondering is resignation what I want. It will be easier if he gives in, stops straining away – but am I going to care much, then, whether he strains away or not?

He's so kind these days, from such a great distance like a warden with a touch of pity in his heart for a prisoner that he's going to hang. Am I condemned then? Has he passed sentence on me? Last night when he came to bed I didn't even pretend to be asleep. He didn't mind, but he wasn't eager either. Kind still, far off, as if he were sorry, understood now, felt it was the least he could do. The least he could do, and the most. That was the hard part, the helplessness and finality about it. He seemed trying to tell me that I must be resigned too.

Wednesday Evening, August 9

It's raining again, and chilly like the fall. I think of sunshine the way you do of dinner when you're hungry. The old, moldy smell seems getting thicker. The drip from the ceiling takes three hours to fill a five-pound sirup-pail. I sit here listening to it, shivering and tense from clink to clink, my skin all wrinkled in the damp, my eyes fixed worming along the rusty water stains that are strung like entrails across the ceiling and down the walls.

A gray, leaden light like early dawn is the best we have all day. The town from the window has a look of sodden disillusionment. The paintless little buildings, the draggled clumps of dried-up grass and weeds, the muddy streets with pools of cold gray rain – it all merges into a November dreariness.

El Greco's tail is like a rat's again. With his wet coat plastered down and clinging to his ribs he looks so gaunt and angular that today when Mrs. Bird dropped in I said a stranger dog might take him for an angel of destruction from the canine lower world. "You *are* ill to think such morbid things," she said triumphantly. "Much more ill, my dear, than you've any idea. I'm going this minute to fetch the doctor."

He tried my lungs with the stethoscope, diagnosed the pains in my neck and arm as neuritis, told Philip to make me wear woolens and keep me in bed till the weather is clear again.

But bed is where I mustn't stay. Philip is anxious about me, does his best to help, but he's not the man to wait on an invalid. I've seen it in him often before, a deep, uncontrollable aversion to any household task ordinarily performed by a woman, and I know it would rouse a loathing in him if he had to be my nurse.

He keeps reminding me dutifully what the doctor said, but I only laugh it off. "The doctor is used to prescribing for fussy old women who like being coddled in their little ailments. Everybody has colds and stiff joints. I'll do far better going round."

Judith came over after the doctor was here, and swept and dusted and got supper ready. The Wenderbys can't afford her any longer, and she's just staying on for her board till she finds another place. Philip suggested that since we still have Mrs. Ellingson's cot she could come and look after me for a few days, but I refused. I didn't explain, I didn't argue. I just drew my lips in tight and said I'd get along all right myself.

She knows now. She cleaned and baked, rubbed my shoulder with liniment till the pain was nearly gone, but she wouldn't look at me. All her activity was just to hide herself. She knows now, and I'm afraid of her.

I don't need to be. Philip paid more attention to her at the supper table than ordinarily he does, but he's been paying more attention to me lately too. Besides he owed her a little. Hadn't she come over and cleaned the house and prepared a good supper for us? I can read him pretty well. It was no more than that.

She's a plain girl – commonplace except for the strange vivid whiteness of her face. When Philip's in the room she's awkward and constrained. She laughs nervously, makes a trite remark, then realizes it was trite and looks embarrassed. I know all that – I know Philip – know too what a short time Steve's been gone – and still I'm afraid of her. I keep shivering, imagining, dreading. It will take a worse ache in my shoulder than this one to keep me in the bedroom while she sits out here alone with him. I suppose it's every woman's lot, dread of what she knows can't be true, of what she knows won't happen.

I wish it were Philip who had been ordered to his bed. I think it's what I've really been wishing ever since we met. He's always been so strong and self-sufficient; his illnesses he's thrown off by sheer stubborn will power rather than lie helpless and dependent upon me. And just for once I'd like to have him helpless enough really to need me, to give me a chance to reach him, prove myself.

It's a weak little wish that ordinarily I wouldn't face; but tonight, sitting here cold and aching, my mind goes probing into itself just as my eyes wind in and out of the rain streaks on the wall.

I face it all – even Philip, and admit that I'm not finding the place in his life I hoped I would once Steve was gone. He keeps kind, out of reach; as if realizing the futility of life anyway, giving up hope of anything better from it, he had decided to accept me and be tolerant.

I said resignation the other day, but there's recklessness there still too. What for him is recklessness, anyway. He laughs without flexing his lips or brightening his eyes. He doesn't draw, he doesn't read. He paces the house as if it were a cage, then goes off with El Greco up the railroad track. He hasn't started to work on his sermon for Sunday yet, and says it doesn't matter. He called Mrs. Finley and Miss Twill in today to look at the leak, asked them were we supposed to be a couple of ducks.

Monday Evening, August 14

Judith's gone at last. I can relax a little and start to think. Philip brought her Thursday after Dr. Bird had been here again and ordered me to bed. There was such a pain in my arm and shoulder I didn't mind. I didn't even worry. She took good care of me. Everything seemed to go on as usual. After supper I would hear Philip go into his study, the familiar stealthy click of the door. For the nights Dr. Bird let them give me sleeping powders.

But last night there was only one left, and trying to take it myself I spilled more than half of it among the bedclothes. Philip had just come in from church and was settled down in his study for the evening. It was raining so hard I didn't want to send him out again. My shoulder seemed a little easier, and I was so tired I thought I'd fall asleep soon anyway.

I did, but in a few hours woke again. There had just been enough of the powder to stupefy me, and for a long time before actually wakening I seemed suffocating and fighting for breath. It was a kind of nightmare. My hands were tied, and someone was stealing Minnie's hay. I could see El Greco sitting on his haunches in the garden, but when I called him he didn't hear me. He seemed a long way off, as if I were looking at him through the wrong end of a telescope. Paul was telling me he was a wolfhound, and wouldn't know how to chase burglars anyway.

I woke at last with a start and sat up. It was dark. Philip wasn't beside me. I remember how I crouched there, cold and frightened, feeling the bedclothes and his pillow. Even though it was dark I didn't look that way, but kept my eyes fixed straight ahead. Then I slipped out of bed and tiptoed stealthily through the living-room to the kitchen. It was raining still, slashing in windy gusts against the windows. I remember the way my mind seized on the thought how cold was the linoleum, that it wasn't right for me to be walking on it in my bare feet. I didn't think of anything else till I reached the door out to the lean-to shed, where we're still keeping Mrs. Ellingson's cot.

Then I heard her laugh. A frightened, soft, half-smothered little laugh, that I've laughed often with him too. There's no other laugh like it. I put my hand out to the door, but didn't open it. I wanted to, but there seemed to be something forbidding it. I just stood there listening a minute, a queer, doomed ache inside me, like a live fly struggling in a block of ice, and then crept back to bed.

It wasn't long till he followed me. I could hear his breath shorten as he came close to the bed, listening to satisfy himself I was asleep. Then he went to the window and stood a long time with a faint ray of light from the street lamp on his face. I could see the regular blink of his eyelids. He looked composed and still. His lips were relaxed. So intently was I watching him, all my muscles tight and drawn, that it seemed he must surely feel me there; and at last to ease the strain I turned and muttered a little, as if I were just about to waken.

He slipped quickly into bed, and lay tense and unbreathing, just as I had been. I stirred again. He spoke to me, and I pushed my face deeper into the pillow. That satisfied him. His set body relaxed, his breathing became deep and even. Half an hour later he was asleep.

It's still the same – to keep it from him that I know. Somehow it's so important that my shoulder even doesn't hurt. There's a high wind, and the rain beats down in hissing scuds against the windows. Like one of the clinks of drip from the ceiling into the pail, as sudden and clear and cold and meaningless, it comes into my mind that what has happened is adultery – that he's been unfaithful to me, that I have a right now to be free.

But I just sit here numb and still, with a kind of dread that I won't be able to keep it from him, that when he looks at me again he'll see I know. I don't know why it's that way. You'd think I couldn't stand him near me, that I'd be crying and storming now, saying the bitterest things I knew. But instead I'm uneasy, afraid, as if I were the guilty one. My rights as a wife somehow don't matter. Like another clink I know I can't be free.

I let her help me out of bed this afternoon. I went to the kitchen and into Philip's study, saying how well she had looked after things. I laughed and held my arms above my head to prove to them that I was better. Then I put my hand on her sleeve a moment and said, "You mustn't mind – Philip says we women are all silly and unreasonable anyway – it's just that I've had my house to myself so long I can't bear anyone else looking after it for me."

I was afraid of her. I just wanted to get her out of the house, be alone a while, and think my way through it. She protested, said I wasn't strong enough, but Philip didn't. And I clung to that, telling myself over and over that he maybe was glad to be finished with her too.

She was there, that was all. She can't really mean anything to him. If she did he would hate me now for standing between them, sending her away, asserting myself. I know if I were married, not to Philip, and then Philip came, I know I would hate the first one. I know that I would never submit to him again. But Philip only says I look tired, keeps a big fire going in the kitchen so it won't be damp or cold. I'd like to cry it out, but I don't dare. He'd ask what was wrong. If I lied and said it was my shoulder he'd send for Judith again. So I just sit here cold, doubled up inside. I just remember how she laughed, when it was over how he came back and went to sleep.

It was different with Steve. He wasn't really a rival. He belonged to a part of Philip's life that was always barred to me anyway. But Judith – another woman – do I mean then so little to him? Does she do just as well?

He's quiet today, but he's often quiet. He doesn't so much as drop his eyes when I'm talking to him. Is it really recklessness, I wonder? Is he just trying to convince himself that with Steve gone nothing matters? The day we were out to the ravine he laughed and threw his pebbles, and said he'd been a long time growing up. Is that it? When a man's grown up is that what a woman means to him? Is it so little, and so easy?

Or Judith – has she been the one? So white and innocent – has it just been a mask? Has she been scheming and contriving behind it all the time, laughing at me? Am I the one who's never grown up, who can't see life for illusions?

I must stop this, though. The rain's so sharp and strong it crackles on the windows just like sand. There's a howl in the wind, and as it tugs at the house and rushes past we seem perched up again all alone somewhere on an isolated little peak.

Somehow I must believe in them, both of them. Because I need him still. This isn't the end. I have to go on, try to win him again. He's hurt me as I didn't know I could be hurt, but still I need him. It's like a finger pointing. It steadies me a little. If only it were morning, something to do again.

Sunday Evening, August 20

It's warm and bright again, and there's a hazy kind of hush and softness just like fall. Everything seems at a pause, listening. You can hear for miles. I slipped out of the house yesterday right after dinner and walked up the railroad track to the ravine and sat there all afternoon with El Greco. I found some straggly stalks of goldenrod, and a little clump of ox-eyed daisies. Judith was out at the gate calling the children for supper when I came past the Wenderbys'. She put her head down to smell the flowers so she wouldn't have to look at me, and I gave her a daisy for her blouse. It was easier than to speak, and it made things between us seem just as usual.

It's a grim, barren fall, though, and this morning out at Partridge Hill it met us stolidly. Philip couldn't talk to them. He stood on the steps watching the old democrats and buggies drive off, his lips white and wincing like they used to be. Steve's gone; it's the old Philip again.

But I'm not going to let it be. It's my turn now to be hard. I still want a thousand dollars – still want to get away from here. I've written Stanley Kirby tonight, asking him to take back Minnie. There's a strip of prairie just a little past the elevators where the grass is fairly good, and if I can persuade

Philip to tether her out for the next few days we can maybe get along without more feed.

There are other letters, too, I'm going to write. Hard ones, that I know now Philip won't. Crow Coulee promised us a hundred dollars the fifteenth of August, and without a word of explanation sent us a check for twenty-five. It won't do. I want the other seventy-five, and as much again by Christmas. Kelby last month missed their payment altogether, and they're no harder up than we are. There wasn't a woman in the congregation whose clothes were as dowdy and plain as mine. They never missed their little teas and bridge parties. Sometimes you've simply got to be hard. Nobody thinks any more of you for keeping quiet and taking what they offer.

I want to get away now more than ever. Horizon hurts. I have a feeling that other streets and houses won't know, that I'll be able to hold my head up again, make another start. Yesterday up at the ravine was the first chance I had to cry it out. I started in as soon as I got there, so that my eyes wouldn't be red by the time I reached home again. It helped a little. It didn't make it hurt any less, but it left me steadier.

If I can just hold myself controlled and quiet like this a few weeks longer – I know it will be all right then. This is the best way, going on as if nothing had happened. I go over it and over it and it always turns out best. With a man like Philip you can't afford rights or pride. I can't, anyway. Last night he didn't wait as usual for me to be asleep, and I was glad. It was weak and contemptible of me maybe, but I didn't care. That's how much he means to me. I'll take him anyway.

As to Judith – she was there, that was all. I know I'm right. The man I see in the pulpit every Sunday isn't Philip. Not the real Philip. However staidly and prosily he lives he's still the artist. He's racked still with the passion of the artist, for seeking, creating, adventuring. That's why it happened. He's restless, cramped. Horizon's too small for him. There's no adventure here among the little false fronts – no more than there is with a woman he's been married to twelve years.

I know I'm right. I watch, listen, thumb it all over, and he's not even remorseful. That's how little she means to him – how little he feels for her. It wasn't intended for me, what I heard the other night. I must forget it. He hasn't seen her since the day she left here. I know – I can account for every minute he's been out of the house. The Philip that night wasn't the real one any more than the preacher is who clasps his hands on the Bible and leads in prayer. If he's quieter even than usual, and strange sometimes in the answers he makes, I must remember that it's not long since they took Steve away. I must keep steady, sane, like him. A few days and it will be easier. Here are seven gone already.

The Ladies Aid meet this Thursday at Mrs. Pratt's, and I'm playing *Autumn* by Chaminade. And Mrs. Bird's having a tea soon, and wants Debussy's *Gollywog's Cake Walk* and *The Sunken Cathedral*. She saw the music on the piano the other day, and when I translated the titles for her decided they were exactly what she needed for atmosphere. It's to be a very elegant tea, with the blinds drawn and yellow candles lit, and star-shaped sandwiches and *petits fours*. I've been neglecting the piano lately; maybe this is the time to start in working again.

Friday Evening, August 25

There was a letter from Steve today. Philip brought it out to the kitchen where I was working, then went quietly into his study and closed the door after him.

He's a strange man. It hurt him because it wasn't a warmer letter, with more of Steve in it. He couldn't read through the bald, matter-of-fact sentences about classes and dormitories and realize that Steve was there. Philip of all people, so ingrown and wary and aloof himself, unable to understand the reticences of a twelve-year-old boy.

I took him in coffee a little while ago, but it was no use. He's drawing again, another little Main Street, bleaker, older, lonelier than ever. He looks older too, tonight, such a white strained rigor to his lips, drawn in that way to keep from wincing. I could see he didn't want to talk to me, and as soon as he finished his coffee came away. Then I called El Greco, opened the study door again, and pushed him inside. They're both in there yet, both quiet, so it must have worked. I've found that El Greco has a way with him sometimes, that ancient look of monkey-grief and wisdom.

Myself, though, the letter has made it easier. I've been right all the time. It really isn't Judith. He was trying to escape that night, trying to prove to himself that Steve after all didn't matter. And she just happened to be there.

Tuesday Evening, September 5

Paul's in town again. He was here for supper tonight, his face more sunburned and his hair more bleached than ever. As he talked I found that I'd almost forgotten about the ranch – I had to keep groping to pick up the threads. We've come such a long way in the last few weeks that Laura and Stanley scarcely seemed real. Paul himself didn't fit in any more. His slow, steady eyes made me fidget as if he were a stranger.

He's a little depressed, too, coming back to Horizon and starting in another year. He finds himself skeptical even of his theories that a boy ought to grow up alone with a horse. "Unless he intends staying among horses. He's not much good afterwards for getting along with people."

He said it in a discouraged, helpless voice, and then sat silent for a while. I think both Philip and I disappointed him. After six weeks of horses and cowboys he'd been looking forward to tonight, and all we could do was agree with everything, and urge him to eat up his supper. He did his best to talk art, but Philip looked patient and wouldn't help him; and in the middle of it I asked was Stanley going to take back Minnie. I think that especially for Philip he's been priming himself on art all this summer, just like I used to do fifteen years ago. For he admires Philip, likes him in a clear, firm, simple way that Philip's incapable of. In Philip's likes and dislikes there's always something troubled and smoldering. It's the artist in him, I suppose. It's what makes getting away from Horizon so important.

After supper I played for Paul. Philip excused himself for a few minutes and stayed out nearly two hours. I told Paul about the thousand dollars I'm trying to save, and took him into the study to see a drawing Philip did last night. It's a string of galloping broncos, done with such a light, deft touch that you can feel space and air and freedom, and hear the ring of their hooves. Fresh from his reading Paul said learnedly that in design and precision it was almost Persian, and agreed with me that Philip ought to make a painting of it. We told him when he came in and caught us there, but he just looked patient and superior again, and made it plain he'd rather be alone.

"They're all like that," Paul tried to put me at my ease when we came out. "Why there was a French artist who decided one day he couldn't stand his business or family any longer, and just walked off and left them. It's a good sign."

"You think that some day Philip will decide he can't stand me any longer?"

"He'd be a fool," Paul said gallantly, and then asked me did I know that *fool* was from a Latin word for *windbag*.

I stood a minute or two at the door, following the sound of his footsteps along the street, hollow and resounding on the wooden sidewalks as if he were walking on a barrel, and then I closed the door softly behind me, and walked as far as the last grain elevator.

Away from the lights it was dark like a cat. I didn't know El Greco was with me till he brushed against my skirt. I didn't know even then for a minute, and just stood petrified. He looked up at me, and his eyes were green and shining like a wolf's. At least like I suppose a wolf's are. I sat down at the elevator on a pile of ties to watch the moon come up, and when it was well above the horizon he went off and howled at it till I was wrinkling to my marrow. There was something wild and ghostly about it, like a skulking, primeval terror, and I was glad to reach the lights again, and the safety of the house.

Philip made an excuse out of his study in a few minutes, and in a somewhat thin voice asked me had I been seeing Paul home. I remembered in time, though, pulled myself together tight and firm, and just said no, that El Greco and I had gone the other way.

Monday Evening, September 11

Dawson's store at the end of Main Street near the station went on fire last night. I had just gone to bed when the bell started ringing, and before I could think to stop him Philip was away in his good Sunday suit.

He was in front of the blaze, struggling to unwind a length of hose, when I got there. I tried to make him go home and change into some old clothes, but he glared dangerously, and ordered me out of the way.

Back with the crowd of women watching from the opposite side of the street I began to be a little proud of him. For all that he's so useless at home he had pretty well taken charge of things, and I could hear his voice above the others shouting orders, and see men running to obey them. I liked that. The fire had got such a start that they had given up Dawson's store, and were trying to save the adjoining ones. There was no wind, fortunately, and the sparks and flaming cinders floated up so slowly that they were out again before they drifted down. Paul was there too. It was his hands and Philip's head. Mrs. Holly edged up to me, and with generous conviction declared it was the first time she'd known them to get the hose working before the fire was out. No one was very excited. There were knowing whispers among the women that Dawson had plenty of insurance anyway.

Mrs. Bird looked up admiringly at the moon and said, "What a lovely night for a fire."

For me, though, before it was over, it turned out a bad one. Next to Dawson's store is Wilson's hardware, and standing with us on the street was Mrs. Wilson, her second baby just a month away. She looked so white and ill that finally I persuaded her to come home with me for coffee, and while we were having it she told me that for the next few months she's getting Judith West to work for her.

It started everything all over again. Just on Friday Mrs. Wenderby told me that Judith couldn't get a place and would have to go back to the farm. And I'd been relieved, years younger. Even Philip noticed it, said how bright I looked, wondered what had come over me.

I've reasoned it out a hundred times, and the answer every time is the same: she doesn't really mean anything to him, she only happened to be there – but even so I can't help thinking that she may be there again some time, and it's such a cold, numbing thought I just sit paralyzed, with a feeling that I can't go on.

Dog in the manger that I am I can stand him indifferent to me, cold and self-sufficient as he so often is, but I can't stand the thought of him with anybody else. I try to be steady and rational and civilized, but it's no use. I just remember listening at the door that night, then leaving them, and slipping back to bed. He came in this morning after the fire was out, flushed and grimy, his sleeves rolled to the elbow, his shirt open at the throat, and looking up at him I was exactly where I was when I first met him, fifteen years ago. I've been scolding today about his good thirty-dollar suit ruined, trying to make him go after the church board again for some of the arrears, but deep inside I know that a thousand dollars and getting away from Horizon isn't nearly so important as I'm pretending to believe. Not so far as I'm concerned, anyway. It will make him think more of himself maybe, but it won't make him think any more of me. Deep inside I even know that it really isn't Judith. She was just there. Another time somebody else will be there.

It's windy tonight, and there's a loose shingle stuttering like it used to in the spring. He got out his oils today to make a painting of the broncos, but it didn't go so well. He blamed the light, and the brushes, and me for coming in to bother him. I got a good supper ready, but it didn't help. He's been in his study since seven o'clock, not reading or drawing, just sitting with his hands clenched, looking straight ahead. I haven't been in, but I know. We've lived together so long that he has no privacy when he's in a mood like this, not even with the study door between us closed.

Thursday Evening, September 14

Minnie's gone at last. One of the cowboys from the ranch arrived last Tuesday night, stayed over to rest his horse and practice pool, and left again early this morning. Philip kept saying what a nuisance she'd been, always time to feed and water her. I nodded, said it was going to be nice now, no more stable or ammonia smells. But he looked downcast, I noticed, and I felt a little hollow in the stomach, too, as I watched her trot away. She was a friendly little thing, and singly we often went out to stroke and talk to her. El Greco was the only honest one. He barked once after her, and she whinnied back; then he sat down forlorn in the middle of the street and howled till we brought him in for breakfast.

He started in again tonight, and later when I let him inside paced round and round so restlessly that at last I put a raincoat on and took him for a walk.

The rain had only started and was just a drizzle still, but you could feel that it was settling down to make a night of it. No one else was out. I stopped and looked up Main Street once, the little false fronts pale and blank and ghostly in the corner light, the night encircling it so dense and wet that the hard gray wheel-packed earth, beginning now to glisten with the rain, was like a single ply of solid matter laid across a chasm. I hesitated a moment and went on dubiously, almost believing that when we reached the darkness we would topple off.

We walked as far as the last grain elevator again, and then sat down on the sheltered side and watched a freight train shunting up and down the yard. A man appeared with a lantern, walking like a pair of legs without a trunk. The headlight for a moment swung on him and made him whole, swung off and left him walking cut in two. The locomotive hissed out clouds of steam that reddened every time the fireman stoked. It started backing up presently, and the dead, clugging sound of car on car ran through the night like a mile of falling dominoes. El Greco all the while sat motionless, his muzzle in my lap. The drizzle thickened till the sound of it on the high expanse of elevator wall was like a great rushing wind.

Then all assembled, the train pulled slowly past us. There seemed something mysterious and important in the gradual, steady quickening of the wheels. It was like a setting forth, and with a queer kind of clutch at my throat, as if I were about to enter it, I felt the wilderness ahead of night and rain. There were two long whistle blasts that instantly the wet put out. The engine left a smell of smoke and distance.

I slipped in quietly by the back door, but Philip heard me and came out of his study. "Just for a little walk with El Greco," I explained. "It started raining hard and we dropped in for a while to see Mrs. Bird."

"Just about ten minutes ago," he said dryly, "Mrs. Bird dropped in here to see you . . .

We stood looking at each other. "I thought it would sound silly," I said, "to tell you I was sitting in the rain with El Greco down by the elevator."

Then I put out a pail to catch the drip from the ceiling, and he went back to his study.

Saturday Evening, September 23

In response to a letter that Philip doesn't know about there was a check for fifty dollars today from Crow Coulee. And twenty-five from Tillsonborough last week, and a promise from Kelby of something substantial early in October. Horizon, though, keeps getting farther behind, and Philip just scowls and won't go after them.

He's back now exactly where he was before Steve came. That's the reason it's so important to save a thousand dollars and get away, and that's the reason he won't help me. We were out visiting among the farmers a few days ago, and I could see how their poverty hurt him. He wouldn't let me catch his eye. Every minute of the time he was thinking what a hypocrite he was. Tonight on the strength of the fifty dollars I had a good steak supper for him, but he ate because I expected him to, and not because he wanted it. Since he started the broncos two weeks ago he hasn't touched his oils. He just sits hour after hour in his study pretending to read, and when I go in tries to hide from me with a look of self-sufficiency and irritation. It makes it hard for even me to believe in the thousand dollars and another life somewhere. Just to keep my head above Horizon and this smelly little house I hunted up the *Italian Concerto* today and went right through it; but it got on Philip's nerves and set him pacing in the kitchen, so that I played the last movement with the soft pedal down, and somewhat furtively.

There's a wind too, tonight, cold and penetrating, that makes me think what we're going to spend for the next six or seven months on fuel. We'll have to get the heater up in the living-room, and the storm windows washed and on. Philip's so useless, it's a dread. I'd ask Paul, only people watch and wonder why Philip can't manage such little jobs himself.

Paul isn't coming round much lately anyway. He rode past on Harlequin this morning, and when he saw me watching at the window gave a nod and then bent over quickly, pretending to try the saddle girths. "What's wrong with Paul these days, he never comes round," I said to Philip, and over his shoulder he withered me, "I'd say that that's one for you to answer."

Friday Evening, September 29

The Ladies Aid met yesterday, and while we were having tea Mrs. Finley said, "Why don't you get a radio, Mrs. Bentley? We hear such splendid sermons – I often think if only Mr. Bentley could listen in – they would be a great help to him I'm sure."

"If he did listen in," I smiled back sweetly, "he might be tempted to borrow from them, and it doesn't do, you know, to go over the heads of your congregation."

I was rather pleased with myself, and this afternoon told Paul. El Greco and I were out walking down past the elevators when he overtook us on Harlequin. "It's a pity, though," he said gravely. "I'm sorry you did it. You must never let yourself become a fly-flap."

I looked mystified. He explained that it was the counsel of some philosopher whose name I can't remember. The market place – Horizon, that is – is swarming with flies. Strike them when they sting you, and others come. Better to run off to the wilderness where there's a strong clean wind blowing. It isn't man's lot to be a fly-flap.

I promised I wouldn't do any more swatting, no matter what the provocation, and he promised to come tomorrow for supper. Philip, when I told him this evening, just looked indifferent and said, "Things are patched up between you then?" But in time I remembered, and fixing on him a stony look of superiority refused to be a fly-flap.

Thursday Evening, October 5

For a week I've been harping at Philip to get the heater up in the living-room, and today at noon it felt so much like snow I lost my temper for a minute and said, "Why can't you take hold and do things like other men?"

He just glared a minute, then put on his hat and coat and disappeared. After a few minutes I put my hat and coat on too, called El Greco, and set off up the railroad track. We went as far as the ravine again. Down in the creek bed the wind didn't reach us, and we stayed there nestled together all afternoon. It was bleak and desolate, but I was in the mood for it. A little clump of dry brown weeds a few feet distant rattled and chattered in the wind, and messages kept running through the grass. A gray shaggy mat of cloud hung so close to earth that looking up from where we sat it seemed to be laid across the ravine. Night fell early. The sunset made the entire sky fierce and red for a minute or two; then you could almost see the darkness slipping in.

As we started for town a coyote howled somewhere. El Greco whined, then bounded off and broke into a long hollow bay that sounded less like defiance than response. All the way home the darkness was alive and slinking. He padded after me so silently that I had to keep turning round to satisfy myself that he was there. Whenever I stopped he stopped. All I could see were his wolfish eyes.

It was after six o'clock when I reached home, and Philip was struggling helplessly to get the heater up. Just before I came in he had made a deep cut in his finger trying to fit two stovepipes together. The blood was smeared on his face and clothes. He had let it drip on the floor, and then gone round tramping it into the soot that had fallen out of the pipes.

It all seemed childish, going off in a pique the way he had after dinner, then coming back to work alone, and now keeping on after he had cut himself. My voice sharp I ordered him out to the kitchen to wash while I got iodine and a bandage. But instead he went on trying to make the stovepipes fit together, and said coolly that he intended to finish. For answer I picked up the lamp and carried it out to the kitchen.

I knew he was just being stubborn, trying to show his independence, and that he would really be glad of an excuse to stop. Without looking at him I snapped that the heater would have to wait till we could get Paul tomorrow after school.

That stung him, but not to temper or indignation. I wouldn't have minded if he had just lost control of himself for a minute. What hurt was the thinness and precision in his voice. He said, "Why not get your mind off Paul, and remember you're a married woman?"

I don't know how I held it back, how I kept from telling him to remember that he was married too. The sneer in his voice made me wheel on him, a hot, sickening feeling at my throat that everything between us was finished now. It was disaster, I knew, and yet I couldn't stop myself. Only the anger itself saved me, the fierceness of it, drawing my lips in stiff and powerless. When the spasm of it passed I was standing there weak and limp, looking up at him with the lamp still in my hand. I felt queerly drained. It was like a finger pointing again, clear and peremptory, to keep on pretending ignorance just as before. I put the lamp on the table and shook up the fire to heat water for his hand. It was a sore, jagged cut, and I kept scolding him for his clumsiness. Strangely enough now he yielded to me, stood quiet and tractable while I washed the soot out of the wound and put a bandage on. "Thank you," he said in a neat, dry voice when I finished, and then, afraid lest I take it for capitulation, strode brusquely off to his study and left the mess he'd made in the living-room to me.

Thinking it over now I know he didn't really mean anything when he spoke of Paul. It was just the stovepipes. His nerves were on edge; the sharp way I spoke when I came in irritated him. I know – I say it over and over to myself – and still I keep wondering is it a sense of guilt that drove him to it.

Unknown to himself even, deeper than his consciousness. Does it mean that I'm becoming a reproach? Guilty himself, is his impulse to find me guilty too? Does the thought that he's been unfaithful rankle? Is he trying to bring us to a level where we must face each other as two of a kind? To do it is he using Paul?

It's hard to believe it of him. It just isn't true of the old Philip, the one I've always known.

It can only mean that the one I've always known hasn't been the real one. I've been a fool like him, just as credulous and blind. I've taken a youth and put him on a pedestal and kept him there. I've taken the extravagances of his boyish dreams and hungers and made a kind of aura of them, through which I've never seen the reality. So that now when he emerges from it into ordinary light I mustn't mind too much. It's just that he's been living all the while, growing, changing, maturing. I must remember, and be fair.

We all change and grow. We don't just happen as we are. We come by way of yesterday. Accounting for what he said tonight is that other night, six or seven weeks ago. Accounting for that one is the void they left when they took Steve away. And his passion for Steve, dark, strange and morbid passion that it was, accounting for that is the tangle of his early years, dark, strange, and morbid most of them too.

I must remember. And if it's finer and stronger to struggle with life than just timidly to submit to it, so, too, when you really come to see and understand them, must the consequences of that struggle be worthier of a man than smug little virtues that have never known trial or soiling. That is right. I know. I must remember.

I must remember it the next time he speaks of Paul. I mustn't let it anger me to flinging Judith at him. Because there's still no way but going on, pretending not to know. Ever since he spoke of Paul tonight I've been questioning myself, standing them up together, side by side and it isn't Paul. Paul could have a hundred virtues and Philip one, but Paul would still just come to Philip's shoulder.

I wish I could go to Philip and tell him that I know just how much and how little Judith has meant to him – that in the last few weeks I've lived through it, left it behind. I wish I could tell him that there's no *guilty* or *not guilty*, but just the two of us as we've always been.

I mustn't, of course. It's his own verdict of guilty that stands between us, not mine. If I accuse him as I so nearly did tonight we'll never face each other again without fear and distrust and antagonism. If I try to let him know that Judith now is behind us both he'll think it just a gesture of smug self-righteousness, will shrink away uneasy, and for having been forgiven will never forgive.

So I'd better just go on. We'll be away this time next year. We'll both forget. I'll ask Paul to come tomorrow after school as if I hadn't heard a word. Philip knows perfectly well that what he said tonight was contemptible, and he'll be relieved if he thinks I didn't understand. Besides it's getting cold. Somebody's got to put the heater up.

Tuesday Evening, October 10

Philip and I are at loggerheads over collections again. We haven't paid for the coal yet that we got last week, and I refuse to take it out of our savings. If Horizon wants a minister they can keep him in at least food and fuel. I rehearsed a little speech on preachers' rights all morning doing my work round the kitchen, and this evening in his study put it over like an orator. At least three-quarters of the way, till he pushed his drawing pad aside and looked at me.

I started spluttering then. I asked him didn't he want to get out of the Church, didn't he admit that saving a thousand dollars was the only way. He smiled a little with his lips and let his eyes stare blank ahead, pulled back his pad to scribble a little dwarf with a conical head and said, "It sounds all right."

He doesn't believe in it, though. He's like a man who's been hungry so long that food no longer tempts him. These last few days he's been quiet and kind again, just as he was for a few days after they took Steve away. A dead, impersonal kindness. I get no more than El Greco.

As a matter of fact I don't get half as much. El Greco's been moody and mopey lately, ever since Minnie left, and Philip has taken to consoling him. It would be funny if it were just a little farther off, the two of them so long and gaunt and hungry-looking, both so desperately in need of being consoled, for the other's sake both trying so hard and so helplessly. For relief yesterday I stood at the door when school was out till Paul came by, and asked him in for supper. When he saw El Greco turning away from his food he said we ought to sell him. He's a wolfhound; he belongs out in the country running down coyotes. Our faces fell a little, and tactfully he hurried on to say that *coyote* means *half-breed*, and to tell me I should pronounce it in three syllables instead of two. But El Greco heard and wouldn't let it drop so easily. He gave a little whine, then started scratching at the door, and rallying to him, Paul spoke up again: "It really isn't right, such a fine dog going to waste, playing in the street and making a fool of himself. He was down by the school the other day, standing stock-still with his legs apart and a string of little youngsters ducking underneath his belly singing *London Bridge Is Falling Down*. I whistled him away, but in a minute or two he was back again. That's why he hasn't any appetite. He's ashamed inside – knows this isn't where he ought to be."

Later, when Paul was going, he slipped out through our legs and disappeared up the street. We stood on the step a minute listening for him, then as his deep bay came back Paul looked at our anxious faces and with a touch of disdain in his voice said, "He's stopped now on the edge of town, afraid to go any farther. You don't need to worry. He'll be back for his blankets and bread and milk."

Wednesday Evening, October 18

There's an old man dying on the other side of town. This is the second night Philip has been away to sit with him.

Last night, after he was gone, I began to think about Judith. On his way out he said he might be late, and it isn't like him to spend many hours at a deathbed. The thought struck me that perhaps he had arranged to meet her somewhere. There was a strong, bitter wind. I went from window to window, came back and sat beside the stove a while, stared out into the night again.

It was starting to snow. I could see the flakes spinning like white, angry flies against the pale light of the corner lamp. I turned away at last and went to the piano – started to read, started to sew. I kept saying to myself how wrong and foolish it was to be suspicious this way, and all the time sat tense, pinched, my head a little forward, my eyes fixed staring on the lamp.

There was a listening, pressed emptiness through the house. It began to hover round me, to dim the room, at last to merge with the yellow lamp flame like a haze. And then on the smooth expanse of it as on a screen my dread began to live and shape itself. I saw them meet. I saw her white face. Over and over. And I couldn't stand it. I paced, shook up the fire – paced, paced – and then I put my hat and coat on, and went outside.

There was no one to see me, but I crept down side streets, in and out of shadows like a fugitive. El Greco started following, and I cuffed him back. When finally I reached the old man's cottage I circled it, crawled through the fence, and at last gathered courage to cross the yard. Then, hugging the walls, I stole from window to window, trying to get a glimpse inside. But the blinds were all drawn. I fancied that I heard voices, but couldn't be sure for the whistle of the wind. A shadow passed the window once where I was standing, but I knew that the old man had a woman looking after him. I came home again, and waited beside the stove. The emptiness returned. I saw them together – over and over – her white face – heard her little laugh – and then it flashed on me why not pay a visit to Mrs. Wilson where Judith was working. I'd know then at least whether she were at home.

She had gone out on an errand for Mrs. Wilson to one of the neighbors. I stayed nearly an hour, waiting for her; then, instead of coming home, I flattened myself against an old shed that stands on a strip of vacant ground beside the Wilson house.

I couldn't return to face the uncertainty, the yellow, lamplit emptiness. I had to see her – see the door close after her. Not that it would tell me anything – she might be alone, and still just have come from him – but though I knew that still I huddled there.

It was colder. The snow was thickening. An automobile swung down from Main Street, revealing me for a moment in its funnel of glare. Then the night was darker than ever, like a slate, and again my dread began to write and shape itself.

It must have been another hour before she came. When at last I reached home Philip was already there. I was inside, shivering beside the stove, when I saw him. He had come to his study door, and was watching me. There was a cold stare like metal in his eyes, and a faint, half-smiling curl to his lips that made me stammer to explain myself, "It was so lonely here by myself – I went out. I went over to see Mrs. Wilson. She's not very well – expecting her baby almost any day."

His eyes shifted to my numb blue hands, then to my shoulders and arms, where there were still tight-packed little wrinkles of snow to tell him how long I had been out of doors. "With Mrs. Wilson – all evening." He spoke in a thin voice. His eyes came back to my face hard and unrelenting. "It was kind of you."

He turned into his study, and on a sharp sudden impulse I ran to him. "No" – I caught his hand and made him look at me. "You mustn't think that – what you're thinking. I haven't seen Paul tonight – I wasn't with him – you must believe me."

"Paul?" He was still cold and hard. "Who mentioned Paul? I thought it was Mrs. Wilson, going to have her baby?"

"I was lying – you know. I haven't seen anyone tonight. Just Mrs. Wilson for a few minutes. It was the wind, and the empty house – I couldn't sit listening to it any longer. I went out and walked up the railroad track. But it's such a cold night to go walking – I thought you wouldn't believe me – and that's the only reason that I lied."

He drew a chair up to the stove and made me sit down. I don't know whether he believed me or not. His mouth softened a little. A look came into his eyes as if he were sorry for me. But he said nothing, and after a minute went back to his study.

And all for nothing. I learned from Mrs. Bird today that he and the doctor were both with the old man till half-past ten – and when I got back it was a quarter to eleven. Tonight while he's there again I'm being sensible, thinking sanely, staying safe beside the fire. But I'm hoping just the same that the old man doesn't last to take him out another night.

Sunday Evening, October 22

Today was my last regular visit to Partridge Hill until the spring. It's been snowing yesterday and today, and tonight there's a cold high wind clamping winter down. Philip says he's going to put the car away this week and ride. He intended hiring a horse from the livery stable, but Paul insists that the exercise will be good for Harlequin. Service at Partridge Hill during the winter is every other week, and only if the roads are clear, and the weather moderate.

Tonight Philip made a sketch of Joe Lawson. One of those strong, passionate little things that crop out of him every now and then with such insight and pity that you turn away silent, somehow purged of yourself. He's sitting at a table, half-hunched over it, his hands lying heavy and inert in front of him like stones. The hands are mostly what you notice. Such big, disillusioned, steadfast hands, so faithful to the earth and seasons that betray them. I didn't know before what drought was really like, watching a crop dry up, going on again. I didn't know that Philip knew either. It makes me feel in contrast fussy and contemptible. There comes over me a kind of urge to do something strong and steadfast too. For what it's worth I sit vowing that I'll never complain about my clothes and furniture again.

It makes the thousand dollars important again. If he can draw like that when he's all shriveled up inside with the guilt of his hypocrisy, what won't he do when he's free of it, able to respect himself again. For his sake I almost wish we still had

Steve. He'd try for him. He'd start to believe in himself, in the thousand dollars, in getting away from here.

Sunday Evening, October 29

It's been a clear, cold, sunny week, but tonight there's a bitter wind again that nicks you when you're facing it with an icy little whip of snow.

After service tonight I slipped out of the house with El Greco and walked up the railroad track nearly to the ravine. I was glad of the cold, because it didn't give me time to think or brood. I saw him talking with her for a minute yesterday in front of Wilson's house, and today he's been unbearable. She sang in church tonight, and watching him in the little mirror over the organ I could see how set and drawn he looked. She wore a soft black dress that made her look whiter even than usual. Holding it together at the throat she had a plain gold brooch, and in the bright light her hair under her hat had a yellow luster too. Because Philip and the others were there I said pleasantly that I thought she had sung especially well, but pretending not to hear she hurried away ahead of us.

I don't know what the outcome's going to be. I'm not so sure of either him or myself as I pretend. Sometimes I wonder should I speak up and put her in her place once and for all. It's all very well going on this way, but where's it getting me? Have I really anything to lose? I feel old and spent tonight. It's a bigger strain than I admit; at last it's beginning to tell. I wake up at night muttering to myself, and then for fear he'll hear me lie awake till morning. At the table, or even when there are callers, I catch myself staring into space, answering at random. I dread the nights, I dread getting up to start another day. There's no escape. I feel as if I were slowly turning to lead.

Friday Evening, November 3

Four weeks from tonight the Ladies Aid are putting on a play in the town hall, and between the second and third acts I'm to play the piano. While the actors change, something loud and brilliant, to keep the audience from becoming too restless.

"It's a rather serious play," Mrs. Bird explained a little while ago. "With drama, and a moral. In the last act I die. At rehearsal last night I discovered it was something I could do very convincingly. In contrast you can be gay and airy if you like."

It's four weeks away. I'm wondering could I get myself in shape to play a rhapsody by Liszt. In the last hour, sitting here staring across at the piano, I've gone right through it half a dozen times. I know the notes well enough, but my wrists aren't strong and supple the way they used to be. There's Philip, too. When I practice he usually looks aggrieved, clumps out to the kitchen and starts his pacing.

It dares me just the same. Not for Horizon – for Philip. He came to a recital once to hear me play it, this same rhapsody, and because he was there I played it well. The desire to reach him, make him really aware of me, it put something into my hands that had never been there before. And I succeeded. He stood waiting for me afterwards, erect and white-lipped with a pride he couldn't conceal. And that was the night he asked me to marry him.

The desire and will to reach him still is there, but I doubt whether it can make up for the rest. I'll have different clothes for one thing. Instead of a big, handsome grand piano it will be an old cracked one with a noisy pedal. Instead of an expectant audience there'll be youngsters in the front rows chewing gum and munching apples. I know all that. And I'm older, and he's had me now twelve years.

I know – and still it dares me. Maybe not to reach him

as I did that night – just to come a little closer, make him stop and look at me again. I can play it all right. It's brilliant, impressive music, with thunder and glitter enough to hide a few missed notes. I can practice on Mrs. Bird's piano. I'll tell her that Philip's painting again and mustn't be disturbed, and she will say, "A genius, my dear – exactly like the doctor. Welcome a hundred times – our piano will be honored."

Such a fool I am. I can't bring back that other night – I know – and yet I'm going to try. His study is cold tonight, but he refuses to come out here where it's warm with me. A while ago when I took him in coffee he nodded for me to set it down, then without a word went on with his book. But he wasn't reading. I could tell that. I could feel his breath a little shorter, all his muscles tense and waiting. It wasn't indifference. He wanted to speak, but there was a barrier. That's why it dares me – to play so that he must speak, so that he forgets himself for a minute or two, breaks through the tangle grown between us. I think everything would be all right then. I'm sure Judith doesn't really matter.

I keep trembling, and for Liszt you need strong hands and steady nerves. The lamp's nearly dry, and I've let the fire go down. El Greco's lying with his muzzle in his paws beside the door. When he sees me raise my head to look at him he gives a little whine. The light now doesn't reach that far; all I can see are his eyes like slits of clear green glass. There's a howl in the wind tonight. The windows are wadded with woolen rags, but still they rattle.

Wednesday Evening, November 15

I forgot last night to take the fuchsias and geraniums out of the windows, and this morning they were frozen stiff as boards. I've never before seen winter set in so early or so hard.

There's half a foot of snow already on the open prairie, and in our back yard it's drifted so deep that Philip twice now in the last four days has had to shovel a path to the woodshed and the Tower of Pisa.

It was clear and glittering today, and when the sun went down the frost-mist made the sky up nearly to the zenith red and savage like a fire. I watched it with El Greco, huddled cold against the last grain elevator. A team and sleigh went past while we were there, the horses snorting at the cold and blowing little clouds of steam. The bells and creaking runners left a white cold silence for a minute, like a field of snow that no one yet has left a footprint on; then a coyote somewhere loped across it with its fluty howl, and El Greco bristled up his back, and pressing close against me bayed off after it in floundering pursuit.

On the way home I bought a pound of sausages, and had them for supper frizzled up and brown, with fried potatoes and tomato sauce. Philip likes them that way, but he was too out of sorts tonight to eat at all, and of the three he took on his plate he slipped two to El Greco, anyway, in covert bites.

That was the reason I went out this afternoon: some posters for the play the Ladies Aid are putting on that they've given him to do. He hates printing and lettering, and yet he couldn't very well refuse. Or at least when Mrs. Bird asked me I couldn't very well refuse for him, seeing that I go now every day to practice on her piano. If I had the things to do, I'd daub the dozen of them off in half an hour, but Philip, of course, isn't built that way. A nice balance and finish is important to him even in a poster; and for all his fuming he plods away conscientiously with rule and eraser, and three or four different-sized brushes.

Realist that I am I was hoping he might like the work.

The advertisements all say that there's money to be made writing show cards, and if ever we do get started in the little store I plan, we'll need every dollar we can get our hands on. This afternoon I tried to tell him what a good job he was doing, but he just pulled his lips in tight and desperate, and glared where I could go. And with Philip there's no use trying to hammer home your point. I knew the signs, and called El Greco and cleared out.

But I'm in queer, high spirits these days, and nothing seems to matter much. It's this rhapsody I'm practicing, the way I'm letting it make such a fool of me again. I know – and still that's how I want it. I'm the kind that never learns, never burns out. I'm all keyed up and tense, the very way a pianist mustn't be, but I know that I'll get through on fever anyway. Fever's a good way if you have enough of it. Right this minute I'm playing as I'm going to play two weeks from Friday – sitting here staring across the room at the piano, playing with every nerve and bone and muscle in my body. El Greco gets up and whines, looks at me for a minute with his glass-green eyes, then lies down again. There's a long swift ripping sound as Philip tears up another poster. Then it's still again, and I go on and play. The fever way. And the whole house has tingles.

Friday Evening, November 24

It's just a week now till the play. I slipped in to listen to rehearsal yesterday, and as Ladies Aid productions go it isn't bad. Mrs. Holly has the leading role – looks attractive – knows it – gives herself airs that make the others furious. Right through she takes the part of a poor, unsophisticated country girl, but insists that in one scene anyway she wear her new blue taffeta. Mrs. Finley who directs has given up – just looks serene now, and refers to her as Jezebel.

In the last act Mrs. Bird spends five minutes dying. Mrs. Finley thinks it could be speeded up to three, but Mrs. Bird took elocution lessons once, and with a tide of bosom says that art is long and Mrs. Finley just a small-town Philistine.

From the second intermission Mrs. Bird has brought me forward to the first – a good sign, since it means she's afraid that the rhapsody would steal her own big scene if it were closer. I spend half an hour at her piano every day – as much and more in snatches at my own. As much as I think Philip's nerves will stand, plus every time he goes uptown or to the Leaning Tower. So that he won't recognize the rhapsody while I'm practicing, I work at the hard parts by themselves, then put them together when I'm alone or at Mrs. Bird's.

My fingers grow stronger, but sometimes in my eagerness and excitement I fail to hold them to the pace that makes for poise and certainty. Each time I play it's the final night. The audience is there, and Philip; and hurrying to keep up with the hammer and tingle in my blood I stumble and exhaust myself. I go up the railroad track sometimes, play it still again, run with El Greco till I'm panting and out of breath like Mrs. Bird. And it's always triumph. There's always applause, always Philip.

At night too I play, while Philip sleeps beside me. I mount the little stairway to the stage, cross to the piano. I begin to play. I feel the hush and stillness as the audience wonders what is coming. The little hall disappears. I play. Then I turn and face them, stand for a moment looking down at Philip. He's waiting for me, erect, white-lipped, and we go home together.

Saturday Evening, December 2

I played Liszt last night.

Philip's been strange and gloomy all this week. He eats nothing, looks past me, leaves his sentences half-finished. He stands brooding at the front windows, then slips furtively into his study if he thinks I'm watching him. Thursday and yesterday I didn't touch the piano. I was overstrung with practice anyway. When it was time to play my hands were clammy. Paul was sitting on one side of me, Philip on the other; I could feel that they were both nervous too. Walking across the stage at last I felt dowdy and ugly and awkward. The stool squeaked when I turned it to the proper height, and promptly all the youngsters in the front rows started squeaking too in imitation.

For all that, though, I played well enough. I was sick and numb when I sat down, scarcely able to see the keyboard for a blaze of heat, but with the first notes I knew the audience was listening. And it brought something like poise and confidence again, even a little of the fever that's been keeping me at breaking-point all these last four weeks.

Anyway it was Liszt, and they liked the brilliant parts, the octave and arpeggio work, and at the end applauded so insistently I had to go back and play another piece. But I was crushed and empty now, and hurried off the stage with an urge to slip away somewhere and cry alone. It was a long way back to my seat, through all the eyes, dowdy and awkward and ugly again. I could tell inside that I had failed. I kept my eyes down, didn't even look for Philip – but I saw Paul suddenly, standing up to let me in to my seat again, his face like a cool white rent in the slowly-wheeling crackle of applause.

I didn't hear or understand what he said – only realized that the applause was fading out, that his voice for a few seats round us must be audible. Some kind of instinct made me smile at random over his shoulder, as if I were unaware of him. Like a child trying to cover her embarrassment I pretended to stumble squeezing past him to my seat.

There was silence now. I glanced up at Philip beside me, and it seemed to be coming from his face. It froze me erect and rigid even though inwardly I was sagging. The play went on. There was laughter and whispering and applause again, but we heard nothing. The silence persisted for us till we were out of the hall and home in here alone. And then, his voice pinched small and sharp in an effort to restrain himself, Philip said I must be satisfied.

I asked him what he meant.

"Your success tonight." His voice began to shake itself out, louder and harsher. "After all your practicing – it would have been a pity if it had gone to waste. I thought the poor fool was going to prostrate himself."

I was too tired and crumpled to be stung. I looked up at him and said quietly he was the one I had done all the practicing for, not Paul.

Then for a minute we watched each other. He knew I was telling the truth – I could see by the way his eyes suddenly tightened and recoiled – but he was too wretched and bitter to admit it. Instead he tried to look contemptuous, and gave a forced, derisive little laugh.

He's a still-faced, sober man; the laughter was unbearable. I buttoned up my coat again and went outside. The play had kept the town up late; all the windows were alight. They seemed to watch me as I went along the street, slant-eyed through a thin raw fog that began to gather on my coat in woolly little knots of rime.

The crunch of footsteps coming towards me made me turn. I came back to the parsonage, hesitated a moment, went on the other way. But still the windows watched me, made me tread uneasily, conscious of myself. Again I turned, again I hesitated, looking at the house. And more vividly than if I had been inside I could see the huddled little rooms, and the old ugly furniture. I felt the strained atmosphere, and the iron, doomlike silence of his study door. And in anticipation of it dread and despondency came up again and filled my throat with stone.

Before the play Philip had locked El Greco in the stable. Now, as if he knew that I was there, he gave a little yelp for me to come and let him out.

But I didn't for a while. Instead when I opened the door and he bounded off to the house I called him back, and then went in and closed the door again, and sat down with him on his pile of straw and blankets.

And in the quiet darkness there I defeated the Philip that a little while before had repelled me with his laughter. Away from him – without the insistence of his voice or face, I was able to restore him to his actual self. El Greco helped. Even the sneer and laughter that stayed with me for a while – it wasn't Philip. I felt no rancor, no affront. Instead the contrast with the real Philip I knew made me uneasy. I understood suddenly that only out of some torture or sickness could such a laugh have come. And I saw him suffering and alone and in need of me, and I went back to him.

He wasn't in need of me, though. As I opened the study door he turned in his chair a moment, and then, as if I had just interrupted him, picked up his pencil and pretended to be working at a little sketch. I went over to him, put a tentative hand on his shoulder. I tightened my fingers, gently and firmly, trying not to obtrude myself, yet to make him understand that if there was anything he might want to share with me I was with him, waiting and willing. But he only went on making aimless little marks on his paper, and presently in a dry, lifeless voice said it was late and that I had better go to bed.

Today it's the same voice, dry and unrevealing. He scarcely speaks. His eyes keep following me, but when I meet them they glance off with what seems a little flash of contention and disdain. Yet I doubt whether he's really aware of me. Out in the yard this morning El Greco leaped up at him, and ill-temperedly he slapped him down. And it's the same with me. Something is wrong. Just the sight of me is enough to set his nerves on edge. Besides, this is a small house for two people. You imagine the other to be listening. Every movement becomes furtive and strained. Then silence at last hardens over you like glass, and you feel it isn't safe to draw a breath.

After the play last night the Ladies Aid should be able to cut the arrears of our salary down by fifty dollars anyway. They'll never give it to us though of their own accord, and with things as they are I don't dare mention it to Philip. We'll see Monday. Our savings now are just three hundred dollars, and this month, with what the other towns have promised us, they should be up to four. I write dunning letters every other week in Philip's name. There's the car, too, to sell if we go, for another hundred surely at the least. We're getting there. If only Philip would believe in it, and show a little heart.

Monday Evening, December 11

Mrs. Bird was here today, and told me that Judith is going to have a baby. I wasn't so shocked or startled as I pretended to be. I haven't admitted it to myself, but for several weeks now I've really known. Philip's such a poor actor. There's not much he keeps me in the dark about.

Judith has gone home to the farm. The doctor says the baby should be born sometime in May. Mrs. Bird wondered if I had any idea who the man might be. Judith and I always seemed such close friends, and Judith herself now won't let slip a word, not even to her own family.

"She talked sometimes about a young farmer who wanted to marry her," I said quickly. "But she didn't like him – and she's the kind of girl that unless she cared a great deal for someone –"

"Well, some seem to think it's Wenderby himself – and the way Mrs. Wenderby is behaving I'd say she thinks so too. Yesterday she slammed the door almost in Mrs. Finley's face. Judith, you know, often used to go back to the office at night, after the children were in bed. Such a willing, conscientious girl."

I told Philip at the supper table, busy with the teacups, so that I wouldn't have to look at him.

"I'm sorry," he said quietly. "It's the kind like that, who slip just once –"

"You can never tell though. Sometimes it's the mild, innocent kind that are the sly ones. A woman usually knows what she's about."

I had to speak that way, just like any other safely married matron. To pity her would have been to condemn him, and glancing at him as he tried to eat I could see he was going through enough just then as it was.

"She's gone back to the farm," I continued casually, and he said, "Yes, she'll be better there." Then for the rest of the meal we were silent, clinking our teacups, listening to the wind.

It's a strong, unflagging wind tonight, mile after mile of it, whistling round the eaves as if it were being throttled by the thick scuds of snow. Winter seems darkening, closing in.

Sunday Evening, December 24

We had a special Christmas service in church tonight. The choir sang an anthem badly, and the congregation *Holy Night* and *0 Come, All Ye Faithful* rather well.

We miss Judith in the choir. Her voice had a strength and fullness that always helped the others. I sat thinking of her during the sermon, hating myself for the little gift I sent her yesterday. I did it deliberately to hurt her, and I'm sorry now. It must be hard enough out there, the long winter months, nothing to fill them but regret and dread. I remember she told me once that the first piece she learned to play was *Holy Night*. They hadn't an instrument of any kind at home. She used to hurry with her chores and reach the schoolhouse in time to practice on the organ half an hour before the others came. The next year she drove a team on the land for her father, and in the fall he bought her an organ of her own. Tonight, Christmas Eve, she'll likely be thinking of it too.

It's cold and clear tonight, with such white, glittering moonlight that the snow-covered landscape against the dark sky looks far brighter than it ever does in daytime. After the service I told Philip I was going home with Mrs. Bird to borrow a book, but instead I went for a walk down past the elevators and then a little way across the prairie.

There was no path or road, but the drifts were so strong they carried me. Two or three times I walked right over fences. It was as if a sea with an angry swell had suddenly been frozen by the moon. The stars looked bright and close, like pictures you see of tropical stars, yet the sky itself was cold and northern. Everything seemed aware of me. Usually when a moonlit winter night is aware of you it's a bitter, implacable awareness, but tonight it was only curious and wondering. It gave me a lost, elemental feeling, as if I were the first of my kind ever to venture there.

The hollows and crests of the drifts made the walking hard, and half a mile from town I perched for a few minutes on a fence post that stood up about a foot above the snow. I sat so still that a rabbit sprinted past not twenty feet in front of me, and a minute later, right at my feet, there was the breathlike shadow of a pursuing owl. I had been climbing a little all the time I walked, so that I could see the dark straggle of Horizon now below me like an island in the snow. A rocky, treacherous island, I told myself, that had to have five lighthouses.

Then I started home, wishing that on such an unearthly, radiant night I might be a little less of a rationalist, able to feel the ecstasy of Christmas. By itself it's a bleak season in a childless home. Coming along the street I kept looking at the houses and thinking of all the suspense and excitement inside. Our little house when I reached it seemed in contrast dead and dry. The perfunctory paper bells and artificial holly wreaths that I had hung round the windows didn't help. It's worse this time because at last there is a child, and it isn't mine. I don't know how much longer I can go on. I don't know either how it can help if I don't go on, but it's like an abscess gathering: you realize that when it breaks the poisons may be fatal, and still you wait for it to break, feeling that then there will be release for a moment anyway.

A while ago, to make the house look a little more festive, I polished a bowl of apples and set out another of oranges; and then I called Philip for coffee and Christmas cake. But it wasn't very successful – our appetites and spirits keep abreast. It's easier when I take the coffee in to him, and then come away and let him have it by himself.

Paul's coming for dinner tomorrow. I have Trench's *On the Study of Words* for him, which Philip says is such an old and standard book it's like giving a cook-book to a chef. I ordered an art magazine for Philip nearly a month ago, but the first number still isn't here. I waited yesterday till the mail was all sorted, then bought him a shirt and a pair of socks. He'd have to get them before long anyway, so it wasn't being extravagant, and I'm counting on the holly box they're in to detract a little from the usefulness.

For me on Christmas morning there's always an envelope with five one-dollar bills in it, which he bends stiffly and lets me kiss him for, and which I conscientiously spend to the last cent on myself. It's a practical arrangement I persuaded him to several years ago, and that now I'm inclined to regret. Perfume atomizers and chocolates done up with ribbons were exasperating when there were so many little things I really needed, but sitting down in cold blood with a mail-order catalogue to pick out stockings and flannelette is worse. There's no way, however, to go back on it. I just can't imagine telling him that I'd like something pretty and foolish again, and he's not sufficiently aware of me ever to guess himself.

Wednesday Evening, January 17

We've lost El Greco. Driven by hunger the coyotes lately have been coming right to the outskirts of the town, and about eleven o'clock last night when they started howling again he answered with such a furious barking that I got frightened and opened the door for him. Philip ran after him, and stayed out so long trying to whistle him back that he froze his ears. There was no more howling from the coyotes, though, so we've concluded that they lured him well away from town, then turned and made an end of him.

Philip, however, was kind about it, said he'd have gone off sooner or later anyway. It's our own fault, keeping such a dog for a pet. He was a wolfhound; we should have let him live like one. Paul kept telling us, but we argued he was better this way than like the poor, clapsided brutes that come to town sometimes with the farmers from the hills. Paul explained that they keep them hungry so they'll be keen for hunting, that in a hound's life bread and milk and safety can never make up for the excitement of a single kill, but Philip and I, of course, decided we knew better. We were attached to El Greco. We meant well.

It always turns out the same when you make up your mind that what's right for you must be right for someone else. I made up my mind about Philip once – and as a result see what he is today. He was so dark and bitter and lonely, struggling away toward such cold, impossible goals, and I was so sure that my little way of sympathy and devotion was the better way. Maybe there would be three of us today a lot happier if I'd had El Greco to teach me his lesson fourteen or fifteen years ago.

Monday Evening, January 29

It's a long winter – two months still ahead. The days repeat themselves without progressing. Sometimes it seems only one morning that I've stood at the door a moment watching the smoke from Horizon's chimneys mount through the frosty air in compact blue and silver plumes. It's only one noon that we've sat down to the table and swallowed a few tasteless morsels in silence – one interminable noon – and one cold, pallid twilight, waiting to light the lamp, that I've watched the night deepen, and the walls melt into the darkness. There have been mornings when the smoke was lost in a blizzard, and days when I lit the lamp early, but the oneness still prevails.

It's snowing again tonight. There's a drift between our house and the church that has climbed up already nearly to the eaves. The face of it is sheer as a wall. It rises close to the study window, darkening it, so that Philip needs a lamp all day. On the other side it mounts with a graceful arch of its back to a thin curling crest, and then poises there like a great breaker, ready to submerge us.

Another drift shores up the woodshed and garage, and the children come sometimes and run right up to the roof, and then climb down again by way of Pisa. When you pause a moment to look across the prairie a queer, lost sensation comes over you of being hung aloft in space, so like a floor of clouds does the unbroken whiteness coil and swell to the horizon.

And week after week, without respite, it keeps cold. Even the sun seems cold, frost in its glitter instead of warmth. I wad up all the windows, hang coats and blankets round the doors, and still the drafts creep in. We have to keep such fires on in the heater that the ashpan's running over twice a day. After supper to save a little I let the kitchen fire go out, and in the morning, even after Philip has it going again, I put on a pair of woolen gloves to handle the breakfast things. You see frost glistening everywhere on the pans and tins, and if I forget to bring in the water pail at night it's frozen solid to the bottom.

Our savings are up to four hundred and thirty dollars now, but with all this extra coal it's hard to keep them there. We've burned over twenty-five dollars' worth since Christmas, and in that time Horizon has paid us thirty. I've made up my mind to mention it to Philip just once again, then on the first of the month pay a visit to the board myself.

It's getting to be an obsession with me, this thousand dollars that I'm trying to save, but at least it steadies a little, gives me focus and direction. It's like being lost, and coming on an old wagon trail. You don't know where it leads, how long or why it's been abandoned, but at least it's a trail. I don't know what difference a thousand dollars will make even if we do get it together, whether we'll be able to leave Horizon as I keep trying to hope, or whether Philip this spring will have other needs for it – but at least it's something to do and think about. A purpose through the days like a spike through a sheaf of little papers. It's easier to calculate than brood, easier to write dunning letters than your thoughts.

And it's about all there is. I was never one for possessions – never set great store on knickknacks – never fretted because my neighbors boasted better rugs or chairs. I do sometimes resent the downright ugliness of our things, but never want new ones just for the sake of owning or displaying them.

It was the piano first, then Philip. They were the essentials; the rest I took casually. One of my teachers used to wonder at what he called my masculine attitude to music. Other girls fluttered about their dresses, what their friends thought about the pieces they played, but I never thought or cared for anything but the music itself. My mother always saw me playing a concerto in white velvet, white to make me conspicuous against the black dress-suits of the orchestra, but I could only edge away from such notions in embarrassment, and think to myself it was like buying wallpaper before you had a house to put it on.

And that's the hard part, remembering how strong and real it used to be, having to admit it means so little now. A few days after Christmas I sent away for some new music, Palmgren and Albéniz, things I'd never tried myself before, that I thought might start me off again – but it just isn't in me any longer. My fingers are wooden. Something's gone dead.

That's what he's done to me, and there are times I can nearly hate him for it. I haven't roots of my own any more. I'm a fungus or parasite whose life depends on his. He throws me off and I dry and wither. My pride's gone.

I'm helpless and weak and spiritless before him. There's nothing left inside me but a panting animal; character and mind against it are of no avail. The way I watch his face for a flicker of awareness or desire; the way I gauge the pressure of my hand against his sleeve, so quick and hungry, all the time so absorbed in the little sketch he's been doing. I sicken, and despise myself, and still keep on. The night comes when he wants me, but it brings no ease or sense of consummation. I'm ashamed afterwards. I lie awake, living again through the night I listened to him with her – wander off to think how white and haggard he looks, to ask myself what's going to happen when the baby's born. So many nights like that – so many days with the fire for company. And still it's only January.

Thursday Evening, February 8

Philip went to see Judith yesterday. I sent him. It was getting unbearable, watching the white silent misery in his face. I thought that if they were alone together for a while it might make things easier.

Maybe I was afraid that alone out there all these months she might weaken and tell her family it was Philip. Maybe I was just sorry, maybe even grateful. When questioned she only sets her lips and moves away, they tell me, and I can't help thinking it's for my sake. When you're the wife at a time like this it's hard to be fair, but I can't believe that there's anything very treacherous about her. I might have done a lot worse had she been the wife.

Anyway I sent him. As we finished breakfast I remarked in an offhand way how long she must be finding the winter. He nodded, and pushed back his chair. I suggested he borrow Harlequin and ride out to see her. There were some magazines Mrs. Bird had given me, and I would go up to the store and get some oranges. For a minute or two he stood frowning, pretending it was too cold for a long ride on horseback. In turn I pretended to believe him, pursed up my lips and said it was never too cold for him to ride to Partridge Hill on Sundays.

It was noon when he went. To keep the oranges from freezing I stuffed a grain sack full of hay and buried them in it. He frowned again, and pretended to grumble about having to carry them like that on horseback.

I spent the afternoon out making calls, and on the way home about five o'clock met Paul and asked him in for supper. He made excuses but I kept insisting. I was afraid of having to talk with Philip alone.

After the meal was ready we sat beside the stove waiting for Philip more than an hour. Paul was nervous and preoccupied. Ordinarily his eyes are disconcerting, the cool, critical examination they make of you, but today he wouldn't look at me at all. He answered in an absent voice when I spoke, and wouldn't go on. When the fire burned down we both made much of putting in another.

Then we had supper without Philip, and then I played for Paul. He sat at the end of the piano watching me. I knew he was watching me, even though I kept my eyes on the keyboard. He spoke once, something about Judith, why had Philip gone to see her, but I pretended not to hear and kept on playing.

While I was still at the piano Philip came in. His eyes were hard as he stood at the fire warming himself, and he wouldn't let me help him off with his coat. He glanced once at Paul, then ignored him. Paul put on his hat and coat, made a sign to me not to come to the door, and went out. As soon as he was gone Philip said in a strident, heavy voice that at least I hadn't been lonely while he was away. He had wondered in the morning why I was so determined to get him out of the house.

I went into the bedroom for a minute, then came out and warmed up his supper. "And Judith?" I asked at last, pouring myself out another cup of tea to drink with him. "How was she? Didn't she send a message?"

It seemed as he looked up at me that something in his eyes broke. "Next time," he said, "you'd better not send oranges." He ate for a moment, looking steadily at the lamp, then went on, "She cried when I told her they were from you – all afternoon, one in each hand, as if that could help."

Monday Evening, February 19

The days are getting longer now, but they're still cold and slow. There was such a blizzard last week that the train from the east was two days late. The farmers are losing heavily in stock. Philip said that on his way to Partridge Hill yesterday he saw two horses frozen on their feet. They had drifted against a fence and perished there, too spent to turn again and face the wind.

Last night he made a sketch of them, and today I persuaded him to try it again in oils. The light went before he could finish, even working out here in the living-room, but he's doing a good job. The way the poor brutes stand with their hindquarters huddled up and their heads thrust over the wire, the tug and swirl of the blizzard, the fence lost in it, only a post or two away – a good job, if it's good in a picture to make you feel terror and pity and desolation.

After supper tonight I went into a trunk and brought out two boxes of his drawings. I started putting the good ones away when we were first married; now there must be three or four hundred of them. Little Main Streets, grain elevators, farmhouses, big bare windy sweeps of prairie – a man beside his plow with his head back drinking out of an earthenware jug – a handsome lad who used to bring us butter when we lived at Kelby – a stooped, hawk-nosed old crone, staring across a wheat field like a sibyl. Twelve years of a deft hand and a penetrating eye. I spread out a dozen of them on the table, then called him.

"Try to forget," I said, "that you did them. Look at them as if you had come across them in a book for the first time. Be detached and fair. Isn't there something there that's important?"

He forgot for a moment to clench his lips in tight and dry. It struck me that if he could have made a drawing of himself right then it would go among the ones I keep. I'd like to see what he'd do with his own expression – if he'd catch it all, the dreams that are there, underneath, like the first writing of a palimpsest, and their paraphrase by life as well.

"You can't be detached about your own work," he said presently. "You feel it too much – and the right way is only to see it. That's your trouble, too. These things all mean something to you because you've lived in these little Main Streets – with me while I was doing them. You're looking at them, but you're not really seeing them. You're only remembering something that happened to you there. But in art, memories and associations don't count. A good way to test a picture is to turn it upside down. That knocks all the sentiment out of it, leaves you with just the design and form."

I gathered them up then, and trying to laugh, said the exhibition was closing for lack of an appreciative public. He went back to his study, and I sat down here with my sewing and a book. But I still believe in them. He does too, I think. He just hasn't the courage to admit it.

Tuesday Evening, March 5

I've fought it out with myself and won at last. We're going to adopt Judith's baby.

He started another picture yesterday in oils, worked hard at it all morning, then left it like that half-finished. I coaxed and admired and upbraided, but it was no use. He just nodded, ran his fingers through his hair, looked past me. The helpless, disillusioned look that always brings me to my judgment. I stood facing him a moment, remembering what a different look it used to be, how hard it was sometimes to get him away from a picture for his meals, and then I put on my hat and coat and overshoes, and walked up the railroad track as far as the ravine.

It seems I'm always doing that. Right to my face Horizon tells me I'm a queer one. They hint that I might go visiting more. Mrs. Bird says call for her – she ought to think about her figure too. It's getting so that I dread starting out. The whole town seems to watch me. The windows stare like eyes. They make me slink – make me feel guilty. Still I go.

It was a cold raw day, with snowdust skimming in little snakes along the drifts, and shooting off the crests at you like musketry of Lilliput. He wasn't old, I told myself. He wasn't dulled, or coarsened, or insensitive. All he needed was something to live for, something to waken and challenge him. Then it would be as before. He would want to paint again.

Steve, I remembered, had nearly brought him back. There were days when he seemed to rouse and shake himself, when his head was high, and his step forthright. I had to ask myself what he might do if it were a son of his own.

Because I still believe in him. I still believe that he's finer and stronger and truer than the run of men. I think that for his son's sake he will be worthy of himself.

He must leave the Church. There are some, no doubt, who belong in it, who find it a comfort, a goal, a field of endeavor. He, though, isn't one of them. In our lives it isn't the Church itself that matters but what he feels about it, the shame and sense of guilt he suffers while remaining a part of it. That's why we're adopting Judith's baby. He'll not dare let his son see him as he sees himself; and he's no dissembler.

"Philip," I said after we had gone to bed. I waited till then, so we wouldn't have to look at each other. "It hasn't been the same since Steve went. Do you never think we might adopt a child legally? This spring there'll be Judith's baby. I've always liked Judith. Better than anyone else's I think I could take her baby and forget it isn't mine."

We both lay still a minute; then he said evenly that since I was the one who would have most of the work and responsibility, it was for me to make the decision.

He had to speak that way. He had to pretend it made no difference to him whether the baby we decided to adopt was Judith's or not – but it was such a heartless, cold response that I had to turn a minute and bite the pillow hard. Only for the darkness, and the long quiet hours to steady myself, I might have failed him.

Nor was it much easier in the morning. Her baby – always with me – a reminder – and Philip in return to think it only a fortunate coincidence that the baby I wanted should be his. I looked ahead and the prospect brought a bitterness. I felt my blood go thin, and my lips set hard and cruel.

I told him he must make her understand that once we take the baby she is never to see it again – that she is never to see even me. I want it to be my baby – my son. I won't let her remind me that it isn't. "Make it clear to her," I said, "that she can't refuse. Tell her that we can give her child opportunity and a name. Tell her how he will suffer if she keeps him, grow up and eventually hate her. You tell her, or I will."

He sat stirring his coffee a minute and biting his lip, then said, "Yes, but later. They say it makes a difference to the child what the mental condition of the mother is before it's born – and since it's to be our child –"

I nodded, drew my lips in again and went on, "I want it to grow up believing us to be its parents. So the sooner we make the break and get away from Horizon –"

He went on stirring his coffee. We didn't mention it again until this evening. Then instead of going off to his study as usual he came out to the kitchen and said, "Do you really think we could make a living in this store you talk about? It sounds like starvation – but another Horizon every three or four years – that's not much of a prospect to look forward to either."

I didn't answer. I think I can leave everything now to him.

Saturday Evening, March 16

The Ladies Aid held a bazaar and tea in the basement of the church yesterday, and Mrs. Bird and Mrs. Finley quarreled because Mrs. Bird said the dishes should be sterilized by boiling twenty minutes, and Mrs. Finley asked her who was running things, and told her not to judge other people's microbes by her own. Apart from that, though, things went well, with all the cakes and baby boots and hand-embroidered dish towels sold, and nearly a hundred in for tea, and the gross takings sixty ninety-five.

Even poor Paul was there, with a hangdog, guilty, miserable look, compelled by the unspoken edict of the Ladies Aid that every man turn out to buy a doily. I saw him finish his two little sandwiches in half a dozen bites, then sit five minutes nibbling a little biscuit trying to spin it out. Later Mrs. Wenderby sold him a dozen doughnuts, a pair of rompers and a cushion top. "You take them –" he squeezed up helplessly to me, and Mrs. Finley who was listening sniffed so nastily I stumped right over to Mr. Finley and sold them to him again for a dollar twenty-five. She was fairly fuming behind her thin little smile when I came back. I held the money up and beamed, "Isn't it wonderful the way they're buying everything."

She's fuming now in earnest, though, for Philip called on her this morning and explained the urgency of coal and grocery bills. We're getting fifty Monday, which apart from this month's payment on the car will leave us clear again. We had twenty-five, too, for our savings from Crow Coulee the other day, and Philip himself now is after Tillsonborough and Kelby. Six hundred he says by the end of the month; seven hundred by the end of April. We're getting there in earnest now. I caught him at the calendar tonight, the leaves turned up to June.

It hurts, of course, seeing the change, and knowing the reason, but it's no use mooning over that. After all that's what I did it for, to make him change. I should be satisfied.

He keeps controlled and unconcerned, but within he's stirring, quickening, like a bed of half-dead coals that someone is blowing on. Last week he went to see Judith again, and though he came back nervous and disturbed, the house ever since has been electric with resolve.

He's kinder, too. So much new life surging up within him that he can afford to be indulgent, bestow a little even on me. But it's all from a great distance still, as if I didn't really count. It's the way, no doubt, with every man. After a year or two he takes a woman for granted. If she's there when he wants her, well and good. If not, there are other things with which he can occupy himself. A woman, I suppose, is like that, too, once she has a child. There's an easing-off on both sides. Neither is hurt too much. But this child now that's coming won't be mine. It will always be a stranger, a reminder how I failed. I'll go on needing Philip just as much as ever.

It's been milder today. I've let the fire go down, and now it's cold again. Philip is quiet, finishing a drawing that he's been working on since suppertime. A file of cattle plowing their way across a field piled deep with snow. Off in the distance there's a farmhouse, erect, small, isolated. It's just a pencil sketch in black and white, but you feel the cold and stillness of a winter's dusk. There's that about Philip, his work is bigger than his moods. He's racked these days with a nervous, half-fearful kind of elation, but the drawing has a heavy calm and brooding. The same brooding that's been in nearly all his drawings for the last four or five years. It may take him as many more to get away from it again.

Monday Evening, March 25

It's been thawing today a little, and tonight there's a strong soft wind from the south that's cold enough still to make you shiver, and that yet you know means spring. We're so tired of the winter it's hard to come in and shut the door on it. We need the fire, yet somehow it's out of season. Philip is restless, bottled-up – thinks that he's keeping it from me by sitting in his study cramped and still.

I'm restless too, expectant and uneasy. I went out after supper and walked myself tired, but it hasn't been much use. On the track between the rails it was nearly bare already. There was a familiar crunch of gravel underfoot. Mrs. Ellingson says her chickens are starting to lay, and tomorrow she's going to bring me over two fresh eggs.

It's just six weeks away. The days seem to hurry, yet they're inert with suspense. I didn't dread when it was my own baby coming as I'm doing now. Philip is white, thin, wide-eyed. Yesterday he went to see Judith again. He suggested hiring a team and taking me, but I couldn't trust myself. Every day my nerves get sharper, tenser. My baby – his baby – all I have of him. It's going to be a boy, of course, and I'm going to call him Philip too.

Tuesday Evening, April 2

I walked up the railroad track this afternoon as far as the ravine with Paul. He was on his way home from school just as I was starting out. He said if I didn't mind he'd come too, and then all the way there and back was silent.

I'd never thought of him like that before, but there was such a strained, helpless look in his eyes that suddenly I felt the windows all accusing me. Somehow it seemed that they all must know now, too. I couldn't refuse him, but I was such a coward I walked in misery till we had left the town behind. All the time I had thought it was only Philip, something he was trying to imagine. Paul had been silent with me often before, thoughtful, masculine, self-sufficient silences, but this time it was just a helpless, numb one of awareness, like a woman's, and I could tell by it that he was suffering.

I kept silent too. It seemed strange that I now should make another suffer who had suffered so much that way myself. We heard some meadowlarks, and saw a flock of crows in clear black scallops on the sky. They cawed a few times over us, hard rasping little strokes of sound that struck on our ears as if when they passed the scallops had fallen, and Paul asked brusquely, "Why is a raven like a writing-desk? "

"A nonsense riddle in *Alice in Wonderland*," I replied. "There isn't an answer, and those are crows, not ravens."

"Once the raven, too, had a croak in his name," he said cryptically, "and there was a time when all pens scratched."

It was a warm, sunny day. There were bare patches big as an acre in the fields, and you could fancy the earth as stretching itself, slowly bursting its way through the snow like a bud through its calyx. The drifts on the bank of the ravine were so sodden and treacherous we didn't dare descend. From the railway bridge we watched the water rushing at the bottom in a frothy yellow flood. Not far upstream an overhanging drift dropped in, shot off with the current crest upwards like a sailboat, then stunned itself to pieces on the trestle of the bridge. Our hands lay side by side on the railing, two or three inches apart. We watched the water and didn't speak, conscious of those inches. There was a smooth, flawless silence, poised between the sky and the thawing fields like a glass bubble. The dull steady bellow of the water was its base.

"It's getting late," I said at last. "There's Philip's supper."

He turned and looked at me a moment, fixedly, humbly, without heed to my response, as if I were asleep, or a curious stranger. Then he said, "He'll be wondering where you are. We'd better go."

It was a kind of avowal. It asked nothing of me. It didn't try to explain or defend itself. We came home leaving it there.

At the supper table Philip said cautiously that he had written Tillsonborough offering them a settlement. They still owe us over a thousand dollars, and the crops there were good last year. He thinks that if we cancel the rest they might make an effort to let us have six hundred dollars within two or three months. I nodded and said what a good idea it was. Then we both went on with our supper, abstractedly.

I went out again afterwards, driven by a feeling that it would be easier to be alone outside than alone in here. As I walked along the pale windy streets and down to the elevators I caught myself wishing Paul were with me. Without knowing it I've relied on him all this last year. A vague, intangible reliance just as without thinking much about them you come to rely on institutions and beliefs. I stood against the south wall of the elevator, letting the wind nail me there. It was dark, deep wind; like a great blind tide it poured to the north again. The earth where I stood was like a solitary rock in it. I cowered there with a sense of being unheeded, abandoned.

I've felt that way so many times in a wind, that it's rushing past me, away from me, that it's leaving me lost and isolated. Back at my table staring into the lamp I think how the winds and tides of life have left me just the same, poured over me, round me, swept north, south, then back again. And I think of Paul, and wonder might it have been different if we had known each other earlier. Then the currents might have taken and fulfilled me. I might not still be nailed by them against a heedless wall.

Friday Evening, April 5

Philip made inquiries recently about a secondhand bookstore in the little city where we used to live, and today there was an answer. He didn't tell me he was writing, but I half-suspected it. A few days before, all in the way of encouragement, I'd made an instance of this particular store, the good business they always seemed to do, their location out by the university. I'd remarked casually, too, that the man who owned it must be getting on. When we used to go there for Philip to browse around, he was all of fifty-five.

Anyway it worked, and since a stock of secondhand books is something you don't want to buy in a poke, Philip is leaving Monday on a business trip. It's two hundred miles southeast of here, but they say the highway there is nearly dry. He's getting the car out tomorrow, and putting it in the garage uptown to be overhauled. His expression keeps so businesslike and nonchalant you'd think he went off like this every spring to buy a store. To me it's such an event I feel a few dramatics would be justified, but just one word to make it sound momentous and he spears me with a look.

I'm uneasy, too, now that things are really under way. Does anybody ever make a living, selling secondhand books? Does Philip know how a business should be run? If we use up our bit of money, then have to close –

I thought at first that we'd put the piano in the store and sell music too, but the more I think about it the more I'm convinced that Philip would be better without me. In workaday matters I'm so much more practical and capable than he is that in a month or two I'd be one of those domineering females that men abominate. Instead I'll try to teach. I still have a few friends there, and there are others who will perhaps remember me. This fall I might even give a recital. There'll be the baby, of course, but maybe I'll be able to find some pupils willing to pay for their lessons minding it. Maybe it will be a good baby.

I think and think, and plan and plan, and every day feel a little shakier. It's raining tonight, and the roof's leaking, and in musty whiffs I smell the past again. We'll be better away. I'll like the baby, too, once I'm used to it, and feel it in my arms. This time next year I'll have forgotten a lot, will be looking ahead. If only the baby were here, and we were away with it. After all she's the mother. I'm busy sewing these days, getting ready, but all the time I have a guilty feeling. You can't just walk in and take a baby. She'll let us have it all right, eventually, but she'll haunt us a long time with that queer white face of hers.

Wednesday Evening, April 10

Judith's baby was born Monday night, a month before its time. Judith died early Tuesday morning.

Philip went to see her Monday after he left here; perhaps he told her we were leaving Horizon, and wanted to take the baby with us. In the afternoon she went for a walk, refusing to let her sister go with her, and promising to be back within an hour. But the fields were soft and sticky, and the hard walking exhausted her. About dusk a neighbor boy out hunting cattle found her resting on a stone pile, cold and ill already, and wandering in her mind.

I didn't know till yesterday afternoon, when Dr. Bird and Judith's mother arrived with the baby. He's a very feeble baby still, and the doctor wanted him in town where he could watch him and see he was being fed properly. Mrs. West spent a long time crying about it, assuring me that their family had never before been brought to shame.

"You and your husband are good people. You're real Christians, and I'm glad you're taking the baby. I was hoping maybe she'd talk to you, so we could find out who it was and make him marry her – but maybe like this it's better. She was always a hard, unfeeling girl. I'm her mother – I had a right to know – but she'd just set her lips and never say a word. I used to tell her it's no use farmers like us trying to be better than we are. Maybe I should have been firmer."

He's a tiny baby, wrinkled and ugly and red. I breathe from my throat and shake a little when I have to pick him up, but I'm not afraid of him. He's helpless, he needs me, and I have an easy, relaxed feeling that the rest now makes no difference. I peer into the puckered little face for signs of Philip, but as yet he isn't there.

I sent Philip a telegram this afternoon, telling him that Judith died and that the baby's a boy. He'll be better to learn it away from me, with time to think it out and find himself again.

For me it's easier this way. It's what I've secretly been hoping for all along. I'm glad she's gone – glad – for her sake as much as ours. What was there ahead of her now anyway? If I lost Philip what would there be ahead of me?

Saturday Evening, April 13

There's been a big windstorm, and Philip's home, and we're leaving Horizon the middle of May.

The wind got up Thursday night, and all day Friday it was a hard, steady gale that you could scarcely stand against. There was dust in it too, for all it's so early, and the sky was dark and ominous and tawny, and you couldn't see beyond the town.

There were some things I needed for the baby from the drugstore, but the way the house was rocking I was afraid to leave him alone, and on such a day there was no one going by. So I watched for Paul on his way home from school, and ran out and asked him to go. The wind got suddenly worse while he was away, the dust so thick that the house went dark. Then our chimney blew down, and the thud of the bricks on the roof sent me running to the bedroom for the baby. He was crying when Paul returned, and I was standing with him at the window sick with fright. Paul made me sit down, then went to the kitchen for a lamp. It was a bad wind, he said dryly. Most of the false fronts were blown down, and Mrs. Ellingson had lost her chicken coop and nearly all her hens.

There was a slow, deliberate quietness in his voice, and he took pains not to look at me. I sent him back to the butcher shop for steak, and while he was away fried potatoes and opened a tin of fruit, and when he said he couldn't stay for supper looked so disappointed that he changed his mind and did.

It wasn't fair to ask him, understanding things now as I did, but with the high wind, and the baby so new on my hands, I was afraid just then to be alone. We talked easily enough, though, philology, and Philip's trip, and secondhand bookstores, and then after the supper things were cleared away I went to the piano and played for him.

But I could feel him watching me all the time, and for escape at last I stopped suddenly and said, "I think I hear the baby." I brought him out of the bedroom to show Paul, but instead of looking at him Paul kept his eyes fixed on me. And the expression in his eyes was so wondering and incredulous that I realized he knew what all along I was certain I was keeping secret.

Then to break the silence I gave the baby to him to hold, and told him that his name was to be Philip too. "It means a love of horses," he said. "You couldn't get a better one."

And the baby, because he wasn't being held right, started to whimper then, and Paul carried him back to the bedroom, and laid him on the bed. Did I know, he asked gravely, that in the early ages of our race it was imitation of just such a little wail as this that had given us some of our noblest words, like father, and patriarch, and paternity. And I shook my head and let him explain, and then motioning him after me went on tiptoe to the living-room again.

And just come in, unheard through the storm and rattling windows, Philip was standing there. He glanced at us, then without a word stalked out to the kitchen to wash. I told Paul to go now, thinking I could explain things better by myself.

But Philip had seen enough, and wouldn't give me the chance. There was a gray bitterness in his face that made me frantic for a moment, but when I spoke to him he started scornfully toward the study, and when I seized his hands to make him listen drew in his lips and wrenched himself away.

And then, slow and deliberate at first, gradually quickening, his contempt and bitterness found words. Words that stung me – that coming from him at such a time I couldn't bear, that made me wheel on him, go blind.

I ran to the bedroom door, flung it open, and showed him the baby. "Your baby!" I cried. "Yours –" and he stopped white a moment, and said in a slow hollow voice, "You were with her then – and she told you –"

I steeled myself, afraid to admit what I had done, then shouted no, she hadn't told me, that I had always known, that I had wanted the baby so that in time his son would be my son too.

And then I couldn't face him any longer, and with a sharp, frightened instinct to escape sprang outside and stumbled down dark side streets out of town. The wind was in my back. I ran with it as far as the last grain elevator.

I went to the sheltered side, and stayed there maybe half an hour. It was a hard half-hour. I was afraid to go back, afraid to think, afraid to ask myself what I had now to look forward to. And then at the engine-house of the next elevator I saw a man with a lantern, and as I watched he came round the corner and into the wind, and the flame flickered sideways for a moment, and went out.

It hurried me home, the thought of the lamp in the living-room, Philip perhaps out looking for me, and the door blown open after him. The baby woke as I lifted him, and at the frightened clutch of my hands began to cry. I hushed him, rocked him, cried with him – and then Philip found us.

I put the baby in his arms, and keeping my eyes down slipped away. In a little while he came to me. He tried to speak, but it was no use. Then he took my hand and held it a minute, but that was no use either. No matter how earnest or contrite, endeavor in a hand is not enough. "You're tired," I said. "Go to bed now and get some sleep. There'll be time to talk tomorrow."

An hour later when I went into the bedroom I heard his breathing suddenly become deep and even. I pretended too, and holding my breath, as if I really thought he were asleep, bent down and kissed him. He stirred a little, lay still again.

I was tired too. I slept at last.

Sunday Evening, May 12

This is our last Sunday in Horizon. Paul helped Philip with the crating yesterday till ten o'clock, and tomorrow we'll get the little things packed, and for the last night go to Mrs. Ellingson's.

After three or four years it's easy to leave a little town. After just one it's hard.

It turns out now that all along they've liked us. Philip, they tell me, was always such an earnest, straightforward man. He's made it hard for his successor. And I minded my own business, came and went willingly, was the sort of woman they could look up to. Last Friday they had a farewell supper for us in the basement of the church, made speeches, sang *God Be With You Till We Meet Again*, presented us with a handsome silver flower basket. It's the way of a little Main Street town – sometimes a rather nice way.

It's blowing tonight, and there's dust again, and the room sways slowly in a yellow smoky haze. The bare, rain-stained walls remind me of our first Sunday here, just a little over a year ago, and in a sentimental mood I keep thinking what an eventful year it's been, what a wide wheel it's run.

We were hanging our shingle out that night, and now we're taking it in. For a few minutes after church tonight I sat talking with Philip about it, staring at the lamp and in the pauses trying to grasp how much the change is going to mean, and then I said I had a little surprise for him, and brought out a pipe and a tin of tobacco.

He turned the pipe over a few times, filled it, struck a match, then looked up dubiously and said, "You're sure it's all right? The smoke won't hurt the boy?"

He's a very small boy yet, mostly lungs and diapers, but we like him. Philip just stands and looks and looks at him, and puts his cheek down close to the little hands, and tells me that way how much I must forget. It takes twelve years without a boy to let you know how much one's worth. He doesn't look like Philip yet, but Philip I'll swear is starting to look like him. It's in the eyes, a stillness, a freshness, a vacancy of beginning.

"Another Philip?" the first one says. "With so many names to pick and choose from you don't need that again. Two of us in the same house you'll get mixed up. Sometimes you won't know which of us is which."

That's right, Philip. I want it so.

This book was previously published under the New Canadian Library imprint.

THE NEW CANADIAN LIBRARY

Founded in 1957 by Malcolm Ross in conjunction with Jack McClelland, the New Canadian Library was, by design, indeed a library, indispensable to a knowledge, understanding, and appreciation of the country itself.

The first paperback series dedicated solely to Canada's literatures, the New Canadian Library acknowledged and celebrated the country's literary achievements. Its attractive and authoritative volumes spanned more than two hundred years of Canadian writing, and confirmed the astonishing diversity, range, and wealth of Canada's literary cultures.

Each volume in the series was met with the unanimous endorsement of all the members of the Advisory Board. The texts have been reprinted in their entirety. Afterwords by distinguished writers, critics, and scholars explained and expanded upon the text. And biographies and bibliographies of the authors completed each book.

The New Canadian Library was synonymous with literary excellence.